THE SILVER CLASSICS

W9-BIF-995

The Adventures of Tom Sawyer
MARK TWAIN

Treasure Island
ROBERT LOUIS STEVENSON

The Call of the Wild and Other Stories
JACK LONDON

Sherlock Holmes, Master Detective
ARTHUR CONAN DOYLE

Tales of Imagination and Suspense
ANTHOLOGY: 16 STORIES

Frankenstein
MARY SHELLEY

Classic Short Stories
ANTHOLOGY: 18 STORIES

Adventures of Huckleberry Finn
MARK TWAIN

The Red Badge of Courage and Other Favorites
STEPHEN CRANE

The Scarlet Letter
NATHANIEL HAWTHORNE

The Turn of the Screw and Washington Square
HENRY JAMES

A Tale of Two Cities
CHARLES DICKENS

A SILVER CLASSIC

Tales of Imagination and Suspense

SILVER BURDETT COMPANY
Morristown, New Jersey
Glenview, Illinois • Palo Alto • Dallas • Atlanta

The stories in this edition are complete and unabridged except for the following: "From the Earth to the Moon" is abridged from *From the Earth to the Moon* and *Round the Moon*. "A Mad Tea Party" is an unabridged excerpt from *Alice in Wonderland*. "The Dancing Doll" is an unabridged excerpt from "The Sandman."

Acknowledgments Pages 32–54: "The Mysterious Death on the Underground Railway" by The Baroness Orczy, from *The Rivals of Sherlock Holmes*. Reprinted by permission of the estate of Baroness Orczy. Pages 113–117: "The Open Window" from *The Complete Stories of Saki* (H. H. Munro). Copyright © 1930 by The Viking Press, Inc., © renewed 1958 by The Viking Press, Inc. Reprinted by permission of Viking Penguin Inc. Pages 263–273: "The Strange Orchid" (original title "The Flowering of the Strange Orchid") by H. G. Wells. Reprinted by permission of the estate of H. G. Wells.

Illustration   Page 180: Edward P. Malsberg.

CONTENTS

TALES OF CRIME AND DETECTION

———

There are two basic kinds of crime stories: stories about crime itself (many of these are told by the criminal or the victim), and stories about how crimes are solved (most of these are detective stories).

People have always been fascinated by crime. One of the first crime stories is in Genesis, the first book of the Bible, when Cain, the son of Adam and Eve, slays his brother Abel.

There are many reasons why people are fascinated by crime and crime stories; among them, the fear of being a victim of crime and the fear of one day committing a crime through overwhelming temptation or impulse. Detective stories have a different sort of allure: The crime is done, the terror is over, and all that remains is the puzzle: Who did it, and how? Watching the fictional detective solve the puzzle reassures us that reason can triumph over evil.

So the crime story often evokes horror, while the detective story presents a puzzle. The two kinds of story are alike in one way, however. Dealing in extremes of behavior, both can reveal a good deal about human nature.

"I knew that sound.... It was the beating of the old man's heart. It increased my fury as the beating of a drum stimulates the soldier...."

THE TELL-TALE HEART

Edgar Allan Poe

True!—nervous—very, very dreadfully nervous I had been and am; but why *will* you say that I am mad? The disease had sharpened my senses—not destroyed—not dulled them. Above all was the sense of hearing acute. I heard all things in the heaven and in the earth. I heard many things in hell. How, then, am I mad? Hearken! and observe how healthily—how calmly I can tell you the whole story.

It is impossible to say how first the idea entered my brain; but once conceived, it haunted me day and night. Object there was none. Passion there was none. I loved the old man. He had never wronged me. He had never given me insult. For his gold I had no desire. I think it was his eye! yes, it was this! One of his eyes resembled that of a vulture—a pale blue eye, with a film over it. Whenever it fell upon me, my blood ran cold; and so by degrees—very gradually—I made up my mind to take the life of the old man, and thus rid myself of the eye forever.

Now this is the point. You fancy me mad. Madmen know nothing. But you should have seen *me*. You should have seen how wisely I proceeded—with what caution— with what foresight—with what dissimulation I went to work! I was never kinder to the old man than during the whole week before I killed him. And every night, about midnight, I turned the latch of his door and opened it— oh, so gently! And then, when I had made an opening suf- ficient for my head, I put in a dark lantern, all closed, closed, so that no light shone out, and then I thrust in my head. Oh, you would have laughed to see how cunningly I thrust it in! I moved it slowly—very, very slowly, so that I might not disturb the old man's sleep. It took me an hour to place my whole head within the opening so far that I could see him as he lay upon his bed. Ha!—would a madman have been so wise as this? And then, when my head was well in the room, I undid the lantern cau- tiously—oh, so cautiously—cautiously (for the hinges creaked)—I undid it just so much that a single thin ray fell upon the vulture eye. And this I did for seven long nights—every night just at midnight—but I found the eye always closed; and so it was impossible to do the work; for it was not the old man who vexed me, but his Evil Eye. And every morning, when the day broke, I went boldly into the chamber, and spoke courageously to him, calling him by name in a hearty tone, and inquiring how he had passed the night. So you see he would have been a very profound old man, indeed, to suspect that every night, just at twelve, I looked in upon him while he slept.

Upon the eighth night I was more than usually cau- tious in opening the door. A watch's minute hand moves more quickly than did mine. Never before that night had

4 I *felt* the extent of my own powers—of my sagacity. I could scarcely contain my feelings of triumph. To think that there I was, opening the door, little by little, and he not even to dream of my secret deeds or thoughts. I fairly chuckled at the idea; and perhaps he heard me; for he moved on the bed suddenly, as if startled. Now you may think that I drew back—but no. His room was as black as pitch with the thick darkness (for the shutters were close fastened, through fear of robbers), and so I knew that he could not see the opening of the door, and I kept pushing it on steadily, steadily.

I had my head in, and was about to open the lantern, when my thumb slipped upon the tin fastening, and the old man sprang up in the bed, crying out—"Who's there?"

I kept quite still and said nothing. For a whole hour I did not move a muscle, and in the meantime I did not hear him lie down. He was still sitting up in the bed listening;—just as I have done, night after night, hearkening to the death watches in the wall.

Presently I heard a slight groan, and I knew it was the groan of mortal terror. It was not a groan of pain or of grief—oh, no!—it was the low stifled sound that arises from the bottom of the soul when overcharged with awe. I knew the sound well. Many a night, just at midnight, when all the world slept, it has welled up from my own bosom, deepening, with its dreadful echo, the terrors that distracted me. I say I knew it well. I knew what the old man felt, and pitied him, although I chuckled at heart. I knew that he had been lying awake ever since the first slight noise, when he had turned in the bed. His fears had

been ever since growing upon him. He had been trying to 5
fancy them causeless, but could not. He had been saying
to himself—"It is nothing but the wind in the chimney—it
is only a mouse crossing the floor," or "it is merely a
cricket which has made a single chirp." Yes, he has been
trying to comfort himself with these suppositions; but he
had found all in vain. *All in vain;* because Death, in approaching him, had stalked with his black shadow before
him, and enveloped the victim. And it was the mournful
influence of the unperceived shadow that caused him to
feel—although he neither saw nor heard—to *feel* the presence of my head within the room.

When I had waited a long time, very patiently, without hearing him lie down, I resolved to open a little—a
very, very little crevice in the lantern. So I opened it—
you cannot imagine how stealthily, stealthily—until, at
length, a single dim ray, like the thread of a spider, shot
from out the crevice and full upon the vulture eye.

It was open—wide, wide open—and I grew furious as I
gazed upon it. I saw it with perfect distinctness—all a dull
blue, with a hideous veil over it that chilled the very mar-
row in my bones; but I could see nothing else of the old
man's face or person: for I had directed the ray as if by
instinct, precisely upon the damned spot.

And now have I not told you that what you mistake for
madness is but over-acuteness of the senses?—now, I say,
there came to my ears a low, dull, quick sound, such as a
watch makes when enveloped in cotton. I knew *that*
sound well too. It was the beating of the old man's heart.
It increased my fury, as the beating of a drum stimulates
the soldier into courage.

6 But even yet I refrained and kept still. I scarcely breathed. I held the lantern motionless. I tried how steadily I could maintain the ray upon the eye. Meantime the hellish tattoo of the heart increased. It grew quicker and quicker, and louder and louder every instant. The old man's terror *must* have been extreme! It grew louder, I say, louder every moment!—do you mark me well? I have told you that I am nervous: so I am. And now at the dead hour of the night, amid the dreadful silence of that old house, so strange a noise as this excited me to uncontrollable terror. Yet, for some minutes longer I refrained and stood still. But the beating grew louder, louder! I thought the heart must burst. And now a new anxiety seized me—the sound would be heard by a neighbor! The old man's hour had come! With a loud yell, I threw open the lantern and leaped into the room. He shrieked once— once only. In an instant I dragged him to the floor, and pulled the heavy bed over him. I then smiled gaily, to find the deed so far done. But, for many minutes, the heart beat on with a muffled sound. This, however, did not vex me; it would not be heard through the wall. At length it ceased. The old man was dead. I removed the bed and examined the corpse. Yes, he was stone, stone dead. I placed my hand upon the heart and held it there many minutes. There was no pulsation. He was stone dead. His eye would trouble me no more.

If still you think me mad, you will think so no longer when I describe the wise precautions I took for the concealment of the body. The night waned, and I worked hastily, but in silence. First of all I dismembered the corpse. I cut off the head and the arms and the legs.

I then took up three planks from the flooring of the

chamber, and deposited all between the scantlings. I then replaced the boards so cleverly, so cunningly, that no human eye—not even *his*—could have detected anything wrong. There was nothing to wash out—no stain of any kind—no blood spot whatever. I had been too wary for that. A tub had caught all—ha! ha!

When I had made an end of these labors, it was four o'clock—still dark as midnight. As the bell sounded the hour, there came a knocking at the street door. I went down to open it with a light heart,—for what had I *now* to fear? There entered three men, who introduced themselves, with perfect suavity, as officers of the police. A shriek had been heard by a neighbor during the night; suspicion of foul play had been aroused; information had been lodged at the police office, and they (the officers) had been deputed to search the premises.

I smiled,—for *what* had I to fear? I bade the gentlemen welcome. The shriek, I said, was my own in a dream. The old man, I mentioned, was absent in the country. I took my visitors all over the house. I bade them search—search *well*. I led them, at length, to *his* chamber. I showed them his treasures, secure, undisturbed. In the enthusiasm of my confidence, I brought chairs into the room, and desired them *here* to rest from their fatigues, while I myself, in the wild audacity of my perfect triumph, placed my own seat upon the very spot beneath which reposed the corpse of the victim.

The officers were satisfied. My *manner* had convinced them. I was singularly at ease. They sat, and while I answered cheerily, they chatted familiar things. But, ere long, I felt myself getting pale and wished them gone. My head ached, and I fancied a ringing in my ears: but still

8 they sat and still chatted. The ringing became more distinct:—it continued and became more distinct: I talked more freely to get rid of the feeling: but it continued and gained definitiveness—until, at length, I found that the noise was *not* within my ears.

No doubt I now grew *very* pale;—but I talked more fluently, and with a heightened voice. Yet the sound increased—and what could I do? It was *a low, dull, quick sound—much such a sound as a watch makes when enveloped in cotton.* I gasped for breath—and yet the officers heard it not. I talked more quickly—more vehemently; but the noise steadily increased. I arose and argued about trifles, in a high key and with violent gesticulations, but the noise steadily increased. Why *would* they not be gone? I paced the floor to and fro with heavy strides, as if excited to fury by the observation of the men—but the noise steadily increased. Oh God! what *could* I do? I foamed—I raved—I swore! I swung the chair upon which I had been sitting, and grated it upon the boards, but the noise arose over all and continually increased. It grew louder—louder—*louder!* And still the men chatted pleasantly, and smiled. Was it possible they heard not? Almighty God!—no, no! They heard!—they suspected!—they *knew!*—they were making a mockery of my horror!—this I thought, and this I think. But anything was better than this agony! Anything was more tolerable than this derision! I could bear those hypocritical smiles no longer! I felt that I must scream or die!—and now—again!—hark! louder! louder! louder! *louder!*—

"Villains!" I shrieked, "dissemble no more! I admit the deed!—tear up the planks!—here, here!—it is the beating of his hideous heart!"

*My blood seemed to stand still. A deadly paralyzing cold-
ness stole all over me as I turned my head round on the
pillow. . . .*

A TERRIBLY STRANGE BED

Wilkie Collins

Shortly after my education at college was finished, I happened to be staying at Paris with an English friend. We
were both young men then, and lived, I am afraid, rather
a wild life, in the delightful city of our sojourn. One night
we were idling about the neighborhood of the Palais
Royal, doubtful to what amusement we should next be-
take ourselves. My friend proposed a visit to Frascati's;
but his suggestion was not to my taste. I knew Frascati's,
as the French saying is, by heart; had lost and won plenty
of five-franc pieces there, merely for amusement's sake,
until it was amusement no longer, and was thoroughly
tired, in fact, of all the ghastly respectabilities of such a
social anomaly as a respectable gambling house. "For
Heaven's sake," said I to my friend, "let us go somewhere
where we can see a little genuine, blackguard, poverty-
stricken gaming with no false gingerbread glitter thrown
over it all. Let us get away from fashionable Frascati's, to
a house where they don't mind letting in a man with a
ragged coat, or a man with no coat, ragged or otherwise."

10   "Very well," said my friend, "we needn't go out of the Palais Royal to find the sort of company you want. Here's the place just before us; as blackguard a place, by all report, as you could possibly wish to see." In another minute we arrived at the door and entered the house.

When we got upstairs, and had left our hats and sticks with the doorkeeper, we were admitted into the chief gambling room. We did not find many people assembled there. But, few as the men were who looked up at us on our entrance, they were all types—lamentably true types—of their respective classes.

We had come to see blackguards; but these men were something worse. There is a comic side, more or less appreciable, in all blackguardism—here there was nothing but tragedy—mute, weird tragedy. The quiet in the room was horrible. The thin, haggard, long-haired young man, whose sunken eyes fiercely watched the turning up of the cards, never spoke; the flabby, fat-faced, pimply player, who pricked his piece of pasteboard perseveringly, to register how often black won, and how often red—never spoke; the dirty, wrinkled old man, with the vulture eyes and the darned greatcoat, who had lost his last *sou*, and still looked on desperately, after he could play no longer—never spoke. Even the voice of the croupier sounded as if it were strangely dulled and thickened in the atmosphere of the room. I had entered the place to laugh, but the spectacle before me was something to weep over. I soon found it necessary to take refuge in excitement from the depression of spirits which was fast stealing on me. Unfortunately I sought the nearest excitement, by going to the table and beginning to play. Still more unfortunately, as the event will show, I won—won prodigiously; won incredibly; won at such a rate that the regular players at the table crowded round me; and staring at my stakes with hungry, superstitious eyes, whispered to one another that the English stranger was going to break the bank.

The game was *Rouge et Noir*. I had played at it in every city in Europe, without, however, the care or the wish to study the Theory of Chances—that philosopher's stone of all gamblers! And a gambler, in the strict sense of the word, I had never been. I was heart-whole from the corroding passion for play. My gaming was a mere idle amusement. I never resorted to it by necessity, because I never knew what it was to want money. I never practiced it so incessantly as to lose more than I could afford, or to gain more than I could coolly pocket without being thrown off my balance by my good luck. In short, I had hitherto frequented gambling tables—just as I frequented ballrooms and opera houses—because they amused me, and because I had nothing better to do with my leisure hours.

But on this occasion it was very different—now, for the first time in my life, I felt what the passion for play really was. My success first bewildered, and then, in the most literal meaning of the word, intoxicated me. Incredible as it may appear, it is nevertheless true, that I only lost when I attempted to estimate chances, and played according to previous calculation. If I left everything to luck, and staked without any care or consideration, I was sure to win—to win in the face of every recognized probability in favor of the bank. At first some of the men present ventured their money safely enough on my color; but I speedily increased my stakes to sums which they dared

12 not risk. One after another they left off playing, and breathlessly looked on at my game.

Still, time after time, I staked higher and higher, and still won. The excitement in the room rose to fever pitch. The silence was interrupted by a deep-muttered chorus of oaths and exclamations in different languages, every time the gold was shoveled across to my side of the table—even the imperturbable croupier dashed his rake on the floor in a (French) fury of astonishment at my success. But one man present preserved his self-possession, and that man was my friend. He came to my side, and whispering in English, begged me to leave the place, satisfied with what I had already gained. I must do him the justice to say that he repeated his warnings and entreaties several times, and only left me and went away after I had rejected his advice (I was to all intents and purposes gambling drunk) in terms which rendered it impossible for him to address me again that night.

Shortly after he had gone, a hoarse voice behind me cried: "Permit me, my dear sir—permit me to restore to their proper place two napoleons which you have dropped. Wonderful luck, sir! I pledge you my word of honor, as an old soldier, in the course of my long experience in this sort of thing, I never saw such luck as yours—never! Go on, sir—*Sacré mille bombes!* Go on boldly, and break the bank!"

I turned round and saw, nodding and smiling at me with inveterate civility, a tall man, dressed in a frogged and braided surtout.

If I had been in my senses, I should have considered him, personally, as being rather a suspicious specimen of an old soldier. He had goggling, bloodshot eyes, mangy mustaches, and a broken nose. His voice betrayed a barrack-room intonation of the worst order, and he had the dirtiest pair of hands I ever saw—even in France. These little personal peculiarities exercised, however, no repelling influence on me. In the mad excitement, the reckless triumph of that moment, I was ready to "fraternize" with anybody who encouraged me in my game. I accepted the old soldier's offered pinch of snuff; clapped him on the back, and swore he was the honestest fellow in the world—the most glorious relic of the Grand Army that I had ever met with. "Go on!" cried my military friend, snapping his fingers in ecstasy—"Go on, and win! Break the bank—*Mille tonnerres!* my gallant English comrade, break the bank!"

And I *did* go on—went on at such a rate, that in another quarter of an hour the croupier called out, "Gentlemen, the bank has discontinued for tonight." All the notes, and all the gold in that "bank," now lay in a heap under my hands; the whole floating capital of the gambling house was waiting to pour into my pockets!

"Tie up the money in your pocket-handkerchief, my worthy sir," said the old soldier, as I wildly plunged my hands into my heap of gold. "Tie it up, as we used to tie up a bit of dinner in the Grand Army; your winnings are too heavy for any breeches pockets that ever were sewed. There! that's it—shovel them in, notes and all! *Credié!* what luck! Stop! another napoleon on the floor! *Ah! sacré petit polisson de Napoleon!* have I found thee at last? Now then, Sir—two tight double knots each way with your honorable permission, and the money's safe. Feel it!

14 feel it, fortunate sir! hard and round as a cannonball—*Ah, bah!* if they had only fired such cannonballs at us at Austerlitz—*nom d'une pipe!* if they only had! And now, as an ancient grenadier, as an ex-brave of the French army, what remains for me to do? I ask what? Simply this, to entreat my valued English friend to drink a bottle of champagne with me, and toast the goddess Fortune in foaming goblets before we part!"

Excellent ex-brave! Convivial ancient grenadier! Champagne by all means! An English cheer for an old soldier! Hurrah! hurrah! Another English cheer for the goddess Fortune! Hurrah! hurrah! hurrah!

"Bravo! the Englishman; the amiable, gracious Englishman, in whose veins circulates the vivacious blood of France! Another glass? *Ah, bah!*—the bottle is empty! Never mind! *Vive le vin!* I, the old soldier, order another bottle, and half a pound of *bonbons* with it!"

"No, no, ex-brave; never—ancient grenadier! *Your* bottle last time; *my* bottle this. Behold it! Toast away! The French Army! the great Napoleon! the present company! the croupier! the honest croupier's wife and daughters—if he has any! the Ladies generally! everybody in the world!"

By the time the second bottle of champagne was emptied, I felt as it I had been drinking liquid fire—my brain seemed all aflame. No excess in wine had ever had this effect on me before in my life. Was it the result of a stimulant acting upon my system when I was in a highly excited state? Was my stomach in a particularly disordered condition? Or was the champagne amazingly strong?

"Ex-brave of the French Army!" cried I, in a mad state of exhilaration, "*I* am on fire! how are *you?* You have set

me on fire. Do you hear, my hero of Austerlitz? Let us
have a third bottle of champagne to put the flame out!"

The old soldier wagged his head, rolled his goggle-
eyes, until I expected to see them slip out of their sockets,
placed his dirty forefinger by the side of his broken nose;
solemnly ejaculated "Coffee!" and immediately ran off
into an inner room.

The word pronounced by the eccentric veteran seemed
to have a magical effect on the rest of the company present. With one accord they all rose to depart. Probably
they had expected to profit by my intoxication; but finding that my new friend was benevolently bent on preventing me from getting dead drunk, had now abandoned
all hope of thriving pleasantly on my winnings. Whatever
their motive might be, at any rate they went away in a
body. When the old soldier returned, and sat down again
opposite to me at the table, we had the room to ourselves. I could see the croupier in a sort of vestibule
which opened out of it, eating his supper in solitude. The
silence was now deeper than ever.

A sudden change, too, had come over the "ex-brave."
He assumed a portentously solemn look; and when he
spoke to me again, his speech was ornamented by no
oaths, enforced by no finger-snapping, enlivened by no
apostrophes or exclamations.

"Listen, my dear sir," said he, in mysteriously confidential tones—"listen to an old soldier's advice. I have
been to the mistress of the house (a very charming
woman, with a genius for cookery!) to impress on her the
necessity of making us some particularly strong and good
coffee. You must drink this coffee in order to get rid of
your little amiable exaltation of spirits before you think

16   of going home—you *must,* my good and gracious friend! With all that money to take home tonight, it is a sacred duty to yourself to have your wits about you. You are known to be a winner to an enormous extent by several gentlemen present tonight, who, in a certain point of view, are very worthy and excellent fellows; but they are mortal men, my dear sir, and they have their amiable weaknesses. Need I say more? Ah, no, no! you understand me! Now, this is what you must do—send for a cabriolet when you feel quite well again—draw up all the windows when you get into it—and tell the driver to take you home only through the large and well-lighted thoroughfares. Do this; and you and your money will be safe. Do this; and tomorrow you will thank an old soldier for giving you a word of honest advice."

Just as the ex-brave ended his oration in very lachrymose tones, the coffee came in, ready poured out in two cups. My attentive friend handed me one of the cups with a bow. I was parched with thirst, and drank it off at a draught. Almost instantly afterward, I was seized with a fit of giddiness, and felt more completely intoxicated than ever. The room whirled round and round furiously; the old soldier seemed to be regularly bobbing up and down before me like a piston of a steam engine. I was half deafened by a violent singing in my ears; a feeling of utter bewilderment, helplessness, idiocy, overcame me. I rose from my chair, holding on by the table to keep my balance; and stammered out that I felt dreadfully unwell—so unwell that I did not know how I was to get home.

"My dear friend," answered the old soldier—and even his voice seemed to be bobbing up and down as he spoke—"my dear friend, it would be madness to go home in *your* state; you would be sure to lose your money; you might be robbed and murdered with the greatest ease. *I* am going to sleep here; do *you* sleep here, too—they make up capital beds in this house—take one; sleep off the effects of the wine, and go home safely with your winnings tomorrow—tomorrow, in broad daylight."

I had but two ideas left: one, that I must never let go hold of my handkerchief full of money; the other, that I must lie down somewhere immediately, and fall off into a comfortable sleep. So I agreed to the proposal about the bed, and took the offered arm of the old soldier, carrying my money with my disengaged hand. Preceded by the croupier, we passed along some passages and up a flight of stairs into the bedroom which I was to occupy. The ex-brave shook me warmly by the hand, proposed that we should breakfast together, and then, followed by the croupier, left me for the night.

I ran to the wash-hand stand; drank some of the water in my jug; poured the rest out, and plunged my face into it; then sat down in a chair and tried to compose myself. I soon felt better. The change for my lungs, from the fetid atmosphere of the gambling room to the cool air of the apartment I now occupied, the almost equally refreshing change for my eyes, from the glaring gaslights of the "salon" to the dim, quiet flicker of one bedroom candle, aided wonderfully the restorative effects of cold water. The giddiness left me, and I began to feel a little like a reasonable being again. My first thought was of the risk of sleeping all night in a gambling house; my second, of the still greater risk of trying to get out after the house was

18 closed, and of going home alone at night through the
streets of Paris with a large sum of money about me. I
had slept in worse places than this on my travels; so I determined to lock, bolt, and barricade my door, and take
my chance till the next morning.

Accordingly, I secured myself against all intrusion;
looked under the bed, and into the cupboard; tried the
fastening of the window; and then, satisfied that I had
taken every proper precaution, pulled off my upper
clothing, put my light, which was a dim one, on the
hearth among a feathery litter of wood ashes, and got
into bed, with the handkerchief full of money under my
pillow.

I soon felt not only that I could not go to sleep, but
that I could not even close my eyes. I was wide awake,
and in a high fever. Every nerve in my body trembled—
every one of my senses seemed to be preternaturally
sharpened. I tossed and rolled, and tried every kind of position, and perseveringly sought out the cold corners of
the bed, and all to no purpose. Now I thrust my arms
over the clothes; now I poked them under the clothes;
now I violently shot my legs straight out down to the bottom of the bed; now I convulsively coiled them up as
near my chin as they would go; now I shook out my
crumpled pillow, changed it to the cool side, patted it
flat, and lay down quietly on my back; now I fiercely
doubled it in two, set it up on end, thrust it against the
board of the bed, and tried a sitting posture. Every effort
was in vain; I groaned with vexation as I felt that I was in
for a sleepness night.

What could I do? I had no book to read. And yet, unless I found out some method of diverting my mind, I felt

certain that I was in the condition to imagine all sorts of horrors; to rack my brain with forebodings of every possible and impossible danger; in short, to pass the night in suffering all conceivable varieties of nervous terror.

I raised myself on my elbow, and looked about the room—which was brightened by a lovely moonlight pouring straight through the window—to see if it contained any pictures or ornaments that I could at all clearly distinguish. While my eyes wandered from wall to wall, a remembrance of Le Maistre's delightful little book, *Voyage autour de ma Chambre*, occurred to me. I resolved to imitate the French author, and find occupation and amusement enough to relieve the tedium of my wakefulness, by making a mental inventory of every article of furniture I could see, and by following up to their sources the multitude of associations which even a chair, a table, or a wash-hand stand may be made to call forth.

In the nervous unsettled state of my mind at that moment, I found it much easier to make my inventory than to make my reflections, and thereupon soon gave up all hope of thinking in Le Maistre's fanciful track—or, indeed, of thinking at all. I looked about the room at the different articles of furniture, and did nothing more.

There was, first, the bed I was lying in; a four-post bed, of all things in the world to meet with in Paris—yes, a thorough clumsy British four-poster, with a regular top lined with chintz—the regular fringed valance all round—the regular stifling, unwholesome curtains, which I remembered having mechanically drawn back against the posts without particularly noticing the bed when I first got into the room. Then there was the marble-topped, wash-hand stand, from which the water I had spilled, in

20 my hurry to pour it out, was still dripping, slowly and more slowly, onto the brick floor. Then two small chairs, with my coat, waistcoat, and trousers flung on them. Then a large elbow chair covered with dirty-white dimity, and my cravat and shirt collar thrown over the back. Then a chest of drawers with two of the brass handles off, and a tawdry, broken china inkstand placed on it by way of ornament for the top. Then the dressing table, adorned by a very small looking glass, and a very large pincushion. Then the window—an unusually large window. Then a dark old picture, which the feeble candle dimly showed me. It was a picture of a fellow in high Spanish hat, crowned with a plume of towering feathers. A swarthy, sinister ruffian, looking upward, shading his eyes with his hand, and looking intently upward—it might be at some tall gallows at which he was going to be hanged. At any rate, he had the appearance of thoroughly deserving it.

This picture put a kind of constraint upon me to look upward too—at the top of the bed. It was a gloomy and not an interesting object, and I looked back at the picture. I counted the feathers in the man's hat—they stood out in relief—three white, two green. I observed the crown of his hat, which was of conical shape, according to the fashion supposed to have been favored by Guido Fawkes. I wondered what he was looking up at. It couldn't be at the stars; such a desperado was neither astrologer nor astronomer. It must be at the high gallows, and he was going to be hanged presently. Would the executioner come into possession of his conical crowned hat and plume of feathers? I counted the feathers again—

three white, two green.

While I still lingered over this very improving and intellectual employment, my thoughts insensibly began to wander. The moonlight shining into the room reminded me of a certain moonlight night in England—the night after a picnic party in a Welsh valley. Every incident of the drive homeward, through lovely scenery, which the moonlight made lovelier than ever, came back to my remembrance, though I had never given the picnic a thought for years; though, if I had *tried* to recollect it, I could certainly have recalled little or nothing of that scene long past. Of all the wonderful faculties that help to tell us we are immortal, which speaks the sublime truth more eloquently than memory? Here was I, in a strange house of the most suspicious character, in a situation of uncertainty, and even of peril, which might seem to make the cool exercise of my recollection almost out of the question; nevertheless, remembering, quite involuntarily, places, people, conversations, minute circumstances of every kind, which I had thought forgotten for ever; which I could not possibly have recalled at will, even under the most favorable auspices. And what cause had produced in a moment the whole of this strange, complicated, mysterious effect? Nothing but some rays of moonlight shining in at my bedroom window.

I was still thinking of the picnic—of our merriment on the drive home—of the sentimental young lady who *would* quote "Childe Harold" because it was moonlight. I was absorbed by these past scenes and past amusement, when, in an instant, the thread on which my memories hung snapped asunder: my attention immediately came

22 back to present things more vividly than ever, and I found myself, I neither knew why nor wherefore, looking hard at the picture again.

Looking for what?

Good God! the man had pulled his hat down on his brows! No! the hat itself was gone! Where was the conical crown? Where the feathers—three white, two green? Not there! In place of the hat and feathers, what dusky object was it that now hid his forehead, his eyes, his shading hand?

Was the bed moving?

I turned on my back and looked up. Was I mad? drunk? dreaming? giddy again? or was the top of the bed really moving down—sinking slowly, regularly, silently, horribly, right down throughout the whole of its length and breadth—right down upon me, as I lay underneath?

My blood seemed to stand still. A deadly paralyzing coldness stole all over me as I turned my head round on the pillow and determined to test whether the bed top was really moving or not, by keeping my eye on the man in the picture.

The next look in that direction was enough. The dull, black, frowzy outline of the valance above me was within an inch of being parallel with his waist. I still looked breathlessly. And steadily and slowly—very slowly—I saw the figure, and the line of frame below the figure, vanish, as the valance moved down before it.

I am, constitutionally, anything but timid. I have been on more than one occasion in peril of my life, and have not lost my self-possession for an instant; but when the conviction first settled on my mind that the bed top was really moving, was steadily and continously sinking down upon me, I looked up shuddering, helpless, panic-stricken, beneath the hideous machinery for murder, which was advancing closer and closer to suffocate me where I lay.

I looked up motionless, speechless, breathless. The candle, fully spent, went out; but the moonlight still brightened the room. Down and down, without pausing and without sounding, came the bed top, and still my panic terror seemed to bind me faster and faster to the mattress on which I lay—down and down it sank, till the dusty odor from the lining of the canopy came stealing into my nostrils.

At that final moment the instinct of self-preservation startled me out of my trance, and I moved at last. There was just room for me to roll myself sidewise off the bed. As I dropped noiselessly to the floor, the edge of the murderous canopy touched me on the shoulder.

Without stopping to draw my breath, without wiping the cold sweat from my face, I rose instantly on my knees to watch the bed top. I was literally spellbound by it. If I had heard footsteps behind me, I could not have turned round; if a means of escape had been miraculously provided for me, I could not have moved to take advantage of it. The whole life in me was, at that moment, concentrated in my eyes.

It descended—the whole canopy, with the fringe round it, came down—down—close down; so close that there was not room now to squeeze my finger between the bed top and the bed. I felt at the sides, and discovered that what had appeared to me from beneath to be the ordinary light canopy of a four-post bed was in reality a thick, broad mattress, the substance of which was con-

24   cealed by the valance and its fringe. I looked up and saw the four posts rising hideously bare. In the middle of the bed top was a huge wooden screw that had evidently worked it down through a hole in the ceiling, just as ordinary presses are worked down on the substance selected for compression. The frightful apparatus moved without making the faintest noise. There had been no creaking as it came down; there was now not the faintest sound from the room above. Amid a dead and awful silence I beheld before me—in the nineteenth century, and in the civilized capital of France—such a machine for secret murder by suffocation as might have existed in the worst days of the Inquisition, in the lonely inns among the Hartz Mountains, in the mysterious tribunals of Westphalia! Still, as I looked on it, I could not move, I could hardly breathe, but I began to recover the power of thinking, and in a moment I discovered the murderous conspiracy framed against me in all its horror.

My cup of coffee had been drugged, and drugged too strongly. I had been saved from being smothered by having taken an overdose of some narcotic. How I had chafed and fretted at the fever fit which had preserved my life by keeping me awake! How recklessly I had confided myself to the two wretches who had led me into this room, determined, for the sake of my winnings, to kill me in my sleep by the surest and most horrible contrivance for secretly accomplishing my destruction! How many men, winners like me, had slept, as I had proposed to sleep, in that bed, and had never been seen or heard of more! I shuddered at the bare idea of it.

But ere long all thought was again suspended by the sight of the murderous canopy moving once more. After it had remained on the bed—as nearly as I could guess—about ten minutes, it began to move up again. The villains who worked it from above evidently believed that their purpose was now accomplished. Slowly and silently, as it had descended, that horrible bed top rose towards its former place. When it reached the upper extremities of the four posts, it reached the ceiling, too. Neither hole nor screw could be seen; the bed became in appearance an ordinary bed again—the canopy an ordinary canopy—even to the most suspicious eyes.

Now, for the first time, I was able to move—to rise from my knees—to dress myself in my upper clothing—and to consider of how I should escape. If I betrayed by the smallest noise that the attempt to suffocate me had failed, I was certain to be murdered. Had I made any noise already? I listened intently, looking towards the door.

No! no footsteps in the passage outside—no sound of a tread, light or heavy, in the room above—absolute silence everywhere. Besides locking and bolting my door, I had moved an only wooden chest against it, which I had found under the bed. To remove this chest (my blood ran cold as I thought of what its contents *might* be!) without making some disturbance was impossible; and, moreover, to think of escaping through the house, now barred up for the night, was sheer insanity. Only one chance was left me—the window. I stole to it on tiptoe.

My bedroom was on the first floor, above an *entresol,* and looked into a back street. I raised my hand to open the window, knowing that on that action hung, by the merest hairbreadth, my chance of safety. They keep vigilant watch in a House of Murder. If any part of the frame

26 cracked, if the hinge creaked, I was a lost man! It must have occupied me at least five minutes, reckoning by time—five *hours*, reckoning by suspense—to open that window. I succeeded in doing it silently—in doing it with all the dexterity of a housebreaker—and then looked down into the street. To leap the distance beneath me would be almost certain destruction! Next, I looked round at the sides of the house. Down the left side ran a thick water pipe—it passed close by the outer edge of the window. The moment I saw the pipe I knew I was saved. My breath came and went freely for the first time since I had seen the canopy of the bed moving down upon me!

To some men the means of escape which I had discovered might have seemed difficult and dangerous enough—to *me* the prospect of slipping down the pipe into the street did not suggest even a thought of peril. I had always been accustomed, by the practice of gymnastics, to keep up my schoolboy powers as a daring and expert climber; and knew that my head, hands, and feet would serve me faithfully in any hazards of ascent or descent. I had already got one leg over the windowsill, when I remembered the handkerchief filled with money under my pillow. I could well have afforded to leave it behind me, but I was revengefully determined that the miscreants of the gambling house should miss their plunder as well as their victim. So I went back to the bed and tied the heavy handkerchief at my back by my cravat.

Just as I had made it tight and fixed it in a comfortable place, I thought I heard a sound of breathing outside the door. The chill feeling of horror ran through me again as I listened. No! dead silence still in the passage—I had only heard the night air blowing softly into the room. The next moment I was on the windowsill—and the next I had a firm grip on the water pipe with my hands and knees.

I slid down into the street easily and quietly, as I thought I should, and immediately set off at the top of my speed to a branch Prefecture of Police, which I knew was situated in the immediate neighborhood. A Sub-prefect, and several picked men among his subordinates, happened to be up, maturing, I believe, some scheme for discovering the perpetrator of a mysterious murder which all Paris was talking of just then. When I began my story, in a breathless hurry and in very bad French, I could see that the Sub-prefect suspected me of being a drunken Englishman who had robbed somebody; but he soon altered his opinion as I went on, and before I had anything like concluded, he shoved all the papers before him into a drawer, put on his hat, supplied me with another (for I was bare-headed), ordered a file of soldiers, desired his expert followers to get ready all sorts of tools for breaking open doors and ripping up brick flooring, and took my arm, in the most friendly and familiar manner possible, to lead me with him out of the house. I will venture to say that when the Sub-prefect was a little boy, and was taken for the first time to the play, he was not half as much pleased as he was now at the job in prospect for him at the gambling house!

Away we went through the streets, the Sub-prefect cross-examining and congratulating me in the same breath as we marched at the head of our formidable *posse comitatus*. Sentinels were placed at the back and front of the house the moment we got to it; a tremendous battery

28 of knocks was directed against the door; a light appeared at a window; I was told to conceal myself behind the police—then came more knocks and a cry of "Open in the name of the law!" At that terrible summons bolts and locks gave way before an invisible hand, and the moment after the Sub-prefect was in the passage, confronting a waiter half dressed and ghastly pale. This was the short dialogue which immediately took place:

"We want to see the Englishman who is sleeping in this house."

"He went away hours ago."

"He did no such thing. His friend went away; *he* remained. Show us to his bedroom!"

"I swear to you, Monsieur le Sous-prefect, he is not here! he—"

"I swear to you, Monsieur le Garçon, he is. He slept here—he didn't find your bed comfortable—he came to us to complain of it—here he is among my men—and here am I ready to look for a flea or two in his bedstead. Renaudin!"—calling to one of the subordinates, and pointing to the waiter—"collar that man and tie his hands behind him. Now, then, gentlemen, let us walk upstairs!"

Every man and woman in the house was secured—the "Old Soldier" the first. Then I identified the bed in which I had slept, and then we went into the room above.

No object that was at all extraordinary appeared in any part of it. The Sub-prefect looked round the place, commanded everybody to be silent, stamped twice on the floor, called for a candle, looked attentively at the spot he had stamped on, and ordered the flooring there to be carefully taken up. This was done in no time. Lights were produced, and we saw a deep raftered cavity between the floor of this room and the ceiling of the room beneath. Through this cavity there ran perpendicularly a sort of case of iron thickly greased; and inside the case appeared the screw, which communicated with the bed top below. Extra lengths of screw, freshly oiled; levers covered with felt; all the complete upper works of a heavy press—constructed with infernal ingenuity so as to join the fixtures below, and when taken to pieces again, to go into the smallest possible compass—were next discovered and pulled out on the floor. After some little difficulty the Sub-prefect succeeded in putting the machinery together, and, leaving his men to work it, descended with me to the bedroom. The smothering canopy was then lowered, but not so noiselessly as I had seen it lowered. When I mentioned this to the Sub-prefect, his answer, simple as it was, had a terrible significance. "My men," said he, "are working down the bed top for the first time—the men whose money you won were in better practice."

We left the house in the sole possession of two police agents—every one of the inmates being removed to prison on the spot. The Sub-prefect, after taking down my *procès verbal* in his office, returned with me to my hotel to get my passport. "Do you think," I asked, as I gave it to him, "that any men have really been smothered in that bed, as they tried to smother *me?*"

"I have seen dozens of drowned men laid out at the Morgue," answered the Sub-prefect, "in whose pocketbooks were found letters stating that they had committed suicide in the Seine, because they had lost everything at the gaming table. Do I know how many of those men entered the same gambling house that *you* entered?

30 won as *you* won? took that bed as *you* took it? slept in it? were smothered in it? and were privately thrown into the river, with a letter of explanation written by the murderers and placed in their pocketbooks? No man can say how many or how few have suffered the fate from which you have escaped. The people of the gambling house kept their bedstead machinery a secret from *us*—even from the police! The dead kept the rest of the secret for them. Good night, or rather good morning, Monsieur Faulkner! Be at my office again at nine o'clock—in the meantime, *au revoir!*"

The rest of my story is soon told. I was examined and re-examined; the gambling house was strictly searched all through from top to bottom; the prisoners were separately interrogated; and two of the less guilty among them made a confession. I discovered that the Old Soldier was the master of the gambling house—*justice* discovered that he had been drummed out of the army as a vagabond years ago; that he had been guilty of all sorts of villainies since; that he was in possession of stolen property, which the owners identified; and that he, the croupier, another accomplice, and the woman who had made my cup of coffee, were all in the secret of the bedstead. There appeared some reason to doubt whether the inferior persons attached to the house knew anything of the suffocating machinery; and they received the benefit of that doubt, by being treated simply as thieves and vagabonds. As for the Old Soldier and his two head myrmidons, they went to the galleys; the woman who had drugged my coffee was imprisoned for I forget how many years; the regular attendants at the gambling house were considered "suspicious" and placed under "surveillance"; and I became, for one whole week (which is a long time) the head "lion" in Parisian society. My adventure was dramatized by three illustrious playmakers, but never saw theatrical daylight; for the censorship forbade the introduction on the stage of a correct copy of the gambling house bedstead.

One good result was produced by my adventure, which any censorship must have approved: it cured me of ever again trying *Rouge et Noir* as an amusement. The sight of a green cloth, with packs of cards and heaps of money on it, will henceforth be forever associated in my mind with the sight of a bed canopy descending to suffocate me in the silence and darkness of the night.

The lady did not move, and the guard stepped into the carriage, thinking that perhaps the lady was asleep. He touched her arm lightly and looked into her face. . . .

THE MYSTERIOUS DEATH ON THE UNDERGROUND RAILWAY

Baroness Orczy

It was all very well for Mr. Richard Frobisher (of the London Mail) to cut up rough about it. Polly did not altogether blame him.

She liked him all the better for that frank outburst of manlike ill temper which, after all said and done, was only a very flattering form of masculine jealousy.

Moreover, Polly distinctly felt guilty about the whole thing. She had promised to meet Dickie—that is Mr. Richard Frobisher—at two o'clock sharp outside the Palace Theatre, because she wanted to go to a Maud Allan matinee, and because he naturally wished to go with her.

But at two o'clock sharp she was still in Norfolk Street, Strand, inside an A.B.C. shop, sipping cold coffee opposite a grotesque old man who was fiddling with a bit of string.

How could she be expected to remember Maud Allan or the Palace Theatre, or Dickie himself for a matter of that? The man in the corner had begun to talk of that mysterious death on the Underground Railway, and Polly had lost count of time, of place, and circumstance.

She had gone to lunch quite early, for she was looking

forward to the matinee at the Palace.

The old scarecrow was sitting in his accustomed place when she came into the A.B.C. shop, but he had made no remark all the time that the young girl was munching her scone and butter. She was just busy thinking how rude he was not even to have said "Good morning," when an abrupt remark from him caused her to look up.

"Will you be good enough," he said suddenly, "to give me a description of the man who sat next to you just now, while you were having your cup of coffee and scone."

Involuntarily Polly turned her head towards the distant door, through which a man in a light overcoat was even now quickly passing. That man had certainly sat at the next table to hers, when she first sat down to her coffee and scone; he had finished his luncheon—whatever it was—a moment ago, had paid at the desk and gone out. The incident did not appear to Polly as being of the slightest consequence.

Therefore she did not reply to the rude old man, but shrugged her shoulders, and called to the waitress to bring her bill.

"Do you know if he was tall or short, dark or fair?" continued the man in the corner, seemingly not the least disconcerted by the young girl's indifference. "Can you tell me at all what he was like?"

"Of course I can," rejoined Polly impatiently, "but I don't see that my description of one of the customers of an A.B.C. shop can have the slightest importance."

He was silent for a minute, while his nervous fingers fumbled about in his capacious pockets in search of the inevitable piece of string. When he had found this necessary "adjunct to thought," he viewed the young girl again

34 through his half-closed lids, and added maliciously:

"But supposing it were of paramount importance that you should give an accurate description of a man who sat next to you for half an hour today, how would you proceed?"

"I should say that he was of medium height—"

"Five foot eight, nine, or ten?" he interrupted quietly.

"How can one tell to an inch of two?" rejoined Polly crossly. "He was between colors."

"What's that?" he inquired blandly.

"Neither fair nor dark—his nose—"

"Well, what was his nose like? Will you sketch it?"

"I am not an artist. His nose was fairly straight—his eyes—"

"Were neither dark nor light—his hair had the same striking peculiarity—he was neither short nor tall—his nose was neither aquiline nor snub—" he recapitulated sarcastically.

"No," she retorted; "he was just ordinary looking."

"Would you know him again—say tomorrow, and among a number of other men who were 'neither tall nor short, dark nor fair, aquiline nor snub-nosed,' etc.?"

"I don't know—I might—he was certainly not striking enough to be specially remembered."

"Exactly," he said, while he leant forward excitedly, for all the world like a jack-in-the-box let loose. "Precisely; and you are a journalist—call yourself one, at least—and it should be part of your business to notice and describe people. I don't mean only the wonderful personage with the clear Saxon features, the fine blue eyes, the noble brow and classic face, but the ordinary person— the person who represents ninety out of every hundred of his own kind—the average Englishman, say, of the middle classes, who is neither very tall nor very short, who wears a mustache which is neither fair nor dark, but which masks his mouth, and a top hat which hides the shape of his head and brow, a man, in fact, who dresses like hundreds of his fellow creatures, moves like them, speaks like them, has no peculiarity.

"Try to describe *him*, to recognize him, say a week hence, among his other eighty-nine doubles; worse still, to swear his life away, if he happened to be implicated in some crime, wherein *your* recognition of him would place the halter round his neck.

"Try that, I say, and having utterly failed you will more readily understand how one of the greatest scoundrels unhung is still at large, and why the mystery on the Underground Railway was never cleared up.

"I think it was the only time in my life that I was seriously tempted to give the police the benefit of my own views upon the matter. You see, though I admire the brute for his cleverness, I did not see that his being unpunished could possibly benefit anyone.

"In these days of tubes and motor traction of all kinds, the old-fashioned 'best, cheapest, and quickest route to City and West End' is often deserted, and the good old Metropolitan Railway carriages cannot at any time be said to be overcrowded. Anyway, when that particular train steamed into Aldgate at about 4 p.m. on March 18th last, the first-class carriages were all but empty.

"The guard marched up and down the platform looking into all the carriages to see if anyone had left a halfpenny evening paper behind for him, and opening the door of one of the first-class compartments, he noticed a

36 lady sitting in the further corner, with her head turned
away towards the window, evidently oblivious of the fact
that on this line Aldgate is the terminal station.

" 'Where are you for, lady?' he said.

"The lady did not move, and the guard stepped into
the carriage, thinking that perhaps the lady was asleep.
He touched her arm lightly and looked into her face. In
his own poetic language, he was 'struck all of a 'eap.' In
the glassy eyes, the ashen color of the cheeks, the rigidity
of the head, there was the unmistakable look of death.

"Hastily the guard, having carefully locked the carriage door, summoned a couple of porters, and sent one
of them off to the police station, and the other in search
of the stationmaster.

"Fortunately at this time of day the up platform is not
very crowded, all the traffic tending westward in the afternoon. It was only when an inspector and two police
constables, accompanied by a detective in plain clothes
and a medical officer, appeared upon the scene, and stood
round a first-class railway compartment, that a few idlers
realized that something unusual had occurred, and
crowded round, eager and curious.

"Thus it was that the later editions of the evening papers, under the sensational heading, 'Mysterious Suicide
on the Underground Railway,' had already an account of
the extraordinary event. The medical officer had very
soon come to the decision that the guard had not been
mistaken, and that life was indeed extinct.

"The lady was young, and must have been very pretty before the look of fright and horror had so terribly
distorted her features. She was very elegantly dressed,
and the more frivolous papers were able to give their

feminine readers a detailed account of the unfortunate woman's gown, her shoes, hat and gloves.

"It appears that one of the latter, the one on the right hand, was partly off, leaving the thumb and wrist bare. That hand held a small satchel, which the police opened, with a view to the possible identification of the deceased, but which was found to contain only a little loose silver, some smelling salts, and a small empty bottle, which was handed over to the medical officer for purposes of analysis.

"It was the presence of that small bottle which had caused the report to circulate freely that the mysterious case on the Underground Railway was one of suicide. Certain it was that neither about the lady's person, nor in the appearance of the railway carriage, was there the slightest sign of struggle or even of resistance. Only the look in the poor woman's eyes spoke of sudden terror, of the rapid vision of an unexpected and violent death, which probably only lasted an infinitesimal fraction of a second, but which had left its indelible mark upon the face, otherwise so placid and so still.

"The body of the deceased was conveyed to the mortuary. So far, of course, not a soul had been able to identify her, or to throw the slightest light upon the mystery which hung around her death.

"Against that, quite a crowd of idlers—genuinely interested or not—obtained admission to view the body, on the pretext of having lost or mislaid a relative or a friend. At about 8:30 p.m. a young man, very well dressed, drove up to the station in a hansom, and sent in his card to the superintendent. It was Mr. Hazeldene, shipping agent, of 11 Crown Lane, E.C., and No. 19 Addison Row, Kensington.

"The young man looked in a pitiable state of mental

distress; his hand clutched nervously a copy of the St. James's Gazette, which contained the fatal news. He said very little to the superintendent except that a person who was very dear to him had not returned home that evening.

"He had not felt really anxious until half an hour ago, when suddenly he thought of looking at his paper. The description of the deceased lady, though vague, had terribly alarmed him. He had jumped into a hansom, and now begged permission to view the body, in order that his worst fears might be allayed.

"You know what followed, of course," continued the man in the corner. "The grief of the young man was truly pitiable. In the woman lying there in a public mortuary before him, Mr. Hazeldene had recognized his wife.

"I am waxing melodramatic," said the man in the corner, who looked up at Polly with a mild and gentle smile, while his nervous fingers vainly endeavored to add another knot on the scrappy bit of string with which he was continually playing, "and I fear that the whole story savors of the penny novelette, but you must admit, and no doubt you remember, that it was an intensely pathetic and truly dramatic moment.

"The unfortunate young husband of the deceased lady was not much worried with questions that night. As a matter of fact, he was not in a fit condition to make any coherent statement. It was at the coroner's inquest on the following day that certain facts came to light, which for the time being seemed to clear up the mystery surrounding Mrs. Hazeldene's death, only to plunge that same mystery, later on, into denser gloom than before.

"The first witness at the inquest was, of course, Mr. Hazeldene himself. I think everyone's sympathy went out to the young man as he stood before the coroner and tried to throw what light he could upon the mystery. He was well dressed, as he had been the day before, but he looked terribly ill and worried, and no doubt the fact that he had not shaved gave his face a careworn and neglected air.

"It appears that he and the deceased had been married some six years or so, and that they had always been happy in their married life. They had no children. Mrs. Hazeldene seemed to enjoy the best of health till lately, when she had had a slight attack of influenza, in which Dr. Arthur Jones had attended her. The doctor was present at this moment, and would no doubt explain to the coroner and the jury whether he thought that Mrs. Hazeldene had the slightest tendency to heart disease, which might have had a sudden and fatal ending.

"The coroner was, of course, very considerate to the bereaved husband. He tried by circumlocution to get at the point he wanted, namely, Mrs. Hazeldene's mental condition lately. Mr. Hazeldene seemed loath to talk about this. No doubt he had been warned as to the existence of the small bottle found in his wife's satchel.

" 'It certainly did seem to me at times,' he at last reluctantly admitted, 'that my wife did not seem quite herself. She used to be very gay and bright, and lately I often saw her in the evening sitting as if brooding over some matters which evidently she did not care to communicate to me.'

"Still the coroner insisted, and suggested the small bottle.

" 'I know, I know,' replied the young man, with a short, heavy sigh. 'You mean—the question of suicide—I

40 cannot understand it at all—it seems so sudden and so terrible—she certainly had seemed listless and troubled
lately—but only at times—and yesterday morning, when I
went to business, she appeared quite herself again, and I
suggested that we should go to the opera in the evening.
She was delighted, I know, and told me she would do
some shopping, and pay a few calls in the afternoon.'

" 'Do you know at all where she intended to go when
she got into the Underground Railway?'

" 'Well, not with certainty. You see, she may have
meant to get out at Baker Street, and go down to Bond
Street to do her shopping. Then, again, she sometimes
goes to a shop in St. Paul's Churchyard, in which case she
would take a ticket to Aldersgate Street; but I cannot
say.'

" 'Now, Mr. Hazeldene,' said the coroner at last very
kindly, 'will you try to tell me if there was anything in
Mrs. Hazeldene's life which you know of, and which
might in some measure explain the cause of the distressed
state of mind, which you yourself had noticed? Did there
exist any financial difficulty which might have preyed
upon Mrs. Hazeldene's mind; was there any friend—to
whose intercourse with Mrs. Hazeldene—you—er—at any
time took exception? In fact,' added the coroner, as if
thankful that he had got over an unpleasant moment,
'can you give me the slightest indication which would
tend to confirm the suspicion that the unfortunate lady,
in a moment of mental anxiety or derangement, may
have wished to take her own life?'

"There was silence in the court for a few moments. Mr.
Hazeldene seemed to everyone there present to be labor-
ing under some terrible moral doubt. He looked very pale

and wretched, and twice attempted to speak before he at last said in scarcely audible tones:

" 'No; there were no financial difficulties of any sort. My wife had an independent fortune of her own—she had no extravagant tastes—'

" 'Nor any friend you at any time objected to?' insisted the coroner.

" 'Nor any friend, I—at any time objected to,' stammered the unfortunate young man, evidently speaking with an effort.

"I was present at the inquest," resumed the man in the corner, after he had drunk a glass of milk and ordered another, "and I can assure you that the most obtuse person there plainly realized that Mr. Hazeldene was telling a lie. It was pretty plain to the meanest intelligence that the unfortunate lady had not fallen into a state of morbid dejection for nothing, and that perhaps there existed a third person who could throw more light on her strange and sudden death than the unhappy, bereaved young widower.

"That the death was more mysterious even than it had at first appeared became very soon apparent. You read the case at the time, no doubt, and must remember the excitement in the public mind caused by the evidence of the two doctors. Dr. Arthur Jones, the lady's usual medical man, who had attended her in a last very slight illness, and who had seen her in a professional capacity fairly recently, declared most emphatically that Mrs. Hazeldene suffered from no organic complaint which could possibly have been the cause of sudden death. Moreover, he had assisted Mr. Andrew Thornton, the district medical officer, in making a postmortem examination, and together

42 they had come to the conclusion that death was due to the action of prussic acid, which had caused instantaneous failure of the heart, but how the drug had been administered neither he nor his colleague were at present able to state.

" 'Do I understand, then, Dr. Jones, that the deceased died, poisoned with prussic acid?'

" 'Such is my opinion,' replied the doctor.

" 'Did the bottle found in her satchel contain prussic acid?'

" 'It had contained some at one time, certainly.'

" 'In your opinion, then, the lady caused her own death by taking a dose of that drug?'

" 'Pardon me, I never suggested such a thing: the lady died poisoned by the drug, but how the drug was administered we cannot say. By injection of some sort, certainly. The drug certainly was not swallowed; there was not a vestige of it in the stomach.'

" 'Yes,' added the doctor in reply to another question from the coroner, 'death had probably followed the injection in this case almost immediately; say within a couple of minutes, or perhaps three. It was quite possible that the body would not have more than one quick and sudden convulsion, perhaps not that; death in such cases is absolutely sudden and crushing.'

"I don't think that at the time anyone in the room realized how important the doctor's statement was, a statement, which, by the way, was confirmed in all its details by the district medical officer, who had conducted the postmortem. Mrs. Hazeldene had died suddenly from an injection of prussic acid, administered no one knew how or when. She had been traveling in a first-class railway carriage in a busy time of the day. That young and elegant woman must have had singular nerve and coolness to go through the process of a self-inflicted injection of a deadly poison in the presence of perhaps two or three other persons.

"Mind you, when I say that no one there realized the importance of the doctor's statement at that moment, I am wrong; there were three persons, who fully understood at once the gravity of the situation, and the astounding development which the case was beginning to assume.

"Of course, I should have put myself out of the question," added the weird old man, with that inimitable self-conceit peculiar to himself. "I guessed then and there in a moment where the police were going wrong, and where they would go on going wrong until the mysterious death on the Underground Railway had sunk into oblivion, together with the other cases which they mismanage from time to time.

"I said there were three persons who understood the gravity of the two doctors' statements—the other two were, firstly, the detective who had originally examined the railway carriage, a young man of energy and plenty of misguided intelligence, the other was Mr. Hazeldene.

"At this point the interesting element of the whole story was first introduced into the proceedings, and this was done through the humble channel of Emma Funnel, Mrs. Hazeldene's maid, who, as far as was known then, was the last person who had seen the unfortunate lady alive and had spoken to her.

" 'Mrs. Hazeldene lunched at home,' explained Emma, who was shy, and spoke almost in a whisper; 'she seemed

44 well and cheerful. She went out at about half-past three, and told me she was going to Spence's, in St. Paul's Churchyard, to try on her new tailor-made gown. Mrs. Hazeldene had meant to go there in the morning, but was prevented as Mr. Errington called.'

" 'Mr. Errington?' asked the coroner casually. 'Who is Mr. Errington?'

"But this Emma found difficult to explain. Mr. Errington was—Mr. Errington, that's all.

" 'Mr. Errington was a friend of the family. He lived in a flat in the Albert Mansions. He very often came to Addison Row, and generally stayed late.'

"Pressed still further with questions, Emma at last stated that latterly Mrs. Hazeldene had been to the theater several times with Mr. Errington, and that on those nights the master looked very gloomy, and was very cross.

"Recalled, the young widower was strangely reticent. He gave forth his answers very grudgingly, and the coroner was evidently absolutely satisfied with himself at the marvelous way in which, after a quarter of an hour of firm yet very kind questionings, he had elicited from the witness what information he wanted.

"Mr. Errington was a friend of his wife. He was a gentleman of means, and seemed to have a great deal of time at his command. He himself did not particularly care about Mr. Errington, but he certainly had never made any observations to his wife on the subject.

" 'But who is Mr. Errington?' repeated the coroner once more. 'What does he do? What is his business or profession?'

" 'He has no business or profession.'

" 'What is his occupation, then?'

" 'He has no special occupation. He has ample private means. But he has a great and very absorbing hobby.'

" 'What is that?'

" 'He spends all his time in chemical experiments, and is, I believe, as an amateur, a very distinguished toxicologist.'

"Did you ever see Mr. Errington, the gentleman so closely connected with the mysterious death on the Underground Railway?" asked the man in the corner as he placed one or two of his little snapshot photos before Miss Polly Burton.

"There he is, to the very life. Fairly good-looking, a pleasant face enough, but ordinary, absolutely ordinary.

"It was this absence of any peculiarity which very nearly, but not quite, placed the halter round Mr. Errington's neck.

"But I am going too fast, and you will lose the thread. The public, of course, never heard how it actually came about that Mr. Errington, the wealthy bachelor of Albert Mansions, of the Grosvenor, and other young dandies' clubs, one fine day found himself before the magistrates at Bow Street, charged with being concerned in the death of Mary Beatrice Hazeldene, late of No. 19 Addison Row.

"I can assure you both press and public were literally flabbergasted. You see, Mr. Errington was a well-known and very popular member of a certain smart section of London society. He was a constant visitor at the opera, the racecourse, the Park, and the Carlton, he had a great many friends, and there was consequently quite a large attendance at the police court that morning. What had happened was this:

"After the very scrappy bits of evidence which came to light at the inquest, two gentlemen bethought themselves that perhaps they had some duty to perform towards the State and the public generally. Accordingly they had come forward offering to throw what light they could upon the mysterious affair on the Underground Railway.

"The police naturally felt that their information, such as it was, came rather late in the day, but as it proved of paramount importance, and the two gentlemen, moreover, were of undoubtedly good position in the world, they were thankful for what they could get, and acted accordingly; they accordingly brought Mr. Errington up before the magistrate on a charge of murder.

"The accused looked pale and worried when I first caught sight of him in the court that day, which was not to be wondered at, considering the terrible position in which he found himself. He had been arrested at Marseilles, where he was preparing to start for Colombo.

"I don't think he realized how terrible his position was until later in the proceedings, when all the evidence relating to the arrest had been heard, and Emma Funnel had repeated her statement as to Mr. Errington's call at 19 Addison Row, in the morning, and Mrs. Hazeldene starting off for St. Paul's Churchyard at 3:30 in the afternoon. Mr. Hazeldene had nothing to add to the statements he had made at the coroner's inquest. He had last seen his wife alive on the morning of the fatal day. She had seemed very well and cheerful.

"I think everyone present understood that he was trying to say as little as possible that could in any way couple his deceased wife's name with that of the accused.

"And yet, from the servant's evidence, it undoubtedly   **47**
leaked out that Mrs. Hazeldene, who was young, pretty,
and evidently fond of admiration, had once or twice an-
noyed her husband by her somewhat open, yet perfectly
innocent flirtation with Mr. Errington.

"I think everyone was most agreeably impressed by
the widower's moderate and dignified attitude. You will
see his photo there, among this bundle. That is just how
he appeared in court. In deep black, of course, but without any sign of ostentation in his mourning. He had allowed his beard to grow lately, and wore it closely cut in
a point.

"After his evidence, the sensation of the day occurred.
A tall, dark-haired man, with the word 'City' written
metaphorically all over him, had kissed the book, and was
waiting to tell the truth, and nothing but the truth.

"He gave his name as Andrew Campbell, head of the
firm of Campbell & Co., brokers, of Throgmorton Street.

"In the afternoon of March 18th Mr. Campbell, traveling on the Underground Railway, had noticed a very
pretty woman in the same carriage as himself. She had
asked him if she was in the right train for Aldersgate. Mr.
Campbell replied in the affirmative, and then buried himself in the Stock Exchange quotations of his evening
paper.

"At Gower Street, a gentleman in a tweed suit and
bowler hat got into the carriage, and took a seat opposite
the lady. She seemed very much astonished at seeing him,
but Mr. Campbell did not recollect the exact words she
said.

"The two talked to one another a good deal, and certainly the lady appeared animated and cheerful. Witness

48 took no notice of them; he was very much engrossed in some calculations, and finally got out at Farringdon Street. He noticed that the man in the tweed suit also got out close behind him, having shaken hands with the lady, and said in a pleasant way: '*Au revoir!* Don't be late tonight.' Mr. Campbell did not hear the lady's reply, and soon lost sight of the man in the crowd.

"Everyone was on tenterhooks, and eagerly waiting for the palpitating moment when witness would describe and identify the man who last had seen and spoken to the unfortunate woman, within five minutes probably of her strange and unaccountable death.

"Personally I knew what was coming before the Scotch stockbroker spoke. I could have jotted down the graphic and lifelike description he would give of a probable murderer. It would have fitted equally well the man who sat and had luncheon at this table just now; it would certainly have described five out of every ten young Englishmen you know.

"The individual was of medium height, he wore a mustache which was not very fair nor yet very dark, his hair was between colors. He wore a bowler hat, and a tweed suit—and—and—that was all—Mr. Campbell might perhaps know him again, but then again, he might not—he was not paying much attention—the gentleman was sitting on the same side of the carriage as himself—and he had his hat on all the time. He himself was busy with his newspaper—yes—he might know him again—but he really could not say.

"Mr. Andrew Campbell's evidence was not worth very much, you will say. No, it was not in itself, and would not have justified any arrest were it not for the additional statements made by Mr. James Verner, manager of Messrs. Rodney & Co., color printers.

"Mr. Verner is a personal friend of Mr. Andrew Campbell, and it appears that at Farringdon Street, where he was waiting for his train, he saw Mr. Campbell get out of a first-class railway carriage. Mr. Verner spoke to him for a second, and then, just as the train was moving off, he stepped into the same compartment which had just been vacated by the stockbroker and the man in the tweed suit. He vaguely recollects a lady sitting in the opposite corner to his own, with her face turned away from him, apparently asleep, but he paid no special attention to her. He was like nearly all businessmen when they are traveling—engrossed in his paper. Presently a special quotation interested him; he wished to make a note of it, took out a pencil from his waistcoat pocket, and seeing a clean piece of pasteboard on the floor, he picked it up, and scribbled on it the memorandum, which he wished to keep. He then slipped the card into his pocketbook.

"'It was only two or three days later,' added Mr. Verner in the midst of breathless silence, 'that I had occasion to refer to these same notes again.

"'In the meanwhile the papers had been full of the mysterious death on the Underground Railway, and the names of those connected with it were pretty familiar to me. It was, therefore, with much astonishment that on looking at the pasteboard which I had casually picked up in the railway carriage I saw the name on it, "Frank Errington."'

"There was no doubt that the sensation in court was almost unprecedented. Never since the days of the Fenchurch Street mystery, and the trial of Smethurst, had I

50 seen so much excitement. Mind you, I was not excited—I knew by now every detail of that crime as if I had committed it myself. In fact, I could not have done it better, although I have been a student of crime for many years now. Many people there—his friends, mostly—believed that Errington was doomed. I think he thought so, too, for I could see that his face was terribly white, and he now and then passed his tongue over his lips, as if they were parched.

"You see he was in the awful dilemma—a perfectly natural one, by the way—of being absolutely incapable of proving an alibi. The crime—if crime there was—had been committed three weeks ago. A man about town like Mr. Frank Errington might remember that he spent certain hours of a special afternoon at his club, or in the Park, but it is very doubtful in nine cases out of ten if he can find a friend who could positively swear as to having seen him there. No! no! Mr. Errington was in a tight corner, and he knew it. You see, there were—besides the evidence—two or three circumstances which did not improve matters for him. His hobby in the direction of toxicology, to begin with. The police had found in his room every description of poisonous substances, including prussic acid.

"Then, again, that journey to Marseilles, the start for Colombo, was, though perfectly innocent, a very unfortunate one. Mr. Errington had gone on an aimless voyage, but the public thought that he had fled, terrified at his own crime. Sir Arthur Inglewood, however, here again displayed his marvelous skill on behalf of his client by the masterly way in which he literally turned all the witnesses for the Crown inside out.

"Having first got Mr. Andrew Campbell to state positively that in the accused he certainly did *not* recognize the man in the tweed suit, the eminent lawyer, after twenty minutes' cross-examination, had so completely upset the stockbroker's equanimity that it is very likely he would not have recognized his own office boy.

"But through all his flurry and all his annoyance Mr. Andrew Campbell remained very sure of one thing; namely, that the lady was alive and cheerful, and talking pleasantly with the man in the tweed suit up to the moment when the latter, having shaken hands with her, left her with a pleasant '*Au revoir!* Don't be late tonight.' He had heard neither scream nor struggle, and in his opinion, if the individual in the tweed suit had administered a dose of poison to his companion, it must have been with her own knowledge and free will; and the lady in the train most emphatically neither looked nor spoke like a woman prepared for a sudden and violent death.

"Mr. James Verner, against that, swore equally positively that he had stood in full view of the carriage door from the moment that Mr. Campbell got out until he himself stepped into the compartment, that there was no one else in that carriage between Farringdon Street and Aldgate, and that the lady, to the best of his belief, had made no movement during the whole of that journey.

"No; Frank Errington was *not* committed for trial on the capital charge," said the man in the corner with one of his sardonic smiles, "thanks to the cleverness of Sir Arthur Inglewood, his lawyer. He absolutely denied his identity with the man in the tweed suit, and swore he had not seen Mrs. Hazeldene since eleven o'clock in the morning of that fatal day. There was no proof that he

52 had; moreover, according to Mr. Campbell's opinion, the man in the tweed suit was in all probability not the murderer. Common sense would not admit that a woman could have a deadly poison injected into her without her knowledge, while chatting pleasantly to her murderer.

"Mr. Errington lives abroad now. He is about to marry. I don't think any of his real friends for a moment believed that he committed the dastardly crime. The police think they know better. They do know this much, that it could not have been a case of suicide, that if the man who undoubtedly traveled with Mrs. Hazeldene on that fatal afternoon had no crime upon his conscience he would long ago have come forward and thrown what light he could upon the mystery.

As to who that man was, the police in their blindness have not the faintest doubt. Under the unshakable belief that Errington is guilty they have spent the last few months in unceasing labor to try and find further and stronger proofs of his guilt. But they won't find them, because there are none. There are no positive proofs against the actual murderer, for he was one of those clever blackguards who think of everything, foresee every eventuality, who know human nature well and can foretell exactly what evidence will be brought against them, and act accordingly.

"This blackguard from the first kept the figure, the personality, of Frank Errington before his mind. Frank Errington was the dust which the scoundrel threw metaphorically in the eyes of the police, and you must admit that he succeeded in blinding them—to the extent even of making them entirely forget the one simple little sentence, overheard by Mr. Andrew Campbell, and which

was, of course, the clue to the whole thing—the only slip
the cunning rogue made—'*Au revoir!* Don't be late
tonight.' Mrs. Hazeldene was going that night to the opera with her husband.

"You are astonished?" he added with a shrug of the
shoulders, "you do not see the tragedy yet, as I have seen
it before me all along. The frivolous young wife, the flirtation with the friend?—all a blind, all pretense. I took
the trouble which the police should have taken immediately, of finding out something about the finances of the
Hazeldene ménage. Money is in nine cases out of ten the
keynote to a crime.

"I found that the will of Mary Beatrice Hazeldene had
been proved by the husband, her sole executor, the estate
being sworn at £15,000. I found out, moreover, that Mr.
Edward Sholto Hazeldene was a poor shipper's clerk
when he married the daughter of a wealthy builder in
Kensington—and then I made note of the fact that the
disconsolate widower had allowed his beard to grow
since the death of his wife.

"There's no doubt that he was a clever rogue," added
the strange creature, leaning excitedly over the table, and
peering into Polly's face. "Do you know how that deadly
poison was injected into the poor woman's system? By
the simplest of all means, one known to every scoundrel
in Southern Europe. A ring—yes! a ring, which has a tiny
hollow needle capable of holding a sufficient quantity of
prussic acid to have killed two persons instead of one.
The man in the tweed suit shook hands with his fair companion—probably she hardly felt the prick, not sufficiently in any case to make her utter a scream. And,
mind you, the scoundrel had every facility, through his

54 friendship with Mr. Errington, of procuring what poison he required, not to mention his friend's visiting card. We cannot gauge how many months ago he began to try and copy Frank Errington in his style of dress, the cut of his mustache, his general appearance, making the change probably so gradual, that no one in his own entourage would notice it. He selected for his model a man his own height and build, with the same colored hair."

"But there was the terrible risk of being identified by his fellow traveler in the Underground," suggested Polly.

"Yes, there certainly was that risk; he chose to take it, and he was wise. He reckoned that several days would in any case elapse before that person, who, by the way, was a businessman absorbed in his newspaper, would actually see him again. The great secret of successful crime is to study human nature," added the man in the corner, as he began looking for his hat and coat. "Edward Hazeldene knew it well."

"But the ring?"

"He may have bought that when he was on his honeymoon," he suggested with a grim chuckle; "the tragedy was not planned in a week, it may have taken years to mature. But you will own that there goes a frightful scoundrel unhung. I have left you his photograph as he was a year ago, and as he is now. You will see he has shaved his beard again, but also his mustache. I fancy he is a friend now of Mr. Andrew Campbell."

He left Miss Polly Burton wondering, not knowing what to believe.

And that is why she missed her appointment with Mr. Richard Frobisher (of the London Mail) to go and see Maud Allan dance at the Palace Theatre that afternoon.

"This is a very singular knife," said Holmes. . . . "I presume, as I see bloodstains upon it, that it is the one which was found in the dead man's grasp."

SILVER BLAZE

Arthur Conan Doyle

"I am afraid, Watson, that I shall have to go," said Holmes as we sat down together to our breakfast one morning.

"Go! Where to?"

"To Dartmoor; to King's Pyland."

I was not surprised. Indeed, my only wonder was that he had not already been mixed up in this extraordinary case, which was the one topic of conversation through the length and breadth of England. For a whole day my companion had rambled about the room with his chin upon his chest and his brows knitted, charging and recharging his pipe with the strongest black tobacco, and absolutely deaf to any of my questions or remarks. Fresh editions of every paper had been sent up by our news agent, only to be glanced over and tossed down into a corner. Yet, silent as he was, I knew perfectly well what it was over which he was brooding. There was but one problem before the public which could challenge his powers of analysis, and that was the singular

56 disappearance of the favorite for the Wessex Cup, and the tragic murder of its trainer. When, therefore, he suddenly announced his intention of setting out for the scene of the drama, it was only what I had both expected and hoped for.

"I should be most happy to go down with you if I should not be in the way," said I.

"My dear Watson, you would confer a great favor upon me by coming. And I think that your time will not be misspent, for there are points about the case which promise to make it an absolutely unique one. We have, I think, just time to catch our train at Paddington, and I will go further into the matter upon our journey. You would oblige me by bringing with you your very excellent field glass."

And so it happened that an hour or so later I found myself in the corner of a first-class carriage flying along a route for Exeter, while Sherlock Holmes, with his sharp, eager face framed in his ear-flapped traveling cap, dipped rapidly into the bundle of fresh papers which he had procured at Paddington. We had left Reading far behind us before he thrust the last one of them under the seat and offered me his cigar case.

"We are going well," said he, looking out of the window and glancing at his watch. "Our rate at present is fifty-three and a half miles an hour."

"I have not observed the quarter-mile posts," said I.

"Nor have I. But the telegraph posts upon this line are sixty yards apart, and the calculation is a simple one. I presume that you have looked into this matter of the murder of John Straker and the disappearance of Silver Blaze?"

"I have seen what the *Telegraph* and the *Chronicle* have to say."

"It is one of those cases where the art of the reasoner should be used rather for the sifting of details than for the acquiring of fresh evidence. The tragedy has been so uncommon, so complete, and of such personal importance to so many people that we are suffering from a plethora of surmise, conjecture, and hypothesis. The difficulty is to detach the framework of fact—of absolute undeniable fact—from the embellishments of theorists and reporters. Then, having established ourselves upon this sound basis, it is our duty to see what inferences may be drawn and what are the special points upon which the whole mystery turns. On Tuesday evening I received telegrams from both Colonel Ross, the owner of the horse, and from Inspector Gregory, who is looking after the case, inviting my cooperation."

"Tuesday evening!" I exclaimed. "And this is Thursday morning. Why didn't you go down yesterday?"

"Because I made a blunder, my dear Watson—which is, I am afraid, a more common occurrence than anyone would think who only knew me through your memoirs. The fact is that I could not believe it possible that the most remarkable horse in England could long remain concealed, especially in so sparsely inhabited a place as the north of Dartmoor. From hour to hour yesterday I expected to hear that he had been found, and that his abductor was the murderer of John Straker. When, however, another morning had come and I found that beyond the arrest of young Fitzroy Simpson nothing had been done, I felt that it was time for me to take action. Yet in some ways I feel that yesterday has not been wasted."

"You have formed a theory, then?"

"At least I have got a grip of the essential facts of the case. I shall enumerate them to you, for nothing clears up a case so much as stating it to another person, and I can hardly expect your cooperation if I do not show you the position from which we start."

I lay back against the cushions, puffing at my cigar, while Holmes, leaning forward, with his long, thin forefinger checking off the points upon the palm of his left hand, gave me a sketch of the events which had led to our journey.

"Silver Blaze," said he, "is from the Somomy stock and holds as brilliant a record as his famous ancestor. He is now in his fifth year and has brought in turn each of the prizes of the turf to Colonel Ross, his fortunate owner. Up to the time of the catastrophe he was the first favorite for the Wessex Cup, the betting being three to one on him. He has always, however, been a prime favorite with the racing public and has never yet disappointed them, so that even at those odds enormous sums of money have been laid upon him. It is obvious, therefore, that there were many people who had the strongest interest in preventing Silver Blaze from being there at the fall of the flag next Tuesday.

"The fact was, of course, appreciated at King's Pyland, where the colonel's training stable is situated. Every precaution was taken to guard the favorite. The trainer, John Straker, is a retired jockey who rode in Colonel Ross's colors before he became too heavy for the weighing chair. He has served the colonel for five years as jockey and for seven as trainer, and has always shown himself to be a zealous and honest servant. Under him were three lads, for the establishment was a small one, containing only four horses in all. One of these lads sat up each night in the stable, while the others slept in the loft. All three bore excellent characters. John Straker, who is a married man, lived in a small villa about two hundred yards from the stables. He has no children, keeps one maidservant, and is comfortably off. The country round is very lonely, but about half a mile to the north there is a small cluster of villas which have been built by a Tavistock contractor for the use of invalids and others who may wish to enjoy the pure Dartmoor air. Tavistock itself lies two miles to the west, while across the moor, also about two miles distant, is the larger training establishment of Mapleton, which belongs to Lord Backwater and is managed by Silas Brown. In every other direction the moor is a complete wilderness, inhabited only by a few roaming gypsies. Such was the general situation last Monday night when the catastrophe occurred.

"On that evening the horses had been exercised and watered as usual, and the stables were locked up at nine o'clock. Two of the lads walked up to the trainer's house, where they had supper as usual, while the third, Ned Hunter, remained on guard. At a few minutes after nine the maid, Edith Baxter, carried down to the stables his supper, which consisted of a dish of curried mutton. She took no liquid, as there was a water tap in the stables, and it was the rule that the lad on duty should drink nothing else. The maid carried a lantern with her, as it was very dark and the path ran across the open moor.

"Edith Baxter was within thirty yards of the stables when a man appeared out of the darkness and called to her to stop. As she stepped into the circle of yellow light

60 thrown by the lantern she saw that he was a person of
gentlemanly bearing, dressed in a gray suit of tweeds,
with a cloth cap. He wore gaiters and carried a heavy
stick with a knob to it. She was most impressed, however,
by the extreme pallor of his face and by the nervousness
of his manner. His age, she thought, would be rather over
thirty than under it.

" 'Can you tell me where I am?' he asked. 'I had almost
made up my mind to sleep on the moor when I saw the
light of your lantern.'

" 'You are close to the King's Pyland training stables,'
said she.

" 'Oh, indeed! What a stroke of luck!' he cried. 'I understand that a stable boy sleeps there alone every night.
Perhaps that is his supper which you are carrying to him.
Now I am sure that you would not be too proud to earn
the price of a new dress, would you?' He took a piece of
white paper folded up out of his waistcoat pocket. 'See
that the boy has this tonight, and you shall have the prettiest frock that money can buy.'

"She was frightened by the earnestness of his manner
and ran past him to the window through which she was
accustomed to hand the meals. It was already opened,
and Hunter was seated at the small table inside. She had
begun to tell him of what had happened when the
stranger came up again.

" 'Good-evening,' said he, looking through the window. 'I wanted to have a word with you.' The girl has
sworn that as he spoke she noticed the corner of the little
paper packet protruding from his closed hand.

" 'What business have you here?' asked the lad.

" 'It's business that may put something into your

pocket,' said the other. 'You've two horses in for the Wessex Cup—Silver Blaze and Bayard. Let me have the straight tip and you won't be a loser. Is it a fact that at the weights Bayard could give the other a hundred yards in five furlongs, and that the stable have put their money on him?'

" 'So you're one of those damned touts!' cried the lad. 'I'll show you how we serve them in King's Pyland.' He sprang up and rushed across the stable to unloose the dog. The girl fled away to the house, but as she ran she looked back and saw that the stranger was leaning through the window. A minute later, however, when Hunter rushed out with the hound he was gone, and though he ran all round the buildings he failed to find any trace of him."

"One moment," I asked. "Did the stable boy, when he ran out with the dog, leave the door unlocked behind him?"

"Excellent, Watson, excellent!" murmured my companion. "The importance of the point struck me so forcibly that I sent a special wire to Dartmoor yesterday to clear the matter up. The boy locked the door before he left it. The window, I may add, was not large enough for a man to get through.

"Hunter waited until his fellow grooms had returned, when he sent a message to the trainer and told him what had occurred. Straker was excited at hearing the account, although he does not seem to have quite realized its true significance. It left him, however, vaguely uneasy, and Mrs. Straker, waking at one in the morning, found that he was dressing. In reply to her inquiries, he said that he could not sleep on account of his anxiety about the horses, and that he intended to walk down to the stables

62 to see that all was well. She begged him to remain at home, as she could hear the rain pattering against the window, but in spite of her entreaties he pulled on his large mackintosh and left the house.

"Mrs. Straker awoke at seven in the morning to find that her husband had not yet returned. She dressed herself hastily, called the maid, and set off for the stables. The door was open; inside, huddled together upon a chair, Hunter was sunk in a state of absolute stupor, the favorite's stall was empty, and there were no signs of his trainer.

"The two lads who slept in the chaff-cutting loft above the harness room were quickly aroused. They had heard nothing during the night, for they are both sound sleepers. Hunter was obviously under the influence of some powerful drug, and as no sense could be got out of him, he was left to sleep it off while the two lads and the two women ran out in search of the absentees. They still had hopes that the trainer had for some reason taken out the horse for early exercise, but on ascending the knoll near the house, from which all the neighboring moors were visible, they not only could see no signs of the missing favorite, but they perceived something which warned them that they were in the presence of a tragedy.

"About a quarter of a mile from the stables John Straker's overcoat was flapping from a furze bush. Immediately beyond there was a bowl-shaped depression in the moor, and at the bottom of this was found the dead body of the unfortunate trainer. His head had been shattered by a savage blow from some heavy weapon, and he was wounded on the thigh, where there was a long, clean cut, inflicted evidently by some very sharp instrument. It was clear, however, that Straker had defended himself vigorously against his assailants, for in his right hand he held a small knife, which was clotted with blood up to the handle, while in his left he clasped a red and black silk cravat, which was recognized by the maid as having been worn on the preceding evening by the stranger who had visited the stables. Hunter, on recovering from his stupor, was also quite positive as to the ownership of the cravat. He was equally certain that the same stranger had, while standing at the window, drugged his curried mutton, and so deprived the stables of their watchman. As to the missing horse, there were abundant proofs in the mud which lay at the bottom of the fatal hollow that he had been there at the time of the struggle. But from that morning he has disappeared, and although a large reward has been offered, and all the gypsies of Dartmoor are on the alert, no news has come of him. Finally, an analysis has shown that the remains of his supper left by the stable lad contained an appreciable quantity of powdered opium, while the people at the house partook of the same dish on the same night without any ill effect.

"Those are the main facts of the case, stripped of all surmise, and stated as baldly as possible. I shall now recapitulate what the police have done in the matter.

"Inspector Gregory, to whom the case has been committed, is an extremely competent officer. Were he but gifted with imagination he might rise to great heights in his profession. On his arrival he promptly found and arrested the man upon whom suspicion naturally rested. There was little difficulty in finding him, for he inhabited one of those villas which I have mentioned. His name, it appears, was Fitzroy Simpson. He was a man of excellent

64 birth and education, who had squandered a fortune upon the turf, and who lived now by doing a little quiet and genteel bookmaking in the sporting clubs of London. An examination of his betting book shows that bets in the amount of five thousand pounds had been registered by him against the favorite. On being arrested he volunteered the statement that he had come down to Dartmoor in the hope of getting some information about the King's Pyland horses, and also about Desborough, the second favorite, which was in charge of Silas Brown at the Mapleton stables. He did not attempt to deny that he had acted as described upon the evening before, but declared that he had no sinister designs and had simply wished to obtain first-hand information. When confronted with his cravat he turned very pale and was utterly unable to account for its presence in the hand of the murdered man. His wet clothing showed that he had been out in the storm of the night before, and his stick, which was a penang-lawyer weighted with lead, was just such a weapon as might, by repeated blows, have inflicted the terrible injuries to which the trainer had succumbed. On the other hand, there was no wound upon his person, while the state of Straker's knife would show that one at least of his assailants must bear his mark upon him. There you have it all in a nutshell, Watson, and if you can give me any light I shall be infinitely obliged to you."

I had listened with the greatest interest to the statement which Holmes, with characteristic clearness, had laid before me. Though most of the facts were familiar to me, I had not sufficiently appreciated their relative importance, nor their connection to each other.

"Is it not possible," I suggested, "that the incised

wound upon Straker may have been caused by his own knife in the convulsive struggles which follow any brain injury?"

"It is more than possible; it is probable," said Holmes. "In that case one of the main points in favor of the accused disappears."

"And yet," said I, "even now I fail to understand what the theory of the police can be."

"I am afraid that whatever theory we state has very grave objections to it," returned my companion. "The police imagine, I take it, that this Fitzroy Simpson, having drugged the lad, and having in some way obtained a duplicate key, opened the stable door and took out the horse, with the intention, apparently, of kidnapping him altogether. His bridle is missing, so that Simpson must have put this on. Then, having left the door open behind him, he was leading the horse away over the moor when he was either met or overtaken by the trainer. A row naturally ensued. Simpson beat out the trainer's brains with his heavy stick without receiving any injury from the small knife which Straker used in self-defense, and then the thief either led the horse on to some secret hiding place, or else it may have bolted during the struggle, and be now wandering out on the moors. That is the case as it appears to the police, and improbable as it is, all other explanations are more improbable still. However, I shall very quickly test the matter when I am once upon the spot, and until then I cannot really see how we can get much further than our present position."

It was evening before we reached the little town of Tavistock, which lies, like the boss of a shield, in the middle of the huge circle of Dartmoor. Two gentlemen

66 were awaiting us in the station—the one a tall, fair man with lionlike hair and beard and curiously penetrating light blue eyes; the other a small, alert person, very neat and dapper, in a frock coat and gaiters, with trim little side-whiskers and an eyeglass. The latter was Colonel Ross, the well-known sportsman; the other, Inspector Gregory, a man who was rapidly making his name in the English detective service.

"I am delighted that you have come down, Mr. Holmes," said the colonel. "The inspector here has done all that could possibly be suggested, but I wish to leave no stone unturned in trying to avenge poor Straker and in recovering my horse."

"Have there been any fresh developments?" asked Holmes.

"I am sorry to say that we have made very little progress," said the inspector. "We have an open carriage outside, and as you would no doubt like to see the place before the light fails, we might talk it over as we drive."

A minute later we were all seated in a comfortable landau and were rattling through the quaint old Devonshire city. Inspector Gregory was full of his case and poured out a stream of remarks, while Holmes threw in an occasional question or interjection. Colonel Ross leaned back with his arms folded and his hat tilted over his eyes, while I listened with interest to the dialogue of the two detectives. Gregory was formulating his theory, which was almost exactly what Holmes had foretold in the train.

"The net is drawn pretty close around Fitzroy Simpson," he remarked, "and I believe myself that he is our man. At the same time I recognize that the evidence is purely circumstantial, and that some new development may upset it."

"How about Straker's knife?"

"We have quite come to the conclusion that he wounded himself in his fall."

"My friend Dr. Watson made that suggestion to me as we came down. If so, it would tell against this man Simpson."

"Undoubtedly. He has neither a knife nor any sign of a wound. The evidence against him is certainly very strong. He had a great interest in the disappearance of the favorite. He lies under suspicion of having poisoned the stable boy; he was undoubtedly out in the storm; he was armed with a heavy stick, and his cravat was found in the dead man's hand. I really think we have enough to go before a jury."

Holmes shook his head. "A clever counsel would tear it all to rags," said he. "Why should he take the horse out of the stable? If he wished to injure it, why could he not do it there? Has a duplicate key been found in his possession? What chemist sold him the powdered opium? Above all, where could he, a stranger to the district, hide a horse, and such a horse as this? What is his own explanation as to the paper which he wished the maid to give to the stable boy?"

"He says that it was a ten-pound note. One was found in his purse. But your other difficulties are not so formidable as they seem. He is not a stranger to the district. He has twice lodged at Tavistock in the summer. The opium was probably brought from London. The key, having

68 served its purpose, would be hurled away. The horse may be at the bottom of one of the pits or old mines upon the moor."

"What does he say about the cravat?"

"He acknowledges that it is his and declares that he had lost it. But a new element has been introduced into the case which may account for his leading the horse from the stable."

Holmes pricked up his ears.

"We have found traces which show that a party of gypsies encamped on Monday night within a mile of the spot where the murder took place. On Tuesday they were gone. Now, presuming that there was some understanding between Simpson and these gypsies, might he not have been leading the horse to them when he was overtaken, and may they not have him now?"

"It is certainly possible."

"The moor is being scoured for these gypsies. I have also examined every stable and outhouse in Tavistock, and for a radius of ten miles."

"There is another training stable quite close, I understand?"

"Yes, and that is a factor which we must certainly not neglect. As Desborough, their horse, was second in the betting, they had an interest in the disappearance of the favorite. Silas Brown, the trainer, is known to have had large bets upon the event, and he was no friend of poor Straker. We have, however, examined the stables, and there is nothing to connect him with the affair."

"And nothing to connect this man Simpson with the interests of the Mapleton stables?"

"Nothing at all."

Holmes leaned back in the carriage, and the conversation ceased. A few minutes later our driver pulled up at a neat little red-brick villa with overhanging eaves which stood by the road. Some distance off, across a paddock, lay a long gray-tiled outbuilding. In every other direction the low curves of the moor, bronze-colored from the fading ferns, stretched away to the skyline, broken only by the steeples of Tavistock, and by a cluster of houses away to the westward which marked the Mapleton stables. We all sprang out with the exception of Holmes, who continued to lean back with his eyes fixed upon the sky in front of him, entirely absorbed in his own thoughts. It was only when I touched his arm that he roused himself with a violent start and stepped out of the carriage.

"Excuse me," said he, turning to Colonel Ross, who had looked at him in some surprise. "I was daydreaming." There was a gleam in his eyes and a suppressed excitement in his manner which convinced me, used as I was to his ways, that his hand was upon a clue, though I could not imagine where he had found it.

"Perhaps you would prefer at once to go on to the scene of the crime, Mr. Holmes?" said Gregory.

"I think that I should prefer to stay here a little and go into one or two questions of detail. Straker was brought back here, I presume?"

"Yes, he lies upstairs. The inquest is tomorrow."

"He has been in your service some years, Colonel Ross?"

"I have always found him an excellent servant."

"I presume that you made an inventory of what he had

70 in his pockets at the time of his death, Inspector?"

"I have the things themselves in the sitting room if you would care to see them."

"I should be very glad." We all filed into the front room and sat round the central table while the inspector unlocked a square tin box and laid a small heap of things before us. There was a box of vestas, two inches of tallow candle, an A. D. P. brier-root pipe, a pouch of sealskin with half an ounce of long-cut Cavendish, a silver watch with a gold chain, five sovereigns in gold, an aluminum pencil case, a few papers, and an ivory-handled knife with a very delicate, inflexible blade marked Weiss & Co., London.

"This is a very singular knife," said Holmes, lifting it up and examining it minutely. "I presume, as I see bloodstains upon it, that it is the one which was found in the dead man's grasp. Watson, this knife is surely in your line?"

"It is what we call a cataract knife," said I.

"I thought so. A very delicate blade devised for very delicate work. A strange thing for a man to carry with him upon a rough expedition, especially as it would not shut in his pocket."

"The tip was guarded by a disc of cork which we found beside his body," said the inspector. "His wife tells us that the knife had lain upon the dressing table, and that he had picked it up as he left the room. It was a poor weapon, but perhaps the best that he could lay his hands on at the moment."

"Very possibly. How about these papers?"

"Three of them are receipted hay dealers' accounts.

One of them is a letter of instructions from Colonel Ross.
This other is a milliner's account for thirty-seven pounds
fifteen made out by Madame Lesurier, of Bond Street, to
William Derbyshire. Mrs. Straker tells us that Derbyshire
was a friend of her husband's and that occasionally his
letters were addressed here."

"Madame Derbyshire had somewhat expensive tastes,"
remarked Holmes, glancing down the account. "Twenty-
two guineas is rather heavy for a single costume. However, there appears to be nothing more to learn, and we
may now go down to the scene of the crime."

As we emerged from the sitting room a woman, who
had been waiting in the passage, took a step forward and
laid her hand upon the inspector's sleeve. Her face was
haggard and thin and eager, stamped with the print of a
recent horror.

"Have you got them? Have you found them?" she
panted.

"No, Mrs. Straker. But Mr. Holmes here has come from
London to help us, and we shall do all that is possible."

"Surely I met you in Plymouth at a garden party some
little time ago, Mrs. Straker?" said Holmes.

"No, sir; you are mistaken."

"Dear me! Why, I could have sworn to it. You wore a
costume of dove-colored silk with ostrich-feather trim-
ming."

"I never had such a dress, sir," answered the lady.

"Ah, that quite settles it," said Holmes. And with an
apology he followed the inspector outside. A short walk
across the moor took us to the hollow in which the body
had been found. At the brink of it was the furze bush

72   upon which the coat had been hung.

"There was no wind that night, I understand," said Holmes.

"None, but very heavy rain."

"In that case the overcoat was not blown against the furze bush, but placed there."

"Yes, it was laid across the bush."

"You fill me with interest. I perceive that the ground had been trampled up a good deal. No doubt many feet have been here since Monday night."

"A piece of matting has been laid here at the side, and we have all stood upon that."

"Excellent."

"In this bag I have one of the boots which Straker wore, one of Fitzroy Simpson's shoes, and a cast horseshoe of Silver Blaze."

"My dear Inspector, you surpass yourself!" Holmes pushed the matting into a more central position. Then stretching himself upon his face and leaning his chin upon his hands, he made a careful study of the trampled mud in front of him. "Hullo!" said he suddenly. "What's this?" It was a wax vesta, half burned, which was so coated with mud that it looked at first like a little chip of wood.

"I cannot think how I came to overlook it," said the inspector with an expression of annoyance.

"It was invisible, buried in the mud. I only saw it because I was looking for it."

"What! you expected to find it?"

"I thought it not unlikely."

He took the boots from the bag and compared the impressions of each of them with marks upon the ground.

Then he clambered up to the rim of the hollow and crawled about among the ferns and bushes.

"I am afraid that there are no more tracks," said the inspector. "I have examined the ground very carefully for a hundred yards in each direction."

"Indeed!" said Holmes, rising. "I should not have the impertinence to do it again after what you say. But I should like to take a little walk over the moor before it grows dark that I may know my ground tomorrow, and I think that I shall put this horseshoe into my pocket for luck."

Colonel Ross, who had shown some signs of impatience at my companion's quiet and systematic method of work, glanced at his watch. "I wish you would come back with me, Inspector," said he. "There are several points on which I should like your advice, and especially as to whether we do not owe it to the public to remove our horse's name from the entries for the cup."

"Certainly not," cried Holmes with decision. "I should let the name stand."

The colonel bowed. "I am very glad to have had your opinion, sir," said he. "You will find us at poor Straker's house when you have finished your walk, and we can drive together into Tavistock."

He turned back with the inspector, while Holmes and I walked slowly across the moor. The sun was beginning to sink behind the stable of Mapleton, and the long, sloping plain in front of us was tinged with gold, deepening into rich, ruddy browns where the faded ferns and brambles caught the evening light. But the glories of the landscape were all wasted upon my companion, who was sunk in the deepest thought.

74   "It's this way, Watson," said he at last. "We may leave the question of who killed John Straker for the instant and confine ourselves to find out what has become of the horse. Now, supposing that he broke away during or after the tragedy, where could he have gone to? The horse is a very gregarious creature. If left to himself his instincts would have been either to return to King's Pyland or go over to Mapleton. Why should he run wild upon the moor? He would surely have been seen by now. And why should gypsies kidnap him? These people always clear out when they hear of trouble, for they do not wish to be pestered by the police. They could not hope to sell such a horse. They would run a great risk and gain nothing by taking him. Surely that is clear."

"Where is he, then?"

"I have already said that he must have gone to King's Pyland or to Mapleton. He is not at King's Pyland. Therefore he is at Mapleton. Let us take that as a working hypothesis and see what it leads us to. This part of the moor, as the inspector remarked, is very hard and dry. But it falls away towards Mapleton, and you can see from here that there is a long hollow over yonder, which must have been very wet on Monday night. If our supposition is correct, then the horse must have crossed that, and there is the point where we should look for his tracks."

We had been walking briskly during this conversation, and a few more minutes brought us to the hollow in question. At Holmes's request I walked down the bank to the right, and he to the left, but I had not taken fifty paces before I heard him give a shout and saw him waving his hand to me. The track of a horse was plainly outlined in the soft earth in front of him, and the shoe which he took from his pocket exactly fitted the impression.

"See the value of imagination," said Holmes. "It is the one quality which Gregory lacks. We imagined what might have happened, acted upon the supposition, and find ourselves justified. Let us proceed."

We crossed the marshy bottom and passed over a quarter of a mile of dry, hard turf. Again the ground sloped, and again we came on the tracks. Then we lost them for half a mile, but only to pick them up once more quite close to Mapleton. It was Holmes who saw them first, and he stood pointing with a look of triumph upon his face. A man's track was visible beside the horse's.

"The horse was alone before," I cried.

"Quite so. It was alone before. Hullo, what is this?"

The double track turned sharp off and took the direction of King's Pyland. Holmes whistled, and we both followed along after it. His eyes were on the trail, but I happened to look a little to one side and saw to my surprise the same tracks coming back again in the opposite direction.

"One for you, Watson," said Holmes when I pointed it out. "You have saved us a long walk, which would have brought us back on our own traces. Let us follow the return track."

We had not to go far. It ended at the paving of asphalt which led up to the gates of the Mapleton stables. As we approached, a groom ran out from them.

"We don't want any loiterers about here," said he.

"I only wished to ask a question," said Holmes, with his finger and thumb in his waistcoat pocket. "Should I be too early to see your master, Mr. Silas Brown, if I were to call at five o'clock tomorrow morning?"

"Bless you, sir, if anyone is about he will be, for he is always the first stirring. But here he is, sir, to answer your questions for himself. No, sir, no, it is as much as my place is worth to let him see me touch your money. Afterwards, if you like."

As Sherlock Holmes replaced the half crown which he had drawn from his pocket, a fierce-looking elderly man strode out from the gate with a hunting crop swinging in his hand.

"What's this, Dawson!" he cried. "No gossiping! Go about your business! And you, what the devil do you want here?"

"Ten minutes' talk with you, my good sir," said Holmes in the sweetest of voices.

"I've no time to talk to every gadabout. We want no strangers here. Be off, or you may find a dog at your heels."

Holmes leaned forward and whispered something in the trainer's ear. He started violently and flushed to the temples.

"It's a lie!" he shouted. "An infernal lie!"

"Very good. Shall we argue about it here in public or talk it over in your parlor?"

"Oh, come in if you wish to."

Holmes smiled. "I shall not keep you more than a few minutes, Watson," said he. "Now, Mr. Brown, I am quite at your disposal."

It was twenty minutes, and the reds had all faded into grays before Holmes and the trainer reappeared. Never have I seen such a change as had been brought about in Silas Brown in that short time. His face was ashy pale, beads of perspiration shone upon his brow, and his hands shook until the hunting crop wagged like a branch in the wind. His bullying, overbearing manner was all gone too, and he cringed along at my companion's side like a dog with its master.

"Your instructions will be done. It shall all be done," said he.

"There must be no mistake," said Holmes, looking round at him. The other winced as he read the menace in his eyes.

"Oh, no, there shall be no mistake. It shall be there. Should I change it first or not?"

Holmes thought a little and then burst out laughing. "No, don't," said he, "I shall write to you about it. No tricks, now, or—"

"Oh, you can trust me, you can trust me!"

"Yes, I think I can. Well, you shall hear from me to-morrow." He turned upon his heel, disregarding the trembling hand which the other held out to him, and we set off for King's Pyland.

"A more perfect compound of the bully, coward, and sneak than Master Silas Brown I have seldom met with," remarked Holmes as we trudged along together.

"He has the horse, then?"

"He tried to bluster out of it, but I described to him so exactly what his actions had been upon that morning that he is convinced that I was watching him. Of course you observed the peculiarly square toes in the impressions, and that his own boots exactly corresponded to them. Again, of course no subordinate would have dared to do such a thing. I described to him how, when according to his custom he was the first down, he perceived a strange horse wandering over the moor. How he went out to it,

78 and his astonishment at recognizing, from the white forehead which has given the favorite its name, that chance had put in his power the only horse which could beat the one upon which he had put his money. Then I described how his first impulse had been to lead him back to King's Pyland, and how the devil had shown him how he could hide the horse until the race was over, and how he had led it back and concealed it at Mapleton. When I told him every detail he gave it up and thought only of saving his own skin."

"But his stables had been searched?"

"Oh, an old horse-faker like him has many a dodge."

"But are you not afraid to leave the horse in his power now, since he has every interest in injuring it?"

"My dear fellow, he will guard it as the apple of his eye. He knows that his only hope of mercy is to produce it safe."

"Colonel Ross did not impress me as a man who would be likely to show much mercy in any case."

"The matter does not rest with Colonel Ross. I follow my own methods and tell as much or as little as I choose. That is the advantage of being unofficial. I don't know whether you observed it, Watson, but the colonel's manner has been just a trifle cavalier to me. I am inclined now to have a little amusement at his expense. Say nothing to him about the horse."

"Certainly not without your permission."

"And of course this is all quite a minor point compared to the question of who killed John Straker."

"And you will devote yourself to that?"

"On the contrary, we both go back to London by the night train."

"I was thunderstruck by my friend's words. We had only been a few hours in Devonshire, and that he should give up an investigation which he had begun so brilliantly was quite incomprehensible to me. Not a word more could I draw from him until we were back at the trainer's house. The colonel and the inspector were awaiting us in the parlor.

"My friend and I return to town by the night express," said Holmes. "We have had a charming little breath of your beautiful Dartmoor air."

The inspector opened his eyes, and the colonel's lip curled in a sneer.

"So you despair of arresting the murderer of poor Straker," said he.

Holmes shrugged his shoulders. "There are certainly grave difficulties in the way," said he. "I have every hope, however, that your horse will start upon Tuesday, and I beg that you will have the jockey in readiness. Might I ask for a photograph of Mr. John Straker?"

The inspector took one from an envelope and handed it to him.

"My dear Gregory, you anticipate all my wants. If I might ask you to wait here for an instant. I have a question which I should like to put to the maid."

"I must say that I am rather disappointed in our London consultant," said Colonel Ross bluntly as my friend left the room. "I do not see that we are any further than when he came."

"At least you have his assurance that your horse will run," said I.

"Yes, I have his assurance," said the colonel with a shrug of his shoulders. "I should prefer to have the

80 horse." I was about to make some reply in defense of my friend when he entered the room again.

"Now, gentlemen," said he, "I am quite ready for Tavistock."

As we stepped into the carriage one of the stable lads held the door open for us. A sudden idea seemed to occur to Holmes, for he leaned forward and touched the lad upon the sleeve.

"You have a few sheep in the paddock," he said. "Who attends to them?"

"I do, sir."

"Have you noticed anything amiss with them of late?"

"Well, sir, not of much account, but three of them have gone lame, sir."

I could see that Holmes was extremely pleased, for he chuckled and rubbed his hands together.

"A long shot, Watson, a very long shot," said he, pinching my arm. "Gregory, let me recommend to your attention this singular epidemic among the sheep. Drive on, coachman!"

Colonel Ross still wore an expression which showed the poor opinion which he had formed of my companion's ability, but I saw by the inspector's face that his attention had been keenly aroused.

"You consider that to be important?" he asked.

"Exceedingly so."

"Is there any point to which you would wish to draw my attention?"

"To the curious incident of the dog in the nighttime."

"The dog did nothing in the nighttime."

"That was the curious incident," remarked Sherlock Holmes.

Four days later Holmes and I were again in the train, bound for Winchester to see the race for the Wessex Cup. Colonel Ross met us by appointment outside the station, and we drove in his drag to the course beyond the town. His face was grave, and his manner was cold in the extreme.

"I have seen nothing of my horse," said he.

"I suppose that you would know him when you saw him?" asked Holmes.

The colonel was very angry. "I have been on the turf for twenty years and never was asked such a question as that before," said he. "A child would know Silver Blaze with his white forehead and his mottled off-foreleg."

"How is the betting?"

"Well, that is the curious part of it. You could have got fifteen to one yesterday, but the price has become shorter and shorter, until you can hardly get three to one now."

"Hum!" said Holmes. "Somebody knows something, that is clear."

As the drag drew up in the enclosure near the grandstand I glanced at the card to see the entries.

Wessex Plate [it ran] 50 sovs. each h ft with 1000 sovs. added, for four and five year olds. Second, £300. Third, £200. New course (one mile and five furlongs).

1. Mr. Heath Newton's The Negro. Red cap. Cinnamon jacket.
2. Colonel Wardlaw's Pugilist. Pink cap. Blue and black jacket.
3. Lord Backwater's Desborough. Yellow cap and sleeves.

4. Colonel Ross's Silver Blaze. Black cap. Red jacket.
5. Duke of Balmoral's Iris. Yellow and black stripes.
6. Lord Singleford's Rasper. Purple cap. Black sleeves.

"We scratched our other one and put all hopes on your word," said the colonel. "Why, what is that? Silver Blaze favorite?"

"Five to four against Silver Blaze!" roared the ring. "Five to four against Silver Blaze! Five to fifteen against Desborough! Five to four on the field!"

"There are the numbers up," I cried. "They are all six there."

"All six there? Then my horse is running," cried the colonel in great agitation. "But I don't see him. My colors have not passed."

"Only five have passed. This must be he."

As I spoke a powerful bay horse swept out from the weighing enclosure and cantered past us, bearing on its back the well-known black and red of the colonel.

"That's not my horse," cried the owner. "That beast has not a white hair upon its body. What is this that you have done, Mr. Holmes?"

"Well, well, let us see how he gets on," said my friend imperturbably. For a few minutes he gazed through my field glass. "Capital! An excellent start!" he cried suddenly. "There they are, coming round the curve!"

From our drag we had a superb view as they came up the straight. The six horses were so close together that a carpet could have covered them, but halfway up the yellow of the Mapleton stable showed to the front. Before they reached us, however, Desborough's bolt was shot, and the colonel's horse, coming away with a rush, passed the post a good six lengths before its rival, the Duke of Balmoral's Iris making a bad third.

"It's my race, anyhow," gasped the colonel, passing his hand over his eyes. "I confess that I can make neither head nor tail of it. Don't you think that you have kept up your mystery long enough, Mr. Holmes?"

"Certainly, Colonel, you shall know everything. Let us all go round and have a look at the horse together. Here he is," he continued as we made our way into the weighing enclosure, where only owners and their friends find admittance. "You have only to wash his face and his leg in spirits of wine, and you will find that he is the same old Silver Blaze as ever."

"You take my breath away!"

"I found him in the hands of a faker and took the liberty of running him just as he was sent over."

"My dear sir, you have done wonders. The horse looks very fit and well. It never went better in its life. I owe you a thousand apologies for having doubted your ability. You have done me a great service by recovering my horse. You would do me a greater still if you could lay your hands on the murderer of John Straker."

"I have done so," said Holmes quietly.

The colonel and I stared at him in amazement. "You have got him! Where is he, then?"

"He is here."

"Here! Where?"

"In my company at the present moment."

The colonel flushed angrily. "I quite recognize that I am under obligations to you, Mr. Holmes," said he, "but I

84 must regard what you have just said as either a very bad joke or an insult."

Sherlock Holmes laughed. "I assure you that I have not associated you with the crime, Colonel," said he. "The real murderer is standing immediatley behind you." He stepped past and laid his hand upon the glossy neck of the thoroughbred.

"The horse!" cried both the colonel and myself.

"Yes, the horse. And it may lessen his guilt if I say that it was done in self-defense, and that John Straker was a man who was entirely unworthy of your confidence. But there goes the bell, and as I stand to win a little on this next race, I shall defer a lengthy explanation until a more fitting time."

We had the corner of a Pullman car to ourselves that evening as we whirled back to London, and I fancy that the journey was a short one to Colonel Ross as well as to myself as we listened to our companion's narrative of the events which had occurred at the Dartmoor training stables upon that Monday night, and the means by which he had unraveled them.

"I confess," said he, "that any theories which I had formed from the newspaper reports were entirely erroneous. And yet there were indications there, had they not been overlaid by other details which concealed their true import. I went to Devonshire with the conviction that Fitzroy Simpson was the true culprit, although, of course, I saw that the evidence against him was by no means complete. It was while I was in the carriage, just as we reached the trainer's house, that the immense significance of the curried mutton occurred to me. You may remember that I was distrait and remained sitting after you had all alighted. I was marveling in my own mind how I could possibly have overlooked so obvious a clue."

"I confess," said the colonel, "that even now I cannot see how it helps us."

"It was the first link in my chain of reasoning. Powdered opium is by no means tasteless. The flavor is not disagreeable, but it is perceptible. Were it mixed with any ordinary dish the eater would undoubtedly detect it and would probably eat no more. A curry was exactly the medium which would disguise this taste. By no possible supposition could this stranger, Fitzroy Simpson, have caused curry to be served in the trainer's family that night, and it is surely too monstrous a coincidence to suppose that he happened to come along with powdered opium upon the very night when a dish happened to be served which would disguise the flavor. That is unthinkable. Therefore Simpson becomes eliminated from the case, and our attention centers upon Straker and his wife, the only two people who could have chosen curried mutton for supper that night. The opium was added after the dish was set aside for the stable boy, for the others had the same for supper with no ill effects. Which of them, then, had access to that dish without the maid seeing them?

"Before deciding that question I had grasped the significance of the silence of the dog, for one true inference invariably suggests others. The Simpson incident had shown me that a dog was kept in the stables, and yet, though someone had been in and had fetched out a horse, he had not barked enough to arouse the two lads in the loft. Obviously the midnight visitor was someone whom

86 the dog knew well.

"I was already convinced, or almost convinced, that John Straker went down to the stables in the dead of the night and took out Silver Blaze. For what purpose? For a dishonest one, obviously, or why should he drug his own stable boy? And yet I was at a loss to know why. There have been cases before now where trainers have made sure of great sums of money by laying against their own horses through agents and then preventing them from winning by fraud. Sometimes it is a pulling jockey. Sometimes it is some surer and subtler means. What was it here? I hoped that the contents of his pockets might help me to form a conclusion.

"And they did so. You cannot have forgotten the singular knife which was found in the dead man's hand, a knife which certainly no sane man would choose for a weapon. It was, as Dr. Watson told us, a form of knife which is used for the most delicate operations known in surgery. And it was to be used for a delicate operation that night. You must know, with your wide experience of turf matters, Colonel Ross, that it is possible to make a slight nick upon the tendons of a horse's ham, and to do it subcutaneously, so as to leave absolutely no trace. A horse so treated would develop a slight lameness, which would be put down to a strain in exercise or a touch of rheumatism, but never to foul play."

"Villain! Scoundrel!" cried the colonel.

"We have here the explanation of why John Straker wished to take the horse out onto the moor. So spirited a creature would have certainly roused the soundest of sleepers when it felt the prick of the knife. It was absolutely necessary to do it in the open air."

"I have been blind!" cried the colonel. "Of course that 87 was why he needed the candle and struck the match."

"Undoubtedly. But in examining his belongings I was fortunate enough to discover not only the method of the crime but even its motives. As a man of the world, Colonel, you know that men do not carry other people's bills about in their pockets. We have most of us quite enough to do to settle our own. I at once concluded that Straker was leading a double life and keeping a second establishment. The nature of the bill showed that there was a lady in the case, and one who had expensive tastes. Liberal as you are with your servants, one can hardly expect that they can buy twenty-guinea walking dresses for their ladies. I questioned Mrs. Straker as to the dress without her knowing it, and, having satisfied myself that it had never reached her, I made a note of the milliner's address and felt that by calling there with Straker's photograph I could easily dispose of the mythical Derbyshire.

"From that time on all was plain. Straker had led out the horse to a hollow where his light would be invisible. Simpson in his flight had dropped his cravat, and Straker had picked it up—with some idea, perhaps, that he might use it in securing the horse's leg. Once in the hollow, he had got behind the horse and had struck a light; but the creature, frightened at the sudden glare, and with the strange instinct of animals feeling that some mischief was intended, had lashed out, and the steel shoe had struck Straker full on the forehead. He had already, in spite of the rain, taken off his overcoat in order to do his delicate task, and so, as he fell, his knife gashed his thigh. Do I make it clear?"

"Wonderful!" cried the colonel. "Wonderful! You

88 might have been there!"

"My final shot was, I confess, a very long one. It struck me that so astute a man as Straker would not undertake this delicate tendon-nicking without a little practice. What could he practice on? My eyes fell upon the sheep, and I asked a question which, rather to my surprise, showed that my surmise was correct.

"When I returned to London I called upon the milliner, who had recognized Straker as an excellent customer of the name of Derbyshire, who had a very dashing wife, with a strong partiality for expensive dresses. I have no doubt that this woman had plunged him over head and ears in debt, and so led him into this miserable plot."

"You have explained all but one thing," cried the colonel. "Where was the horse?"

"Ah, it bolted, and was cared for by one of your neighbors. We must have an amnesty in that direction, I think. This is Clapham Junction, if I am not mistaken, and we shall be in Victoria in less than ten minutes. If you care to smoke a cigar in our rooms, Colonel, I shall be happy to give you any other details which might interest you."

GHOST STORIES

Do you believe in ghosts? Over the centuries, many people have. Ghosts are part of the folklore of many cultures. Some North American Indians created ghost dances. In damp, gloomy English castles, people think they have seen ghosts rattling chains and howling, some carrying their heads under their arms (a sign that they were beheaded). In America, ghosts have been sighted in New England, in deserted mining towns of the Southwest, and even in Hollywood where some dead movie stars are said to have come back as ghosts!

Ghosts have played important roles in literature. They appear in Shakespeare's plays—Macbeth, Julius Caesar, Hamlet—to threaten, warn, or demand revenge from the living. In Charles Dickens's "A Christmas Carol," four ghosts force Ebenezer Scrooge to change his miserly ways. Many kinds of ghosts are possible in fiction: ghosts that scare, ghosts that surprise, even ghosts that make us laugh.

Even people who don't believe in ghosts can enjoy ghost stories. Reading them is a bit like sitting by an open fire on a stormy evening: No matter how the storm rages, you won't get wet; and being scared by ghosts is good fun—as long as you're safe.

Suddenly the rosebush was agitated violently as if by a gust of wind, yet it was a remarkably still day....
"What on earth—" began Rebecca, then she stopped with a gasp....

THE WIND IN THE ROSEBUSH

Mary Wilkins Freeman

Ford Village has no railroad station, being on the other side of the river from Porter's Falls, and accessible only by the ford which gives it its name, and a ferry line.

The ferryboat was waiting when Rebecca Flint got off the train with her bag and lunch basket. When she and her small trunk were safely embarked she sat stiff and straight and calm in the ferryboat as it shot swiftly and smoothly across stream. There was a horse attached to a light country wagon on board, and he pawed the deck uneasily. His owner stood near, with a wary eye upon him, although he was chewing, with as dully reflective an expression as a cow. Beside Rebecca sat a woman of about her own age, who kept looking at her with furtive curiosity; her husband, short and stout and saturnine, stood near her. Rebecca paid no attention to either of them. She was tall and spare and pale, the type of a spinster, yet with rudimentary lines and expressions of matronhood. She all unconsciously held her shawl, rolled up in a canvas bag, on her left hip, as if it had been a child.

She wore a settled frown of dissent at life, but it was the frown of a mother who regarded life as a froward child, rather than as an overwhelming fate.

The other woman continued staring at her; she was mildly stupid, except for an overdeveloped curiosity which made her at times sharp beyond belief. Her eyes glittered, red spots came on her flaccid cheeks; she kept opening her mouth to speak, making little abortive motions. Finally she could endure it no longer; she nudged Rebecca boldly.

"A pleasant day," said she.

Rebecca looked at her and nodded coldly.

"Yes, very," she assented.

"Have you come far?"

"I have come from Michigan."

"Oh!" said the woman, with awe. "It's a long way," she remarked presently.

"Yes, it is," replied Rebecca, conclusively.

Still the other woman was not daunted; there was something which she determined to know, possibly roused thereto by a vague sense of incongruity in the other's appearance. "It's a long ways to come and leave a family," she remarked with painful slyness.

"I ain't got any family to leave," returned Rebecca shortly.

"Then you ain't—"

"No, I ain't."

"Oh!" said the woman.

Rebecca looked straight ahead at the race of the river.

It was a long ferry. Finally Rebecca herself waxed unexpectedly loquacious. She turned to the other woman and inquired if she knew John Dent's widow who lived in

92 Ford Village. "Her husband died about three years ago," said she, by way of detail.

The woman started violently. She turned pale, then she flushed; she cast a strange glance at her husband, who was regarding both women with a sort of stolid keenness.

"Yes, I guess I do," faltered the woman finally.

"Well, his first wife was my sister," said Rebecca with the air of one imparting important intelligence.

"Was she?" responded the other woman feebly. She glanced at her husband with an expression of doubt and terror, and he shook his head forbiddingly.

"I'm going to see her, and take my niece Agnes home with me," said Rebecca.

Then the woman gave such a violent start that she noticed it.

"What is the matter?" she asked.

"Nothin', I guess," replied the woman, with eyes on her husband, who was slowly shaking his head, like a Chinese toy.

"Is my niece sick?" asked Rebecca with quick suspicion.

"No, she ain't sick," replied the woman with alacrity, then she caught her breath with a gasp.

"When did you see her?"

"Let me see; I ain't seen her for some little time," replied the woman. Then she caught her breath again.

"She ought to have grown up real pretty, if she takes after my sister. She was a real pretty woman," Rebecca said wistfully.

"Yes, I guess she did grow up pretty," replied the woman in a trembling voice.

"What kind of a woman is the second wife?"

The woman glanced at her husband's warning face.
She continued to gaze at him while she replied in a choking voice to Rebecca:

"I—guess she's a nice woman," she replied. "I—don't know, I—guess so. I—don't see much of her."

"I felt kind of hurt that John married again so quick," said Rebecca; "but I suppose he wanted his house kept, and Agnes wanted care. I wasn't so situated that I could take her when her mother died. I had my own mother to care for, and I was school teaching. Now Mother has gone, and my uncle died six months ago and left me quite a little property, and I've given up my school, and I've come for Agnes. I guess she'll be glad to go with me, though I suppose her stepmother is a good woman, and has always done for her."

The man's warning shake at his wife was fairly portentous.

"I guess so," said she.

"John always wrote that she was a beautiful woman," said Rebecca.

Then the ferryboat grated on the shore.

John Dent's widow had sent a horse and wagon to meet her sister-in-law. When the woman and her husband went down the road, on which Rebecca in the wagon with her trunk soon passed them, she said reproachfully:

"Seems as if I'd ought to have told her, Thomas."

"Let her find it out herself," replied the man. "Don't you go to burnin' your fingers in other folks' puddin', Maria."

"Do you s'pose she'll see anything?" asked the woman with a spasmodic shudder and a terrified roll of her eyes.

"See!" returned her husband with stolid scorn. "Better be sure there's anything to see."

"Oh, Thomas, they say—"

"Lord, ain't you found out that what they say is mostly lies?"

"But if it should be true, and she's a nervous woman, she might be scared enough to lose her wits," said his wife, staring uneasily after Rebecca's erect figure in the wagon disappearing over the crest of the hilly road.

"Wits that's so easy upset ain't worth much," declared the man. "You keep out of it, Maria."

Rebecca in the meantime rode on in the wagon, beside a flaxen-headed boy, who looked, to her understanding, not very bright. She asked him a question, and he paid no attention. She repeated it, and he responded with a bewildered and incoherent grunt. Then she let him alone, after making sure that he knew how to drive straight.

They had traveled about half a mile, passed the village square, and gone a short distance beyond, when the boy drew up with a sudden Whoa! before a very prosperous-looking house. It had been one of the aboriginal cottages of the vicinity, small and white, with a roof extending on one side over a piazza, and a tiny "L" jutting out in the rear, on the right hand. Now the cottage was transformed by dormer windows, a bay window on the piazzaless side, a carved railing down the front steps, and a modern hardwood door.

"Is this John Dent's house?" asked Rebecca.

The boy was as sparing of speech as a philosopher. His only response was in flinging the reins over the horse's back, stretching out one foot to the shaft, and leaping out of the wagon, then going around to the rear for the trunk.

Rebecca got out and went toward the house. Its white
paint had a new gloss; its blinds were an immaculate
apple green; the lawn was trimmed as smooth as velvet,
and it was dotted with scrupulous groups of hydrangeas
and cannas.

"I always understood that John Dent was well-to-do,"
Rebecca reflected comfortably. "I guess Agnes will have
considerable. I've got enough, but it will come in handy
for her schooling. She can have advantages."

The boy dragged the trunk up the fine gravel walk, but
before he reached the steps leading up to the piazza, for
the house stood on a terrace, the front door opened and a
fair, frizzled head of a very large and handsome woman
appeared. She held up her black silk skirt, disclosing vo-
luminous ruffles of starched embroidery, and waited for
Rebecca. She smiled placidly, her pink, double-chinned
face widened and dimpled, but her blue eyes were wary
and calculating. She extended her hand as Rebecca
climbed the steps.

"This is Miss Flint, I suppose," said she.

"Yes, ma'am," replied Rebecca, noticing with bewilderment a curious expression compounded of fear and de-
fiance on the other's face.

"Your letter only arrived this morning," said Mrs.
Dent, in a steady voice. Her great face was a uniform
pink, and her china-blue eyes were at once aggressive
and veiled with secrecy.

"Yes, I hardly thought you'd get my letter," replied
Rebecca. "I felt as if I could not wait to hear from you
before I came. I supposed you would be so situated that
you could have me a little while without putting you out
too much, from what John used to write me about his cir-

96 cumstances, and when I had that money so unexpected I felt as if I must come for Agnes. I suppose you will be willing to give her up. You know she's my own blood, and of course she's no relation to you, though you must have got attached to her. I know from her picture what a sweet girl she must be, and John always said she looked like her own mother, and Grace was a beautiful woman, if she was my sister."

Rebecca stopped and stared at the other woman in amazement and alarm. The great handsome blonde creature stood speechless, livid, gasping, with her hand to her heart, her lips parted in a horrible caricature of a smile.

"Are you sick!" cried Rebecca, drawing near. "Don't you want me to get you some water!"

Then Mrs. Dent recovered herself with a great effort. "It is nothing," she said. "I am subject to—spells. I am over it now. Won't you come in, Miss Flint?"

As she spoke, the beautiful deep rose color suffused her face, her blue eyes met her visitor's with the opaqueness of turquoise—with a revelation of blue, but a concealment of all behind.

Rebecca followed her hostess in, and the boy, who had waited quiescently, climbed the steps with the trunk. But before they entered the door a strange thing happened. On the upper terrace, close to the piazza post, grew a great rosebush, and on it, late in the season though it was, one small red, perfect rose.

Rebecca looked at it, and the other woman extended her hand with a quick gesture. "Don't you pick that rose!" she brusquely cried.

Rebecca drew herself up with stiff dignity.

"I ain't in the habit of picking other folks' roses without leave," said she.

As Rebecca spoke she started violently, and lost sight of her resentment, for something singular happened. Suddenly the rosebush was agitated violently as if by a gust of wind, yet it was a remarkably still day. Not a leaf of the hydrangea standing on the terrace close to the rose trembled.

"What on earth—" began Rebecca, then she stopped with a gasp at the sight of the other woman's face. Although a face, it gave somehow the impression of a desperately clutched hand of secrecy.

"Come in!" said she in a harsh voice, which seemed to come forth from her chest with no intervention of the organs of speech. "Come into the house. I'm getting cold out here."

"What makes that rosebush blow so when there isn't any wind?" asked Rebecca, trembling with vague horror, yet resolute.

"I don't see as it is blowing," returned the woman calmly. And as she spoke, indeed the bush was quiet.

"It was blowing," declared Rebecca.

"It isn't now," said Mrs. Dent. "I can't try to account for everything that blows out-of-doors. I have too much to do."

She spoke scornfully and confidently, with defiant, unflinching eyes, first on the bush, then on Rebecca, and led the way into the house.

"It looked queer," persisted Rebecca, but she followed, and also the boy with the trunk.

Rebecca entered an interior, prosperous, even elegant, according to her simple ideas. There were Brussels carpets, lace curtains, and plenty of brilliant upholstery and polished wood.

"You're real nicely situated," remarked Rebecca, after she had become a little accustomed to her new surroundings and the two women were seated at the tea table.

Mrs. Dent stared with a hard complacency from behind her silver-plated service. "Yes, I be," said she.

"You got all the things new?" said Rebecca hesitatingly, with a jealous memory of her dead sister's bridal furnishings.

"Yes," said Mrs. Dent; "I was never one to want dead folks' things, and I had money enough of my own, so I wasn't beholden to John. I had the old duds put up at auction. They didn't bring much."

"I suppose you saved some for Agnes. She'll want some of her poor mother's things when she is grown up," said Rebecca with some indignation.

The defiant stare of Mrs. Dent's blue eyes waxed more intense. "There's a few things up garret," said she.

"She'll be likely to value them," remarked Rebecca. As she spoke she glanced at the window. "Isn't it most time for her to be coming home?" she asked.

"Most time," answered Mrs. Dent carelessly; "but when she gets over to Addie Slocum's she never knows when to come home."

"Is Addie Slocum her intimate friend?"

"Intimate as any."

"Maybe we can have her come out to see Agnes when she's living with me," said Rebecca wistfully. "I suppose she'll be likely to be homesick at first."

"Most likely," answered Mrs. Dent.

"Does she call you mother?" Rebecca asked.

"No, she calls me Aunt Emeline," replied the other

woman shortly. "When did you say you were going home?"

"In about a week, I thought, if she can be ready to go so soon," answered Rebecca with a surprised look.

She reflected that she would not remain a day longer than she could help after such an inhospitable look and question.

"Oh, as far as that goes," said Mrs. Dent, "it wouldn't make any difference about her being ready. You could go home whenever you felt that you must, and she could come afterward."

"Alone?"

"Why not? She's a big girl now, and you don't have to change cars."

"My niece will go home when I do, and not travel alone; and if I can't wait here for her, in the house that used to be her mother's and my sister's home, I'll go and board somewhere," returned Rebecca with warmth.

"Oh, you can stay here as long as you want to. You're welcome," said Mrs. Dent.

Then Rebecca started. "There she is!" she declared in a trembling, exultant voice. Nobody knew how she longed to see the girl.

"She isn't as late as I thought she'd be," said Mrs. Dent, and again that curious, subtle change passed over her face, and again it settled into that stony impassiveness.

Rebecca stared at the door, waiting for it to open. "Where is she?" she asked presently.

"I guess she's stopped to take off her hat in the entry," suggested Mrs. Dent.

Rebecca waited. "Why don't she come? It can't take her all this time to take off her hat."

For answer Mrs. Dent rose with a stiff jerk and threw open the door.

"Agnes!" she called. "Agnes." Then she turned and eyed Rebecca. "She ain't there."

"I saw her pass the window," said Rebecca in bewilderment.

"You must have been mistaken."

"I know I did," persisted Rebecca.

"You couldn't have."

"I did. I saw first a shadow go over the ceiling, then I saw her in the glass there"—she pointed to a mirror over the sideboard opposite—"and then the shadow passed the window."

"How did she look in the glass?"

"Little and light-haired, with the light hair kind of tossing over her forehead."

"You couldn't have seen her."

"Was that like Agnes?"

"Like enough; but of course you didn't see her. You've been thinking so much about her that you thought you did."

"You thought *you* did."

"I thought I saw a shadow pass the window, but I must have been mistaken. She didn't come in, or we would have seen her before now. I knew it was too early for her to get home from Addie Slocum's, anyhow."

When Rebecca went to bed Agnes had not returned. Rebecca had resolved that she would not retire until the girl came, but she was very tired, and she reasoned with herself that she was foolish. Besides, Mrs. Dent suggested that Agnes might go to the church social with Addie Slocum. When Rebecca suggested that she be sent for and told that her aunt had come, Mrs. Dent laughed meaningly.

"I guess you'll find out that a young girl ain't so ready to leave a sociable, where there's boys, to see her aunt," said she.

"She's too young," said Rebecca incredulously and indignantly.

"She's sixteen," replied Mrs. Dent; "and she's always been great for the boys."

"She's going to school four years after I get her before she thinks of boys," declared Rebecca.

"We'll see," laughed the other woman.

After Rebecca went to bed, she lay awake a long time listening for the sound of girlish laughter and a boy's voice under her window; then she fell asleep.

The next morning she was down early. Mrs. Dent, who kept no servants, was busily preparing breakfast.

"Don't Agnes help you about breakfast?" asked Rebecca.

"No, I let her lay," replied Mrs. Dent shortly.

"What time did she get home last night?"

"She didn't get home."

"What?"

"She didn't get home. She stayed with Addie. She often does."

"Without sending you word?"

"Oh, she knew I wouldn't worry."

"When will she be home?"

"Oh, I guess she'll be along pretty soon."

Rebecca was uneasy, but she tried to conceal it, for she knew of no good reason for uneasiness. What was there to occasion alarm in the fact of one young girl staying over-

102 night with another? She could not eat much breakfast. Afterward she went out on the little piazza, although her hostess strove furtively to stop her.

"Why don't you go out back of the house? It's real pretty—a view over the river," she said.

"I guess I'll go out here," replied Rebecca. She had a purpose: to watch for the absent girl.

Presently Rebecca came hustling into the house through the sitting room, into the kitchen where Mrs. Dent was cooking.

"That rosebush!" she gasped.

Mrs. Dent turned and faced her.

"What of it?"

"It's a-blowing."

"What of it?"

"There isn't a mite of wind this morning."

Mrs. Dent turned with an inimitable toss of her fair head. "If you think I can spend my time puzzling over such nonsense as—" she began, but Rebecca interrupted her with a cry and a rush to the door.

"There she is now!" she cried.

She flung the door wide open, and curiously enough a breeze came in and her own gray hair tossed, and a paper blew off the table to the floor with a loud rustle, but there was nobody in sight.

"There's nobody here," Rebecca said.

She looked blankly at the other woman, who brought her rolling pin down on a slab of piecrust with a thud.

"I didn't hear anybody," she said calmly.

"I saw somebody pass that window!"

"You were mistaken again."

"I *know* I saw somebody."

"You couldn't have. Please shut that door."

Rebecca shut the door. She sat down beside the window and looked out on the autumnal yard, with its little curve of footpath to the kitchen door.

"What smells so strong of roses in this room?" she said presently. She sniffed hard.

"I don't smell anything but these nutmegs."

"It is not nutmeg."

"I don't smell anything else."

"Where do you suppose Agnes is?"

"Oh, perhaps she has gone over the ferry to Porter's Falls with Addie. She often does. Addie's got an aunt over there, and Addie's got a cousin, a real pretty boy."

"You suppose she's gone over there?"

"Mebbe. I shouldn't wonder."

"When should she be home?"

"Oh, not before afternoon."

Rebecca waited with all the patience she could muster. She kept reassuring herself, telling herself that it was all natural, that the other woman could not help it, but she made up her mind that if Agnes did not return that afternoon she should be sent for.

When it was four o'clock she started up with resolution. She had been furtively watching the onyx clock on the sitting-room mantel; she had timed herself. She had said that if Agnes was not home by that time she should demand that she be sent for. She rose and stood before Mrs. Dent, who looked up coolly from her embroidery.

"I've waited just as long as I'm going to," she said. "I've come 'way from Michigan to see my own sister's daughter and take her home with me. I've been here ever since yesterday—twenty-four hours—and I haven't seen

104 her. Now I'm going to. I want her sent for."

Mrs. Dent folded her embroidery and rose.

"Well, I don't blame you," she said. "It is high time she came home. I'll go right over and get her myself."

Rebecca heaved a sigh of relief. She hardly knew what she had suspected or feared, but she knew that her position had been one of antagonism if not accusation, and she was sensible of relief.

"I wish you would," she said gratefully, and went back to her chair, while Mrs. Dent got her shawl and her little white head tie. "I wouldn't trouble you, but I do feel as if I couldn't wait any longer to see her," she remarked apologetically.

"Oh, it ain't any trouble at all," said Mrs. Dent as she went out. "I don't blame you; you have waited long enough."

Rebecca sat at the window watching breathlessly until Mrs. Dent came stepping through the yard alone. She ran to the door and saw, hardly noticing it this time, that the rosebush was again violently agitated, yet with no wind evident elsewhere.

"Where is she?" she cried.

Mrs. Dent laughed with stiff lips as she came up the steps over the terrace. "Girls will be girls," said she. "She's gone with Addie to Lincoln. Addie's got an uncle who's conductor on the train, and lives there, and he got 'em passes, and they're goin' to stay to Addie's Aunt Margaret's a few days. Mrs. Slocum said Agnes didn't have time to come over and ask me before the train went, but she took it on herself to say it would be all right, and—"

"Why hadn't she been over to tell you?" Rebecca was angry, though not suspicious. She even saw no reason for her anger.

"Oh, she was putting up grapes. She was coming over just as soon as she got the black off her hands. She heard I had company, and her hands were a sight. She was holding them over sulphur matches."

"You say she's going to stay a few days?" repeated Rebecca dazedly.

"Yes; till Thursday, Mrs. Slocum said."

"How far is Lincoln from here?"

"About fifty miles. It'll be a real treat to her. Mrs. Slocum's sister is a real nice woman."

"It is goin' to make it pretty late about my goin' home."

"If you don't feel as if you could wait, I'll get her ready and send her on just as soon as I can," Mrs. Dent said sweetly.

"I'm going to wait," said Rebecca grimly.

The two women sat down again, and Mrs. Dent took up her embroidery.

"Is there any sewing I can do for her?" Rebecca asked finally in a desperate way. "If I can get her sewing along some—"

Mrs. Dent arose with alacrity and fetched a mass of white from the closet. "Here," she said, "if you want to sew the lace on this nightgown. I was going to put her to it, but she'll be glad enough to get rid of it. She ought to have this and one more before she goes. I don't like to send her away without some good underclothing."

Rebecca snatched at the little white garment and sewed feverishly.

That night she wakened from a deep sleep a little after midnight and lay a minute trying to collect her faculties

106 and explain to herself what she was listening to. At last she discovered that it was the then popular strains of "The Maiden's Prayer" floating up through the floor from the piano in the sitting room below. She jumped up, threw a shawl over her nightgown, and hurried downstairs trembling. There was nobody in the sitting room; the piano was silent. She ran to Mrs. Dent's bedroom and called hysterically:

"Emeline! Emeline!"

"What is it?" asked Mrs. Dent's voice from the bed. The voice was stern, but had a note of consciousness in it.

"Who—who was that playing 'The Maiden's Prayer' in the sitting room, on the piano?"

"I didn't hear anybody."

"There was someone."

"I didn't hear anything."

"I tell you there was someone. But—*there ain't anybody there.*"

"I didn't hear anything."

"I did—somebody playing 'The Maiden's Prayer' on the piano. Has Agnes got home? I *want to know.*"

"Of course Agnes hasn't got home," answered Mrs. Dent with rising inflection. "Be you gone crazy over that girl? The last boat from Porter's Falls was in before we went to bed. Of course she ain't come."

"I heard—"

"You were dreaming."

"I wasn't; I was broad awake."

Rebecca went back to her chamber and kept her lamp burning all night.

The next morning her eyes upon Mrs. Dent were wary and blazing with suppressed excitement. She kept opening her mouth as if to speak, then frowning, and setting her lips hard. After breakfast she went upstairs, and came down presently with her coat and bonnet.

"Now, Emeline," she said, "I want to know where the Slocums live."

Mrs. Dent gave a strange, long, half-lidded glance at her. She was finishing her coffee.

"Why?" she asked.

"I'm going over there and find out if they have heard anything from her daughter and Agnes since they went away. I don't like what I heard last night."

"You must have been dreaming."

"It don't make any odds whether I was or not. Does she play 'The Maiden's Prayer' on the piano? I want to know."

"What if she does? She plays it a little, I believe. I don't know. She don't half play it, anyhow; she ain't got an ear."

"That wasn't half played last night. I don't like such things happening. I ain't superstitious, but I don't like it. I'm going. Where do the Slocums live?"

"You go down the road over the bridge past the old grist mill, then you turn to the left; it's the only house for half a mile. You can't miss it. It has a barn with a ship in full sail on the cupola."

"Well, I'm going. I don't feel easy."

About two hours later Rebecca returned. There were red spots on her cheeks. She looked wild. "I've been there," she said, "and there isn't a soul at home. Something *has* happened."

"What has happened?"

"I don't know. Something. I had a warning last night.

108 There wasn't a soul there. They've been sent for to Lincoln."

"Did you see anybody to ask?" asked Mrs. Dent with thinly concealed anxiety.

"I asked the woman that lives on the turn of the road. She's stone deaf. I suppose you know. She listened while I screamed at her to know where the Slocums were, and then she said, 'Mrs. Smith don't live here.' I didn't see anybody on the road, and that's the only house. What do you suppose it means?"

"I don't suppose it means much of anything," replied Mrs. Dent coolly. "Mr. Slocum is conductor on the railroad, and he'd be away anyway, and Mrs. Slocum often goes early when he does, to spend the day with her sister in Porter's Falls. She'd be more likely to go away than Addie."

"And you don't think anything has happened?" Rebecca asked with diminishing distrust before the reasonableness of it.

"Land, no!"

Rebecca went upstairs to lay aside her coat and bonnet. But she came hurrying back with them still on.

"Who's been in my room?" she gasped. Her face was pale as ashes.

Mrs. Dent also paled as she regarded her.

"What do you mean?" she asked slowly.

"I found when I went upstairs that—little nightgown of—Agnes's on—the bed, laid out. It was—*laid out*. The sleeves were folded across the bosom, and there was that little red rose between them. Emeline, what is it? Emeline, what's the matter? Oh!"

Mrs. Dent was struggling for breath in great, choking

gasps. She clung to the back of a chair. Rebecca, trembling herself so she could scarcely keep on her feet, got her some water.

As soon as she recovered herself Mrs. Dent regarded her with eyes full of the strangest mixture of fear and horror and hostility.

"What do you mean talking so?" she said in a hard voice.

"It *is there.*"

"Nonsense. You threw it down and it fell that way."

"It was folded in my bureau drawer."

"It couldn't have been."

"Who picked that red rose?"

"Look on the bush," Mrs. Dent replied shortly.

Rebecca looked at her; her mouth gaped. She hurried out of the room. When she came back her eyes seemed to protrude. (She had in the meantime hastened upstairs, and come down with tottering steps, clinging to the banisters.)

"Now I want to know what all this means?" she demanded.

"What what means?"

"The rose is on the bush, and it's gone from the bed in my room! Is this house haunted, or what?"

"I don't know anything about a house being haunted. I don't believe in such things. Be you crazy?" Mrs. Dent spoke with gathering force. The color flashed back to her cheeks.

"No," said Rebecca shortly. "I ain't crazy yet, but I shall be if this keeps on much longer. I'm going to find out where that girl is before night."

Mrs. Dent eyed her.

"What be you going to do?"

"I'm going to Lincoln."

A faint triumphant smile overspread Mrs. Dent's large face.

"You can't," said she; "there ain't any train."

"No train?"

"No; there ain't any afternoon train from the Falls to Lincoln."

"Then I'm going over to the Slocums' again tonight."

However, Rebecca did not go; such a rain came up as deterred even her resolution and she had only her best dresses with her. Then in the evening came the letter from the Michigan village which she had left nearly a week ago. It was from her cousin, a single woman, who had come to keep her house while she was away. It was a pleasant unexciting letter enough, all the first of it, and related mostly how she missed Rebecca; how she hoped she was having pleasant weather and kept her health; and how her friend, Mrs. Greenaway, had come to stay with her since she had felt lonesome the first night in the house; how she hoped Rebecca would have no objections to this, although nothing had been said about it, since she had not realized that she might be nervous alone. The cousin was painfully conscientious, hence the letter. Rebecca smiled in spite of her disturbed mind as she read it, then her eye caught the postscript. That was in a different hand, purporting to be written by the friend, Mrs. Hannah Greenaway, informing her that the cousin had fallen down the cellar stairs and broken her hip, and was in a dangerous condition, and begging Rebecca to return at once, as she herself was rheumatic and unable to nurse her properly, and no one else could be obtained.

Rebecca looked at Mrs. Dent, who had come to her
room with the letter quite late; it was half past nine, and
she had gone upstairs for the night.

"Where did this come from?" she asked.

"Mr. Amblecrom brought it," she replied.

"Who's he?"

"The postmaster. He often brings the letters that come
on the late mail. He knows I ain't anybody to send. He
brought yours about your coming. He said he and his wife
came over on the ferryboat with you."

"I remember him," Rebecca replied shortly. "There's
bad news in this letter."

Mrs. Dent's face took on an expression of serious
inquiry.

"Yes, my Cousin Harriet has fallen down the cellar
stairs—they were always dangerous—and she's broken her
hip, and I've got to take the first train home tomorrow."

"You don't say so. I'm dreadfully sorry."

"No, you ain't sorry!" said Rebecca, with a look as if
she leaped. "You're glad. I don't know why, but you're
glad. You've wanted to get rid of me for some reason ever
since I came. I don't know why. You're a strange woman.
Now you've got your way, and I hope you're satisfied."

"How you talk."

Mrs. Dent spoke in a faintly injured voice, but there
was a light in her eyes.

"I talk the way it is. Well, I'm going tomorrow morning, and I want you, just as soon as Agnes Dent comes
home, to send her out to me. Don't you wait for anything.
You pack what clothes she's got, and don't wait even to
mend them, and you buy her ticket. I'll leave the money,
and you send her along. She don't have to change cars.

112 You start her off, when she gets home, on the next train!"

"Very well," replied the other woman. She had an expression of covert amusement.

"Mind you do it."

"Very well, Rebecca."

Rebecca started on her journey the next morning. When she arrived, two days later, she found her cousin in perfect health. She found, moreover, that the friend had not written the postscript in the cousin's letter. Rebecca would have returned to Ford Village the next morning, but the fatigue and nervous strain had been too much for her. She was not able to move from her bed. She had a species of low fever induced by anxiety and fatigue. But she could write, and she did, to the Slocums, and she received no answer. She also wrote to Mrs. Dent; she even sent numerous telegrams, with no response. Finally she wrote to the postmaster, and an answer arrived by the first possible mail. The letter was short, curt, and to the purpose. Mr. Amblecrom, the postmaster, was a man of few words, and especially wary as to his expressions in a letter.

"Dear Madam," (he wrote,) "your favor rec'ed. No Slocums in Ford's Village. All dead. Addie ten years ago, her mother two years later, her father five. House vacant. Mrs. John Dent said to have neglected stepdaughter. Girl was sick. Medicine not given. Talk of taking action. Not enough evidence. House said to be haunted. Strange sights and sounds. Your niece, Agnes Dent, died a year ago, about this time.

"Yours truly,
"THOMAS AMBLECROM."

"Out through that window, three years ago to a day, her husband and her two young brothers went off for their day's shooting. They never came back. . . ."

THE OPEN WINDOW

Saki

"My aunt will be down presently, Mr. Nuttel," said a very self-possessed young lady of fifteen; "in the meantime you must try and put up with me."

Framton Nuttel endeavoured to say the correct something which should duly flatter the niece of the moment without unduly discounting the aunt that was to come. Privately he doubted more than ever whether these formal visits on a succession of total strangers would do much towards helping the nerve cure which he was supposed to be undergoing.

"I know how it will be," his sister had said when he was preparing to migrate to this rural retreat; "you will bury yourself down there and not speak to a living soul, and your nerves will be worse than ever from moping. I shall just give you letters of introduction to all the people I know there. Some of them, as far as I can remember, were quite nice."

Framton wondered whether Mrs. Sappleton, the lady to whom he was presenting one of the letters of introduction, came into the nice division.

"Do you know many of the people round here?" asked the niece, when she judged that they had had sufficient silent communion.

"Hardly a soul," said Framton. "My sister was staying here, at the rectory, you know, some four years ago, and she gave me letters of introduction to some of the people here."

He made the last statement in a tone of distinct regret.

"Then you know practically nothing about my aunt?" pursued the self-possessed young lady.

"Only her name and address," admitted the caller. He was wondering whether Mrs. Sappleton was in the married or widowed state. An undefinable something about the room seemed to suggest masculine habitation.

"Her great tragedy happened just three years ago," said the child; "that would be since your sister's time."

"Her tragedy?" asked Framton; somehow in this restful country spot tragedies seemed out of place.

"You may wonder why we keep that window wide open on an October afternoon," said the niece, indicating a large French window that opened onto a lawn.

"It is quite warm for the time of the year," said Framton; "but has that window got anything to do with the tragedy?"

"Out through that window, three years ago to a day, her husband and her two young brothers went off for their day's shooting. They never came back. In crossing the moor to their favourite snipe-shooting ground they were all three engulfed in a treacherous piece of bog. It had been that dreadful wet summer, you know, and places that were safe in other years gave way suddenly without warning. Their bodies were never recovered. That was the dreadful part of it." Here the child's voice lost its self-possessed note and became falteringly human. "Poor aunt always thinks that they will come back some day, they and the little brown spaniel that was lost with them, and walk in at that window just as they used to do. That is why the window is kept open every evening till it is quite dusk. Poor dear aunt, she has often told me how they went out, her husband with his white waterproof coat over his arm, and Ronnie, her youngest brother, singing, 'Bertie, why do you bound?' as he always did to tease her, because she said it got on her nerves. Do you know, sometimes on still, quiet evenings like this, I almost get a creepy feeling that they will all walk in through that window—"

She broke off with a little shudder. It was a relief to Framton when the aunt bustled into the room with a whirl of apologies for being late in making her appearance.

"I hope Vera has been amusing you?" she said.

"She has been very interesting," said Framton.

"I hope you don't mind the open window," said Mrs. Sappleton briskly; "my husband and brothers will be home directly from shooting, and they always come in this way. They've been out for snipe in the marshes today, so they'll make a fine mess over my poor carpets. So like you menfolk, isn't it?"

She rattled on cheerfully about the shooting and the scarcity of birds, and the prospects for duck in the winter. To Framton it was all purely horrible. He made a desperate but only partially successful effort to turn the talk on

116 to a less ghastly topic; he was conscious that his hostess was giving him only a fragment of her attention, and her eyes were constantly straying past him to the open window and the lawn beyond. It was certainly an unfortunate coincidence that he should have paid his visit on this tragic anniversary.

"The doctors agree in ordering me complete rest, an absence of mental excitement, and avoidance of anything in the nature of violent physical exercise," announced Framton, who labored under the tolerably widespread delusion that total strangers and chance acquaintances are hungry for the least detail of one's ailments and infirmities, their cause and cure. "On the matter of diet they are not so much in agreement," he continued.

"No?" said Mrs. Sappleton, in a voice which only replaced a yawn at the last moment. Then she suddenly brightened into alert attention—but not to what Framton was saying.

"Here they are at last!" she cried. "Just in time for tea, and don't they look as if they were muddy up to the eyes!"

Framton shivered slightly and turned towards the niece with a look intended to convey sympathetic comprehension. The child was staring out through the open window with dazed horror in her eyes. In a chill shock of nameless fear Framton swung round in his seat and looked in the same direction.

In the deepening twilight three figures were walking across the lawn towards the window; they all carried guns under their arms, and one of them was additionally burdened with a white coat hung over his shoulders. A tired brown spaniel kept close at their heels. Noiselessly they neared the house, and then a hoarse young voice chanted out of the dusk: "I said, Bertie, why do you bound?"

Framton grabbed wildly at his stick and hat; the hall door, the gravel drive, and the front gate were dimly noted stages in his headlong retreat. A cyclist coming along the road had to run into the hedge to avoid imminent collision.

"Here we are, my dear," said the bearer of the white mackintosh, coming in through the window; "fairly muddy, but most of it's dry. Who was that who bolted out as we came up?"

"A most extraordinary man, a Mr. Nuttel," said Mrs. Sappleton; "could only talk about his illnesses, and dashed off without a word of good-bye or apology when you arrived. One would think he had seen a ghost."

"I expect it was the spaniel," said the niece calmly; "he told me he had a horror of dogs. He was once hunted into a cemetery somewhere on the banks of the Ganges by a pack of pariah dogs, and had to spend the night in a newly dug grave with the creatures snarling and grinning and foaming just above him. Enough to make any one lose their nerve."

Romance at short notice was her speciality.

The phantom of this black hound is what the fishermen see.... His jaws drip angry foam and his eyes are lit with crimson fire.

GHOSTS ON THE JERSEY COAST

Stephen Crane

Asbury Park, N.J., Nov. 9.—Of all the brightly attired city people who throng this place during the summer months not one seems to care a penny for the ghosts that line New Jersey's famous stretch of seacoast. It is only in the fall, when the marshes around Barnegat turn a dreary brown and the gray autumn rains sweep among the sand hills that the slightest attention is paid to the numerous phantoms that dwell here. However, some parts of this coast are fairly jammed with hobgoblins—white ladies, grave lights, phantom ships, prowling corpses. In his cabin many an old fisherman, wagging his head solemnly, can tell sincere and fierce tales, well calculated to freeze the blood. Around the gay modern resorts these stories have lost weight, but in the little villages of the fishermen south of here, near the salt marshes of Barnegat, a man had better think three times before he openly scorns the legends of the phantoms. Even at Branchburg, too, there are people who will pummel your features well if you deny the dim bluish light that floats above the long grave wherein lie the dead of the *New Era,* flickering and sputtering in spectral wrath whenever any attempt is made after the gold which is said to have been buried with the bodies of the unfortunate sailors and emigrants. Too, if you go into the huckleberry region back of Shark River you had better not scorn the story of the great pirate ship that sails without trouble in twelve inches of water, and has skeletons dangling at the mastheads. Terrible faces peer over the bulwarks, and confound the visions of any who would witness the phantom movements from the shore.

In this region there is also an old Indian, dead a hundred years, who stalks through the land at night. He is looking, it is said, for his fair young bride, whom he buried in a previous century because she put too much salt in his muskrat stew. This ghost was once followed on his shadowy pilgrimage by some young men who had greatly fortified themselves with applejack, but when his pursuers came too near the ghostly Indian simply turned and looked at them. He had a stilettolike glance, they asserted, which went straight through them as if they had been made of paper. So they ran away.

At Deal Beach a youth and a maiden, impalpable as sea mist, perambulate to and fro on the bluff, keeping their lovers' tryst while the wind swirls in the branches of the solitary tree and the stars shine through their forms of air.

Near Barnegat Light, wicked fishermen engaged in doing that which they ought not to do, hear low chuckles, and upon looking up quickly see an old crone, who chuckles at them for a moment and then goes off, looking back occasionally to chuckle.

120   At Long Beach, where men deep in slumber were killed by brave Refugees and Tories from New York, few fishermen care to lie and sleep, for then the gray specter of the Tory captain, hideous from the ancient crimes, comes and holds a knife at the throat. When they flee they hear feet crunch in the sand at their heels, and no matter how fast they run they cannot shake off this invisible pursuer, who follows them to their threshold.

In fact, it can truly be said that more hair has risen on the New Jersey shore than at any other place of the same geographical dimensions in the world. The fishermen are never low in their imaginative faculties. They are poets, and although they create more ghosts than any other known place they turn no butchers into specters. No dead jeweler in these villages ever comes back to wind up his clocks. No departed cobbler returns to peg at his trade. It would be incompatible with the taste of the people. To make a good ghost a man has to be old and sinister; a crone, wrinkled and wicked; a maiden, beautiful and fragile. When such die, a serviceable phantom is added to the list.

An example of the discernment of the people in their choice of specters may be had in the famous legend of the black dog. They created a spectral black hound in this tale and they gave him red eyes. It was genius. No one knew better than they that a ghostly Yorkshire terrier could have no effect upon even the most timid. The specter must be a hound, and it must be black; no yellow dog would answer the purpose, nor a speckled one, nor a striped one. It must be black. Thus was built the legend.

The tradition of the black dog has been much obscured because of its great age. It relates away back prior to the

Revolution, when the New Jersey coast was for the most part unpeopled. It was a desolate stretch of sand, pine forest and salt marsh. Upon the narrow strip of land that separates Barnegat Bay from the ocean there then lived men who were so villainous that they had made a business of luring ships to the shore by means of false lights, that in stormy weather shone afar out to the jaded sailors, precisely as bright as the brightest beacons of hope. When a vessel would be wrecked, the pirates gayly plundered it. It was their habit to murder the crews.

One night there came a great storm which tossed the vessels upon the sea like little chips. The Jersey coast was strewn with wreckage and many strong ships lay dying upon the bar. No coast has proved so formidable to navigation as this New Jersey shore, just a brown lip of land rearing from the sea. From a vessel the coast looks so low that one wonders why each wave has not swallowed it.

During this storm a fine full-rigged ship struck the bar directly opposite the stronghold of the band of pirates. They ran down to the beach and cheered and caroused, for they had not even been put to the trouble of deceiving the pilot and decoying the ship upon the bar. The thing had happened without labor or plan. They gathered in a crowd at the edge of the surf and watched the ship's people clinging to the rigging and looking toward the shore. They clung in bunches, lines, irregular groups, reminding one of some kind of insects. Sometimes a monstrous white wave would thunder over the ship, bearing off perhaps two or three sailors whose grasp it had torn away and tumbling the bodies into the wide swirl of foam that covered the sea. Soon they grew so weary that they began to drop off one by one into the water, unable to stand the strain of the terrific rushes of the waves. The pirates on the shore laughed when they saw a mass of men try to launch the boats, for they knew that none could live in that sea. Presently, the bodies of sailors and passengers began to wash up at the feet of the pirates, who searched them for jewels and money. The hull of the ship was hidden in the white smothering riot of water, but the rigging, with its lessening burden of men, was faintly outlined upon the dead black sky. The pirates became busily engaged in overhauling the corpses.

At last a fine black hound emerged slowly from the water and crawled painfully up the beach. He was dragging the body of a young man by the shirt collar. The dog had fought a tremendous battle. It seemed incredible that he could have forced his way to shore with the body through the wild surf. The young man's face was ghastly in death. There was a grievous red wound in his temple where, perhaps, he had been flung against some wreckage by the waves. The dog hauled the body out of reach of the water and then went to whine and sniff at the dead man's hand. He wagged his tail expectantly. At last he settled, shivering, back upon his haunches and gave vent to a long howl, a dog's cry of death and despair and fear, that cry that is in the most indescribable key of woe. It made the pirates turn their heads instantly, startled. They gathered about the dead body and the dog to stare curiously. At the approach of this band of assassins, vagabonds and outcasts the hound braced himself, the hair on his neck ruffled and his teeth gleaming. For a moment they confronted each other, the pirates and the dog, guardian of his master's corpse. There stood the dog, a tempest of water behind him and the evil crowd of men before him, and not even a caress possible from the pallid hand at his feet. No doubt he did not comprehend the odds of his battle. He only knew one thing—to be faithful until he was dead.

Then one particularly precious villain perceived the glitter of gems upon the dead man's hand. He reached covetously forward, and the dog lunged for his throat. An instant later there were many curses and the thud of blows and then, suddenly, a humanlike scream from the dog. He crawled until he could lay his head upon the dead man's chest, and there he died, as the robbers were pulling the rings from his master's fingers.

The phantom of this black hound is what the fishermen see as they return home from their boats and nets late at night. There is a dreadful hatchet wound in the animal's head, and from it the phantom blood bubbles. His jaws drip angry foam and his eyes are lit with crimson fire. He gallops continually with his nose to the ground as if he were trailing someone. If you are ever down upon the New Jersey coast at midnight and meet this specter, you had better run.

"I never aspired to be a shower bath," said the ghost,
"but it is my doom."

THE WATER GHOST
OF HARROWBY HALL

John Kendrick Bangs

The trouble with Harrowby Hall was that it was haunted,
and, what was worse, the ghost did not content itself with
merely appearing at the bedside of the afflicted person
who saw it, but persisted in remaining there for one mortal hour before it would disappear.

It never appeared except on Christmas Eve, and then
as the clock was striking twelve, in which respect alone
was it lacking in that originality which in these days is a
sine qua non of success in spectral life. The owners of
Harrowby Hall had done their utmost to rid themselves
of the damp and dewy lady who rose up out of the best
bedroom floor at midnight, but without avail. They had
tried to stop the clock, so that the ghost would not know
when it was midnight; but she made her appearance just
the same, with that fearful miasmatic personality of hers,
and there she would stand until everything about her was
thoroughly saturated.

Then the owners of Harrowby Hall calked up every
crack in the floor with the very best quality of hemp, and
over this were placed layers of tar and canvas; the walls

were made waterproof, and the doors and windows like-wise, the proprietors having conceived the notion that the unexorcised lady would find it difficult to leak into the room after these precautions had been taken; but even this did not suffice. The following Christmas Eve she appeared as promptly as before, and frightened the occupant of the room quite out of his senses by sitting down alongside of him and gazing with her cavernous blue eyes into his; and he noticed, too, that in her long, aqueously bony fingers bits of dripping seaweed were entwined, the ends hanging down, and these ends she drew across his forehead until he became like one insane. And then he swooned away, and was found unconscious in his bed the next morning by his host, simply saturated with seawater and fright, from the combined effects of which he never recovered, dying four years later of pneumonia and nervous prostration at the age of seventy-eight.

The next year the master of Harrowby Hall decided not to have the best spare bedroom opened at all, thinking that perhaps the ghost's thirst for making herself disagreeable would be satisfied by haunting the furniture, but the plan was as unavailing as the many that had preceded.

The ghost appeared as usual in the room—that is, it was supposed she did, for the hangings were dripping wet the next morning, and in the parlor below the haunted room a great damp spot appeared on the ceiling. Finding no one there, she immediately set out to learn the reason why, and she chose none other to haunt than the owner of the Harrowby himself. She found him in his own cozy room drinking whiskey—whiskey undiluted—and felicitating himself upon having foiled her ghostship, when all

126 of a sudden the curl went out of his hair, his whiskey bottle filled and overflowed, and he was himself in a condition similar to that of a man who had fallen into a water butt. When he had recovered from the shock, which was a painful one, he saw before him the lady of the cavernous eyes and the seaweed fingers. The sight was so unexpected and so terrifying that he fainted, but immediately came to, because of the vast amount of water in his hair, which, trickling down over his face, restored his consciousness.

Now it so happened that the master of Harrowby was a brave man, and while he was not particularly fond of interviewing ghosts, especially such quenching ghosts as the one before him, he was not to be daunted by an apparition. He had paid the lady the compliment of fainting from the effects of his first surprise, and now that he had come to, he intended to find out a few things he felt he had a right to know. He would have liked to put on a dry suit of clothes first, but the apparition declined to leave him for an instant until her hour was up, and he was forced to deny himself that pleasure. Every time he would move she would follow him, with the result that everything she came in contact with got a ducking. In an effort to warm himself up, he approached the fire, an unfortunate move as it turned out, because it brought the ghost directly over the fire, which immediately was extinguished. The whiskey became utterly valueless as a comforter to his chilled system, because it was by this time diluted to a proportion of ninety per cent of water. The only thing he could do to ward off the evil effects of his encounter he did, and that was to swallow ten two-grain quinine pills, which he managed to put into his mouth

before the ghost had time to interfere. Having done this,
he turned with some asperity to the ghost, and said:

"Far be it from me to be impolite to a woman, madam,
but I'm hanged if it wouldn't please me better if you'd
stop these infernal visits of yours to this house. Go sit out
on the lake, if you like that sort of thing; soak the water
butt, if you wish; but do not, I implore you, come into a
gentleman's house and saturate him and his possessions in
this way. It is disagreeable."

"Henry Hartwick Oglethorpe," said the ghost, in a
gurgling voice, "you don't know what you are talking
about."

"Madam," returned the unhappy householder, "I wish
that remark were strictly truthful. I was talking about
you. It would be shillings and pence—nay, pounds, in my
pocket, madam, if I did not know you."

"That is a bit of specious nonsense," returned the
ghost, throwing a quart of indignation into the face of the
master of Harrowby. "It may rank high as repartee, but
as a comment upon my statement that you do not know
what you are talking about, it savors of irrelevant impertinence. You do not know that I am compelled to
haunt this place year after year by inexorable fate. It is
no pleasure to me to enter this house, and ruin and mil-
dew everything I touch. I never aspired to be a shower
bath, but it is my doom. Do you know who I am?"

"No, I don't," returned the master of Harrowby. "I
should say you were the Lady of the Lake, or Little Sallie
Waters."

"You are a witty man for your years," said the ghost.

"Well, my humor is drier than yours will ever be," returned the master.

"No doubt. I'm never dry. I am the Water Ghost of Harrowby Hall, and dryness is a quality entirely beyond my wildest hope. I have been the incumbent of this highly unpleasant office for two hundred years tonight."

"How the deuce did you ever come to get elected?" asked the master.

"Through a suicide," replied the specter. "I am the ghost of that fair maiden whose picture hangs over the mantelpiece in the drawing room. I should have been your great-great-great-great-great-aunt if I had lived, Henry Hartwick Oglethorpe, for I was the own sister of your great-great-great-great-grandfather."

"But what induced you to get this house into such a predicament?"

"I was not to blame, sir," returned the lady. "It was my father's fault. He it was who built Harrowby Hall, and the haunted chamber was to have been mine. My father had it furnished in pink and yellow, knowing well that blue and gray formed the only combination of color I could tolerate. He did it merely to spite me, and with what I deem a proper spirit, I declined to live in the room; whereupon my father said I could live there or on the lawn, he didn't care which. That night I ran from the house and jumped over the cliff into the sea."

"That was rash," said the master of Harrowby.

"So I've heard," returned the ghost. "If I had known what the consequences were to be I should not have jumped; but I really never realized what I was doing until after I was drowned. I had been drowned a week when a sea nymph came to me and informed me that I was to be one of her followers forever afterwards, adding that it should be my doom to haunt Harrowby Hall for one hour every Christmas Eve throughout the rest of eternity. I was to haunt that room on such Christmas Eves as I found it inhabited; and if it should turn out not to be inhabited, I was and am to spend the allotted hour with the head of the house."

"I'll sell the place."

"That you cannot do, for it is also required of me that I shall appear as the deeds are to be delivered to any purchaser, and divulge to him the awful secret of the house."

"Do you mean to tell me that on every Christmas Eve that I don't happen to have somebody in that guest chamber, you are going to haunt me wherever I may be, ruining my whiskey, taking all the curl out of my hair, extinguishing my fire, and soaking me through to the skin?" demanded the master.

"You have stated the case, Oglethorpe. And what is more," said the water ghost, "it doesn't make the slightest difference where you are; if I find that room empty, wherever you may be I shall douse you with my spectral pres—"

Here the clock struck one, and immediately the apparition faded away. It was perhaps more of a trickle than a fade, but as a disappearance it was complete.

"By Saint George and his Dragon!" ejaculated the master of Harrowby, wringing his hands. "It is guineas to hot cross buns that next Christmas there's an occupant of the spare room, or I spend the night in a bathtub."

But the master of Harrowby would have lost his wager had there been any one there to take him up, for when Christmas Eve came again he was in his grave, never having recovered from the cold contracted that awful night. Harrowby Hall was closed, and the heir to the estate was

130 in London, where to him in his chambers came the same experience that his father had gone through, saving only that, being younger and stronger, he survived the shock. Everything in his room was ruined—his clocks were rusted in the works; a fine collection of water-color drawings was entirely obliterated by the onslaught of the water ghost; and, what was worse, the apartments below his were drenched with the water soaking through the floors, a damage for which he was compelled to pay, and which resulted in his being requested by his landlady to vacate the premises immediately.

The story of the visitation inflicted upon his family had gone abroad, and no one could be got to invite him out to any function save afternoon teas and receptions. Fathers of daughters declined to permit him to remain in their houses later than eight o'clock at night, not knowing but that some emergency might arise in the supernatural world which would require the unexpected appearance of the water ghost in this on nights other than Christmas Eve, and before the mystic hour when weary church-yards, ignoring the rules which are supposed to govern polite society, begin to yawn. Nor would the maids themselves have aught to do with him, fearing the destruction by the sudden incursion of aqueous femininity of the costumes which they held most dear.

So the heir of Harrowby Hall resolved, as his ancestors for several generations before him had resolved, that something must be done. His first thought was to make one of his servants occupy the haunted room at the crucial moment; but in this he failed, because the servants themselves knew the history of the room and rebelled. None of his friends would consent to sacrifice their personal comfort to his, nor was there to be found in all England a man so poor as to be willing to occupy the doomed chamber on Christmas Eve for pay.

Then the thought came to the heir to have the fireplace in the room enlarged, so that he might evaporate the ghost at its first appearance, and he was felicitating himself upon the ingenuity of his plan, when he remembered what his father had told him—how that no fire could withstand the lady's extremely contagious dampness. And then he bethought him of steampipes. These, he remembered, could lie hundreds of feet deep in water, and still retain sufficient heat to drive the water away in vapor; and as a result of this thought the haunted room was heated by steam to a withering degree, and the heir for six months attended daily the Turkish baths, so that when Christmas Eve came he could himself withstand the awful temperature of the room.

The scheme was only partially successful. The water ghost appeared at the specified time, and found the heir of Harrowby prepared; but hot as the room was, it shortened her visit by no more than five minutes in the hour, during which time the nervous system of the young master was well-nigh shattered, and the room itself was cracked and warped to an extent which required the outlay of a large sum of money to remedy. And worse than this, as the last drop of the water ghost was slowly sizzling itself out on the floor, she whispered to her would-be conqueror that his scheme would avail him nothing, because there was still water in great plenty where she came from, and that next year would find her rehabilitated and as exasperatingly saturating as ever.

It was then that the natural action of the mind, in

132 going from one extreme to the other, suggested to the ingenious heir of Harrowby the means by which the water ghost was ultimately conquered, and happiness once more came within the grasp of the house of Oglethorpe.

The heir provided himself with a warm suit of fur underclothing. Donning this with the furry side in, he placed over it a rubber garment, tight-fitting, which he wore just as a woman wears a jersey. On top of this he placed another set of underclothing, this suit made of wool, and over this was a second rubber garment like the first. Upon his head he placed a light and comfortable diving helmet, and so clad, on the following Christmas Eve he awaited the coming of his tormentor.

It was a bitterly cold night that brought to a close this twenty-fourth day of December. The air outside was still, but the temperature was below zero. Within all was quiet, the servants of Harrowby Hall awaiting with beating hearts the outcome of their master's campaign against his supernatural visitor.

The master himself was lying on the bed in the haunted room, clad as has already been indicated, and then—

The clock clanged out the hour of twelve.

There was a sudden banging of doors, a blast of cold air swept through the halls, the door leading into the haunted chamber flew open, a splash was heard, and the water ghost was seen standing at the side of the heir of Harrowby, from whose outer dress there streamed rivulets of water, but whose own person deep down under the various garments he wore was as dry and as warm as he could have wished.

"Ha!" said the young master of Harrowby. "I'm glad to see you."

"You are the most original man I've met, if that is true," returned the ghost. "May I ask where did you get that hat?"

"Certainly, madam," returned the master, courteously. "It is a little portable observatory I had made just for such emergencies as this. But, tell me, is it true that you are doomed to follow me about for one mortal hour—to stand where I stand, to sit where I sit?"

"That is my delectable fate," returned the lady.

"We'll go out on the lake," said the master, starting up.

"You can't get rid of me that way," returned the ghost. "The water won't swallow me up; in fact, it will just add to my present bulk."

"Nevertheless," said the master firmly, "we will go out on the lake."

"But, my dear sir," returned the ghost, with a pale reluctance, "it is fearfully cold out there. You will be frozen hard before you've been out ten minutes."

"Oh, no, I'll not," replied the master. "I am very warmly dressed. Come!" This last in a tone of command that made the ghost ripple.

And they started.

They had not gone far before the water ghost showed signs of distress.

"You walk too slowly," she said. "I am nearly frozen. My knees are so stiff now I can hardly move. I beseech you to accelerate your step."

"I should like to oblige a lady," returned the master courteously, "but my clothes are rather heavy, and a

134 hundred yards an hour is about my speed. Indeed, I think we would better sit down here on this snowdrift, and talk matters over."

"Do not! Do not do so, I beg!" cried the ghost. "Let me move on. I feel myself growing rigid as it is. If we stop here, I shall be frozen stiff."

"That, madam," said the master slowly, and seating himself on an ice cake—"that is why I have brought you here. We have been on this spot just ten minutes; we have fifty more. Take your time about it, madam, but freeze, that is all I ask of you."

"I cannot move my right leg now," cried the ghost, in despair, "and my overskirt is a solid sheet of ice. Oh, good, kind Mr. Oglethorpe, light a fire, and let me go free from these icy fetters."

"Never, madam. It cannot be. I have you at last."

"Alas!" cried the ghost, a tear trickling down her frozen cheek. "Help me, I beg. I congeal."

"Congeal, madam, congeal!" returned Oglethorpe coldly. "You have drenched me and mine for two hundred and three years, madam. Tonight you have had your last drench."

"Ah, but I shall thaw out again, and then you'll see. Instead of the comfortably tepid, genial ghost I have been in my past, sir, I shall be iced water," cried the lady threateningly.

"No, you won't, either," returned Oglethorpe; "for when you are frozen quite stiff, I shall send you to a cold-storage warehouse, and there shall you remain an icy work of art forever more."

"But warehouses burn."

"So they do, but this warehouse cannot burn. It is

made of asbestos and surrounding it are fireproof walls, and within those walls the temperature is now and shall forever be 416 degrees below the zero point; low enough to make an icicle of any flame in the world—or the next," the master added, with an ill-suppressed chuckle.

"For the last time let me beseech you. I would go on my knees to you, Oglethorpe, were they not already frozen. I beg of you do not doo—"

Here even the words froze on the water ghost's lips and the clock struck one. There was a momentary tremor throughout the ice-bound form, and the moon, coming out from behind a cloud, shone down on the rigid figure of a beautiful woman sculptured in clear, transparent ice. There stood the ghost of Harrowby Hall, conquered by the cold, a prisoner for all time.

The heir of Harrowby had won at last, and today in a large storage house in London stands the frigid form of one who will never again flood the house of Oglethorpe with woe and seawater.

As for the heir of Harrowby, his success in coping with a ghost has made him famous, a fame that still lingers about him, although his victory took place some twenty years ago; and so far from being unpopular with the fair sex, as he was when we first knew him, he has not only been married twice, but is to lead a third bride to the altar before the year is out.

FANTASY

———

Magic, fabulous creatures, wizards, strange worlds—
these are the stuff of fantasy. Fantasy begins by asking
What if? What if a genie granted three wishes? What if
each tree in a forest were inhabited by a spirit? What if
gods and demons roamed the earth disguised as mortals?
(Would we recognize them?)

Fantasy appeals because it deals with extreme situations. It traffics with dreams and nightmares, the wonderful and the horrible, the beautiful and the grotesque. It
crystalizes our hopes and gives a shape to our fears.

But, like all fiction, fantasy must follow rules. Once an
author creates a world of fantasy, what happens within
that world must be consistent. A person riding on a magic
carpet cannot attach an outboard motor to it. If an author
goes too far, readers stop believing, and the delicate, special world that has been created falls apart.

Each fantasy does create its own special world, and
even at its most fantastic, each fantasy makes its own
kind of sense.

At last the great egg burst. "Peep! peep!" said the little
one, and crept forth. It was very large and very ugly.

THE UGLY DUCKLING

Hans Christian Andersen

It was so glorious out in the country. It was summer; the cornfields were yellow, the oats were green, the hay had been put up in stacks in the green meadows, and the stork went about on his long red legs and chattered Egyptian, for this was the language he had learned from his mother. All around the fields and meadows were great forests, and in the midst of these forests lay deep lakes. Yes, it was certainly glorious out in the country. In the midst of the sunshine there lay an old farm with deep canals about it, and from the wall down to the water grew great burdocks, so high that little children could stand upright under the loftiest of them. It was just as wild there as in the deepest wood, and here sat a duck upon her nest. She had to hatch her ducklings; but she was almost tired out before the little ones came; and then she so seldom had visitors. The other ducks liked better to swim about in the canals than to run up to sit down under a burdock and cackle with her.

At last one eggshell after another burst open. "Peep! peep!" they cried; and in all the eggs there were little

138 creatures that stuck out their heads.

"Quack! quack!" they said; and they all came quacking out as fast as they could, looking all around them under the green leaves; and the mother let them look as much as they chose, for green is good for the eye.

"How wide the world is!" said all the young ones, for they certainly had much more room now than when they were in the eggs.

"Do you think this is all the world?" said the mother. "That stretches far across the other side of the garden, quite into the parson's field; but I have never been there yet. I hope you are all together," and she stood up. "No, I have not all. The largest egg still lies there. How long is that to last? I am really tired of it." And she sat down again.

"Well, how goes it?" asked an old duck who had come to pay her a visit.

"It lasts a long time with that one egg," said the duck who sat there. "It will not burst. Now, only look at the others; are they not the prettiest little ducks one could possibly see? They are all like their father: the rogue, he never comes to see me."

"Let me see the egg which will not burst," said the old visitor. "You may be sure it is a turkey's egg. I was once cheated in that way and had much anxiety and trouble with the young ones, for they are afraid of the water. Must I say it to you, I could not get them to venture in. I quacked and I clacked, but it was no use. Let me see the egg. Yes, that's a turkey's egg. Let it lie there, and teach the other children to swim."

"I think I will sit on it a little longer," said the duck.

"I've sat so long now that I can sit a few days more."

"Just as you please," said the old duck; and she went away.

At last the great egg burst. "Peep! peep!" said the little one, and crept forth. It was very large and very ugly. The duck looked at it.

"He's a very large duckling," said she; "none of the others look like that: can he really be a turkey chick? Well, we shall soon find out. He must go into the water, even if I have to kick him in myself."

The next day, it was bright, beautiful weather; the sun shone on all the green trees. The mother duck went down to the canal with all her family. Splash! she jumped into the water. "Quack! quack!" she said, and one duckling after another plunged in. The water closed over their heads, but they came up in an instant and swam beautifully; their legs went of themselves. They were all in the water, and the ugly gray duckling swam with them.

"No, he's not a turkey," said she; "look how well he can use his legs, and how straight he holds himself. He is my own child! On the whole he's quite handsome, if one looks at him rightly. Quack! quack! come with me, and I'll lead you out into the great world and present you in the duck yard; but keep close to me, so that no one may tread on you, and take care of the cats!"

And so they came into the duck yard. There was a terrible riot going on in there, for two families were quarreling about an eel's head, and the cat got it after all.

"See, that's how it goes in the world!" said the mother duck; and she whetted her beak, for she too had wanted the eel's head. "Now come along," she said; "and see that

140 you bow your heads before the old duck yonder. She's the grandest of all here; she's of Spanish blood—that's why she's so fat; and do you see? she has a red rag around her leg. That's something particularly fine, and the greatest distinction a duck can enjoy: it signifies that one does not want to lose her, and that she's to be known by the animals and by men too. Shake yourselves—don't turn in your toes; a well-brought-up duck turns its toes quite out, just like father and mother—so! Now bend your necks and say 'Quack!' "

And they did so: but the other ducks round about looked at them, and said quite boldly—

"Look there! now we're to have these hanging on, as if there were not enough of us already! And—fie!—how that duckling yonder looks; we won't stand that!" And one duck flew up at him and bit him in the neck.

"Let him alone," said the mother; "he does no harm to anyone."

"Yes, but he's too large and peculiar," said the duck who had bitten him; "and therefore he must be put down."

"Those are pretty children that the mother has there," said the old duck with the rag around her leg. "They're all pretty but that one; that was rather unlucky. I wish she could make him over again."

"That cannot be done, my lady," replied the mother duck. "He is not pretty, but he has a really good disposition and swims as well as any other; yes, I may even say he swims better. I think he will grow up handsome and become smaller in time; he has lain too long in the egg and therefore is not properly shaped." And then she

pinched him in the neck, and smoothed his feathers.
"Moreover it is a drake," she said, "and therefore it is not
so much consequence. I think he will be very strong: he
makes his way already."

"The other ducklings are graceful enough," said the
old duck. "Make yourself at home; and if you find an eel's
head, you may bring it to me."

And now they were at home. But the poor duckling
which had crept last out of the egg and looked so ugly
was bitten and pushed and jeered, as much by the ducks
as by the chickens.

"He is too big!" they all said. And the turkey cock,
who had been born with spurs and therefore thought
himself an emperor, blew himself up like a ship in full
sail, and bore straight down upon him; then he gobbled
and grew quite red in the face. The poor duckling did not
know where he should stand or walk. He was quite melancholy because he looked ugly and was the butt of the
whole duck yard.

So it went on the first day; and afterwards it became
worse and worse. The poor duckling was hunted about by
everyone; even his brothers and sisters were quite angry
with him and said, "If the cat would only catch you, you
ugly creature!" And the mother said, "If you were only
far away!" And the ducks bit him, and the chickens beat
him, and the girl who had to feed the poultry kicked at
him with her foot.

Then he ran and flew over the fence, and the little
birds in the bushes flew up in fear.

"That is because I am so ugly!" thought the duckling;
and he shut his eyes, but flew on further; and so he came

142 out into the great moor, where the wild ducks lived. Here he lay the whole night long; and he was weary and downcast.

Towards morning the wild ducks flew up and looked at their new companion.

"What sort of a one are you?" they asked; and the duckling turned in every direction and bowed as well as he could. "You are remarkably ugly!" said the wild ducks. "But that is nothing to us, so long as you do not marry into our family."

Poor thing! he certainly did not think of marrying and only hoped to obtain leave to lie among the reeds and drink some of the swamp water.

Thus he lay two whole days; then came thither two wild geese, or, properly speaking, two wild ganders. It was not long since each had crept out of an egg, and that's why they were so saucy.

"Listen, comrade," said one of them. "You're so ugly that I like you. Will you go with us, and become a bird of passage? Near here, in another moor, there are a few sweet lovely wild geese, all unmarried, and all able to say 'Rap!' you've a chance of making your fortune, ugly as you are."

"Bang! bang!" resounded through the air; and the two ganders fell down dead in the swamp, and the water became blood red. "Bang! bang!" it sounded again, and the whole flock of wild geese rose up from the reeds. And then there was another report. A great hunt was going on. The sportsmen were lying in wait all around the moor, and some were even sitting up in the branches of the trees, which spread far over the reeds. The blue smoke rose up like clouds among the dark trees and was wafted far away across the water; and the hunting dogs came—splash, splash!—into the swamp, and the rushes and the reeds bent down on every side. That was a fright for the poor duckling! He turned his head and put it under his wing; but at that moment a frightful great dog stood close by the duckling. His tongue hung far out of his mouth, and his eyes gleamed horrible and ugly; he thrust out his nose close against the duckling, showed his sharp teeth, and—splash, splash!—on he went without seizing him.

"Oh, Heaven be thanked!" sighed the duckling. "I am so ugly that even the dog does not like to bite me!"

And so he lay quite quiet while the shots rattled through the reeds and gun after gun was fired. At last, late in the day, all was still; but the poor duckling did not dare to rise up; he waited several hours before he looked around, and then hastened away out of the moor as fast as he could. He ran on over field and meadow, but there was such a storm raging that it was difficult to get from one place to another.

Towards evening the duckling came to a little miserable peasant's hut. This hut was so dilapidated that it did not itself know on which side it should fall; and that's why it remained standing. The storm whistled round the duckling in such a way that the poor creature was obliged to sit down to resist it; and the wind blew worse and worse. Then the duckling noticed that one of the hinges of the door had given way, and the door hung so slanting that the duckling could slip through the crack into the room; and that is what he did.

Here lived a woman with her cat and her hen. And the cat, whom she called Sonnie, could arch his back and

144 purr; he could even give out sparks, but for that one had to stroke his fur the wrong way. The hen had quite little short legs, and therefore she was called Chickabiddy Shortshanks; she laid good eggs, and the woman loved her as her own child.

In the morning the strange duckling was at once noticed, and the cat began to purr and the hen to cluck.

"What's this?" said the woman, and looked all around; but she could not see well, and therefore she thought the duckling was a fat duck that had strayed. "This is a rare prize!" she said. "Now I shall have duck's eggs. I hope it is not a drake. We must wait and see about that."

And so the duckling was admitted on trial for three weeks; but no eggs came. And the cat was master of the house, and the hen was the lady and always said "We and the world!" for she thought they were half the world and by far the better half. The duckling thought one might have a different opinion, but the hen would not allow it.

"Can you lay eggs?" she asked.

"No."

"Then hold your tongue!"

And the cat said, "Can you curve your back, and purr, and give out sparks?"

"No."

"Then you had better have no opinion of your own when sensible folks are speaking."

And the duckling sat in a corner and was melancholy. Then the fresh air and the sunshine streamed in; and he was seized with such a strange longing to swim on the water that he could not help telling the hen of it.

"What are you thinking of?" cried the hen. "You have nothing to do, that's why you have these fancies. Lay eggs, or purr, and they will pass over."

"But it is so charming to swim on the water!" said the duckling, "so refreshing to let it close above one's head and to dive down to the bottom."

"Yes, that must certainly be amusing," said the hen. "You must have gone crazy. Ask the cat about it—he's the cleverest animal I know—ask him if he likes to swim on the water or to dive down. I won't speak about myself. Ask our mistress, the old woman; no one in the world is cleverer than she. Do you think she has any desire to swim and to let the water close above her head?"

"You don't understand me," said the duckling.

"We don't understand you? Then pray who is to understand you? You surely don't pretend to be cleverer than the cat and the woman—I won't say anything of myself. Don't be conceited, child, and thank your Maker for all the kindness you have received. Did you not get into a warm room, and have you not fallen into company from which you may learn something? But you are a chatterer, and it is not pleasant to associate with you. You may believe me, I speak for your good. I tell you disagreeable things, and by that one may always know one's true friends! Only take care that you learn to lay eggs or to purr and give out sparks!"

"I think I will go out into the wide world," said the duckling.

"Yes, do go," replied the hen.

And so the duckling went away. He swam on the water, and dived, but he was slighted by every creature because of his ugliness.

Now came the autumn. The leaves in the forest turned yellow and brown; the wind caught them so that they

146 danced about; and up in the air it was very cold. The clouds hung low, heavy with hail and snowflakes, and on the fence stood the raven, crying, "Croak! croak!" for mere cold; yes, it was enough to make one feel cold to think of this. The poor little duckling certainly had not a good time. One evening—the sun was just setting in its beauty—there came a whole flock of great, handsome birds out of the bushes; they were dazzlingly white, with long, flexible necks; they were swans. They uttered a very peculiar cry, spread forth their glorious great wings, and flew away from that cold region to warmer lands, to fair open lakes. They mounted so high, so high! and the ugly duckling felt quite strange as he watched them. He turned around and around in the water like a wheel, stretched out his neck towards them, and uttered such a strange, loud cry as frightened himself. Oh! he could not forget those beautiful, happy birds; and so soon as he could see them no longer, he dived down to the very bottom, and when he came up again, he was quite beside himself. He did not know the name of those birds, and did not know whither they were flying; but he loved them more than he had ever loved any one. He was not at all envious of them. How could he think of wishing to possess such loveliness as they had? He would have been glad if only the ducks would have endured his company—the poor, ugly creature!

And the winter grew cold, very cold! The duckling was forced to swim about in the water to prevent the surface from freezing entirely; but every night the hole in which he swam about became smaller and smaller. It froze so hard that the icy covering cracked again; and the duckling was obliged to use it continually to prevent the hole from freezing up. At last he became exhausted and lay quite still and thus froze fast into the ice.

Early in the morning a peasant came by, and when he saw what had happened, he took his wooden shoe, broke the ice crust to pieces, and carried the duckling home to his wife. Then he came to himself again. The children wanted to play with him; but the duckling thought they wanted to hurt him and in his terror fluttered up into the milk pan so that the milk spurted down into the room. The woman clasped her hands, at which the duckling flew down into the butter tub and then into the meal barrel and out again. How he looked then! The woman screamed and struck at him with the fire tongs; the children trumbled over one another in their efforts to catch the duckling; and they laughed and they screamed! Well it was that the door stood open, and the poor creature was able to slip out between the shrubs into the newly-fallen snow. There he lay, quite exhausted.

But it would be too melancholy if I were to tell all the misery and care which the duckling had to endure in the hard winter. He lay out on the moor among the reeds when the sun began to shine again and the larks to sing: it was a beautiful spring.

Then all at once the duckling could flap his wings: they beat the air more strongly than before and bore him strongly away; and before he well knew how all this happened, he found himself in a great garden where the elder trees smelled sweet and bent their long green branches down to the canal that wound through the region. Oh, here it was so beautiful, such a gladness of spring! and from the thicket came three glorious white swans; they rustled their wings, and swam lightly on the

148 water. The duckling knew the splendid creatures and felt oppressed by a peculiar sadness.

"I will fly away to them, to the royal birds! and they will beat me, because I, that am so ugly, dare to come near them. But it is all the same. Better to be killed by *them* than to be pursued by ducks, and beaten by fowls, and pushed about by the girl who takes care of the poultry yard, and to suffer hunger in winter!" And he flew out into the water and swam towards the beautiful swans. These looked at him and came sailing down upon him with outspread wings. "Kill me!" said the poor creature, and bent his head down upon the water, expecting nothing but death. But what was this that he saw in the clear water? He beheld his own image; and, lo! he was no longer a clumsy dark-gray bird, ugly and hateful to look at, but a—swan!

It matters nothing if one is born in a duck yard, if one has only lain in a swan's egg.

He felt quite glad at all the need and misfortune he had suffered, now that he realized his happiness in all the splendor that surrounded him. And the great swans swam around him and stroked him with their beaks.

Into the garden came little children, who threw bread and corn into the water; and the youngest cried, "There is a new one!" and the other children shouted joyously, "Yes, a new one has arrived!" And they clapped their hands and danced about and ran to their father and mother; and bread and cake were thrown into the water; and they all said, "The new one is the most beautiful of all! so young and handsome!" and the old swans bowed their heads before him.

Then he felt quite ashamed and hid his head under his

wings, for he did not know what to do; he was so happy, and yet not at all proud. He thought how he had been persecuted and despised; and now he heard them saying that he was the most beautiful of all birds. Even the elder tree bent its branches straight down into the water before him, and the sun shone warm and mild. Then his wings rustled, he lifted his slender neck and cried rejoicingly from the depths of his heart—

"I never dreamed of so much happiness when I was the ugly duckling!"

"Do you love me, do you love me, Olympia? Only one word! Do you love me?"

THE DANCING DOLL

from "The Sandman"

E.T.A. Hoffmann

The story begins when Nathanael, as a small child, hears fairy stories about the sandman. In his childish confusion, he gets the idea that the sandman is a monster that steals children's eyes. He also decides that a stranger who often visits his father at night is the sandman. One night, he hides in his father's study to see, but the "sandman" turns out to be his father's friend, Coppelius. Hidden, Nathanael is horrified to see his father and Coppelius doing strange experiments with what seem to be human faces with empty eyeholes. One night, there is an explosion; Nathanael's father is found dead; Coppelius has vanished.

Now grown up, Nathanael meets a peddler of barometers called Coppola, whom he believes to be Coppelius in disguise—Coppelius who caused his father's death, Coppelius come back to destroy his happiness. Nathanael's sweetheart, Clara, tells him he must put these nightmarish ideas out of his mind. His professor, Spalanzani, reassures him that Coppola is just an Italian peddler whom he has known for years. Finally, Nathanael promises Clara to give up his notion that Coppola the peddler is really the evil Coppelius.

Then one day Nathanael catches a glimpse of Olympia, the daughter of Professor Spalanzani. But Olympia's father keeps her locked up, and no man is ever allowed to come near her. . . .

How surprised Nathanael was when he returned to the house where he lived to find it burned down, with only the bare walls standing amid the ashes. However, although the fire had broken out in the laboratory of the chemist who lived on the ground floor and had therefore consumed the house from top to bottom, some bold, active friends had succeeded in getting into Nathanael's room in the upper story in time to save his books, manuscripts, and instruments. They carried everything safe and sound to another house where they rented a room which Nathanael moved into at once.

He did not think it all remarkable that he now lived just across from Professor Spalanzani; nor did it appear strange when he perceived that his window looked straight into the room where Olympia often sat alone, so that he could plainly recognize her figure although the features of her face were indistinct and confused. At last it struck him that Olympia often remained for hours in that position in which he had once seen her through the glass door, sitting at a little table without any occupation, and that she was plainly gazing over at him constantly. He was forced to confess that he had never seen a more lovely form, but with Clara in his heart, he remained indifferent to the stiff and listless Olympia. Occasionally, to

152 be sure, he gave her a glance over the top of his textbook, but that was all.

He was just writing to Clara when he heard a light tap at the door; it stopped as he answered, and the repulsive face of Coppola peeped in. Nathanael's heart trembled with fear, but remembering what Spalanzani had told him about his fellow countryman, and also the firm promise he had made to Clara with respect to the sandman Coppelius, he felt ashamed of his childish fear and, collecting himself with all his might, said as softly and calmly as he could, "I do not want a barometer, my good friend. Please go away."

Upon this, Coppola came right into the room, his wide mouth twisted into a hideous smile and his little eyes darting fire from beneath their long gray lashes. "Eh, eh—no barometer—no barometer?" he said in a hoarse voice. "I have pretty eyes too—pretty eyes!" "Madman!" cried Nathanael in horror. "How can you have eyes—eyes?" But Coppola had already put his barometer aside and plunged his hand into his wide coat-pocket, from which he drew lorgnettes and spectacles which he placed upon the table. "There—there—spectacles on the nose, those are my eyes—pretty eyes!" he gabbled, drawing out more and more spectacles until the whole table began to glisten and sparkle in the most extraordinary manner. A thousand eyes stared and quivered, their gaze fixed upon Nathanael. Yet he could not look away from the table where Coppola kept laying down still more and more spectacles, and all those flaming eyes leaped in wilder and wilder confusion, shooting their blood-red light into Nathanael's heart.

At last, overwhelmed with horror, he shrieked out,

"Stop! Stop! you fiend!" and seized Coppola's arm which
he had just thrust back into his pockets to bring out still
more spectacles, although the whole table was already
covered. Coppola gently pulled himself free with a
hoarse, repulsive laugh, and with the words, "Ah! Nothing for you—but here are pretty glasses!" collected all the
spectacles, packed them away, and from the breast
pocket of his coat drew forth a number of telescopes
large and small. As soon as the spectacles were removed,
Nathanael felt quite relieved and, thinking of Clara, perceived that the nightmare illusion was but the product of
his own mind, that this Coppola was an honest optician
and could not possibly be the accursed double of Coppelius. Moreover, in all the glasses which Coppola now
placed on the table there was nothing remarkable, or at
least nothing as weird as in the spectacles; and to make
up for his behavior Nathanael decided to buy something.
He took up a small, very neatly-constructed pocket telescope and looked through the window to try it.

Never in his life had he come across a glass which
brought objects so clearly and sharply before his eyes. Involuntarily he looked into Spalanzani's room. Olympia
was sitting as usual before the little table with her arms
laid upon it and her hands folded. For the first time he
could see the wondrous beauty in the shape of her face.
Only her eyes seemed to him peculiarly still and dead.
Nevertheless, as he looked more keenly through the glass,
it seemed to him as if moist moonbeams were rising in
Olympia's eyes. It was as if the power of seeing were
being kindled for the first time. Her glances flashed with
constantly increasing life.

As if spellbound, Nathanael reclined against the win-

154 dow, gazing upon the charming Olympia. A coughing
and shuffling of feet aroused him as if from a dream. Coppola was standing behind him. "*Tre zechini*—three ducats!" He had quite forgotten the optician and quickly
paid him what he asked. "Is it not so? A pretty glass—a
pretty glass?" asked Coppola in his hoarse, repulsive
voice and with his malicious smile. "Yes—yes," replied
Nathanael peevishly. "Good-bye, friend." Coppola left
the room, but not without casting many strange glances
at Nathanael. He heard him laugh loudly on the stairs.

"Ah," thought Nathanael, "he is laughing at me because, no doubt, I have paid him too much for this little
glass." While he softly uttered these words, it seemed as
if a deep and mournful sigh like the sigh of a dying man
were sounding through the room, and he was so frightened he stopped breathing. He realized, however, that he
himself had sighed. "Clara is right," he said to himself,
"in taking me for a hopeless illusion-seer, but it is pure
madness—no, more than madness—that the stupid
thought of having paid Coppola too much for the glass
still upsets me so strangely. I can see no reason for it."

He now sat down to finish his letter to Clara; but a
glance through the window assured him that Olympia
was still sitting there, and he sprang up at once, as if im-
pelled by an irresistible power, seized Coppola's glass,
and could not tear himself away from the seductive sight
of Olympia till his friend Siegmund called for him to go
to Professor Spalanzani's lecture. The curtains were
drawn shut before the fatal room, and he could no longer
see Olympia, nor could he on the next day or the next, although he scarcely ever left his window and constantly
looked through Coppola's glass.

On the third day, the windows were completely covered. In utter despair, filled with a longing and a burning desire, he ran out of the town gate. Olympia's form floated before him in the air, stepped forth from the bushes, and peeped at him with large, beaming eyes from the clear brook. Clara's image had completely vanished from his mind; he thought of nothing but Olympia and complained aloud in a tearful voice, "Ah, noble, sublime star of my love, have you only risen upon me to vanish immediately and leave me in the dark, hopeless night?"

As he returned home, however, he perceived a great bustle in Spalanzani's house. The doors were wide open, all sorts of equipment was being carried in, the windows of the first floor were being taken out, maid servants were rushing to and fro, sweeping and dusting with great hair brooms, and carpenters and upholsterers were knocking and hammering within. Nathanael was still standing in the street in a state of perfect wonder when Siegmund came up to him laughing and said, "Now, what do you say to our old Spalanzani?" Nathanael assured him that he could say nothing because he knew nothing about the professor, but he perceived with astonishment the mad proceedings in a house usually so quiet and gloomy. He then learned from Siegmund that Spalanzani intended to give a grand party on the following day—a concert and ball—and that half the university was invited. It was rumored that Spalanzani, who had so long kept his daughter so carefully guarded from every human eye, would now let her appear for the first time.

Nathanael received an invitation, and with heart beating high he went at the appointed hour to the professor's, where the coaches were already arriving and the lights

156 shining in the decorated rooms. The company was numerous and brilliant. Olympia appeared dressed with great richness and taste. Her beautifully-shaped face and her figure roused general admiration. The somewhat strange arch of her back and the wasp-like thinness of her waist seemed to be produced by too-tight lacing. In her step and deportment there was something measured and stiff which struck many as unpleasant, but it was ascribed to the constraint produced by the company.

The concert began. Olympia played the harpsichord with great skill and sang a virtuoso piece with a voice like the sound of a glass bell, clear and almost piercing. Nathanael was quite enraptured. He stood in the back row and could not quite make out Olympia's features in the dazzling light; so, quite unnoticed, he took out Coppola's glass and looked towards the fair creature. Ah! then he saw with what a longing glance she gazed towards him, and how every note of her song plainly sprang from that loving glance, whose fire penetrated his inmost soul. Her skillful roulades seemed to Nathanael the exultation of a mind transformed by love, and when at last, after the cadenza, the long trill sounded shrilly through the room, he felt as if he were clutched by burning arms. He could restrain himself no longer, but with mingled pain and rapture shouted out, "Olympia!" Everyone looked at him, and many laughed. The organist of the cathedral made a sourer face than usual and simply said, "Well, well."

The concert had finished and the ball began. "To dance with her—with her!" That was the aim of all Nathanael's desire, of all his efforts; but how to gain courage to ask her, the queen of the ball? Nevertheless—he himself did

not know how it happened—no sooner had the dancing
begun than he was standing close to Olympia, who had
not yet been asked to dance. Scarcely able to stammer
out a few words, he had seized her hand. Olympia's hand
was as cold as ice. He felt a horrible deathly chill thrilling
through him. He looked into her eyes, which beamed
back full of love and desire, and at the same time it
seemed as though her pulse began to beat and her life's
blood to flow into her cold hand. And in Nathanael's soul
the joy of love rose still higher. He clasped the beautiful
Olympia and whirled her through the dance.

He thought that his dancing was usually correct as to
time, but the peculiarly steady rhythm with which Olympia moved, and which often quite threw him off, soon
showed him that his time was most defective. However,
he would dance with no other lady, and would like to
have murdered anyone who approached Olympia for the
purpose of asking her. But this only happened twice, and
to his astonishment Olympia remained seated until the
next dance when he lost no time in leading her out again.
Had he had eyes for anything but the fair Olympia, all
sorts of unfortunate quarrels would have been inevitable.
For the quiet, scarcely suppressed laughter which arose
among the young people in every corner was plainly directed towards Olympia, whom they followed with very
curious glances—one could not tell why.

Heated by the dance and by the wine, of which he had
freely partaken, Nathanael had laid aside all his ordinary
shyness. He sat by Olympia with her hand in his and, in a
high state of inspiration, told her of his passion in words
which neither he nor Olympia understood. Yet perhaps
she did; for she looked steadfastly into his face and sighed

158 several times, "Ah, ah!" Upon this, Nathanael said, "Oh splendid, heavenly lady! Ray from the promised land of love—deep soul in whom all my being is reflected!" with much more stuff of that kind. But Olympia merely went on sighing, "Ah, ah!"

Professor Spalanzani occasionally passed the happy pair and smiled on them with a look of peculiar satisfaction. To Nathanael, although he felt in quite another world, it seemed suddenly as though it was growing considerably darker here in Professor Spalanzani's house, and when he looked around he perceived, to his no-small horror, that the last two candles in the empty room had burned down to their sockets and were just going out. The music and dancing had ceased long ago. "Parting—parting!" he cried in wild despair. He kissed Olympia's hand, he bent towards her mouth, but his burning lips were met by lips as cold as ice! Just as when he had touched her cold hand, he felt himself overcome by horror. The legend of the dead bride darted suddenly through his mind, but Olympia pressed him to her, and his kiss seemed to warm her lips into life.

Professor Spalanzani strode through the empty hall, his steps making a hollow echo, and his figure, with a flickering shadow playing around it, had a fearful, ghostly appearance. "Do you love me, do you love me, Olympia? Only one word! Do you love me?" whispered Nathanael; but as she rose Olympia only sighed, "Ah, ah!" "Yes, my gracious, my beautiful star of love," said Nathanael, "You have risen upon me, and you will shine, forever lighting my inmost soul." "Ah, ah!" replied Olympia as she departed. Nathanael followed her. They both stood before the professor.

"You have had a very animated conversation with my daughter," said he, smiling. "So, dear Mr. Nathanael, if you have any pleasure in talking with a silly girl, your visits shall be welcome."

Nathanael departed with a whole heaven blazing in his heart.

Nathanael is now completely in love with Olympia and spends all his time with her, although she never speaks and only listens to him. One day he goes to the Professor's house intending to declare his love for Olympia and make her say, at last, that she loves him, too. But as he enters the house, he hears a terrible clattering and banging and the voices of Professor Spalanzani and the sandman Coppelius in a furious argument—"Let go!" "I made the eyes!" "I made the clockwork!" Forcing his way into the professor's laboratory, Nathanael finds the professor and Coppelius pulling Olympia back and forth between them. At last Coppelius seizes her and throws her over his shoulder. He carries her out and down the stairs, her lifeless feet banging each step. Nathanael sees that her eye sockets are black and empty. Then he sees two bloody glass eyes on the laboratory floor. Olympia was only a doll.

Madness overcomes Nathanael, and although his old sweetheart Clara tries to help him, he sinks deeper and deeper into insanity. At last he throws himself from a tower and dies.

"I'll never go there again!" said Alice. "It's the stupidest tea party I ever was at in all my life!"

A MAD TEA PARTY

from *Alice in Wonderland*

Lewis Carroll

Once, there was a little girl named Alice who fell down a rabbit hole into a strange underground world where she had many adventures. Among other creatures, she met the March Hare and the Mad Hatter. Eventually, she came to the March Hare's house which had chimneys "shaped like ears" and a roof "thatched with fur."...

There was a table set out under a tree in front of the house, and the March Hare and the Hatter were having tea at it: a Dormouse was sitting between them, fast asleep, and the other two were using it as a cushion, resting their elbows on it, and talking over its head. "Very uncomfortable for the Dormouse," thought Alice; "only as it's asleep, I suppose it doesn't mind."

The table was a large one, but the three were all crowded together at one corner of it. "No room! No room!" they cried out when they saw Alice coming. "There's *plenty* of room!" said Alice indignantly, and she sat down in a large armchair at one end of the table.

"Have some wine," the March Hare said in an encour- aging tone.

Alice looked all round the table, but there was nothing on it but tea. "I don't see any wine," she remarked.

"There isn't any," said the March Hare.

"Then it wasn't very civil of you to offer it," said Alice angrily.

"It wasn't very civil of you to sit down without being invited," said the March Hare.

"I didn't know it was *your* table," said Alice: "it's laid for a great many more than three."

"Your hair wants cutting," said the Hatter. He had been looking at Alice for some time with great curiosity, and this was his first speech.

"You should learn not to make personal remarks," Alice said with some severity: "it's very rude."

The Hatter opened his eyes very wide on hearing this; but all he *said* was, "Why is a raven like a writing desk?"

"Come, we shall have some fun now!" thought Alice. "I'm glad they've begun asking riddles—I believe I can guess that," she added aloud.

"Do you mean that you think you can find out the answer to it?" said the March Hare.

"Exactly so," said Alice.

"Then you should say what you mean," the March Hare went on.

"I do," Alice hastily replied; "at least—at least I mean what I say—that's the same thing, you know."

"Not the same thing a bit!" said the Hatter. "Why, you might just as well say that 'I see what I eat' is the same thing as 'I eat what I see'!"

"You might just as well say," added the March Hare,

162 "that 'I like what I get' is the same thing as 'I get what I like'!"

"You might just as well say," added the Dormouse, which seemed to be talking in its sleep, "that 'I breathe when I sleep' is the same thing as 'I sleep when I breathe'!"

"It *is* the same thing with you," said the Hatter, and here the conversation dropped, and the party sat silent for a minute, while Alice thought over all she could remember about ravens and writing desks, which wasn't much.

The Hatter was the first to break the silence. "What day of the month is it?" he said, turning to Alice: he had taken his watch out of his pocket, and was looking at it uneasily, shaking it every now and then, and holding it to his ear.

Alice considered a little, and then said "The fourth."

"Two days wrong!" sighed the Hatter. "I told you butter wouldn't suit the works!" he added, looking angrily at the March Hare.

"It was the *best* butter," the March Hare meekly replied.

"Yes, but some crumbs must have got in as well," the Hatter grumbled: "you shouldn't have put it in with the bread knife."

The March Hare took the watch and looked at it gloomily; then he dipped it into his cup of tea, and looked at it again: but he could think of nothing better to say than his first remark, "It was the *best* butter, you know."

Alice had been looking over his shoulder with some curiosity. "What a funny watch!" she remarked. "It tells the day of the month, and doesn't tell what o'clock it is!"

"Why should it?" muttered the Hatter. "Does *your* watch tell you what year it is?"

"Of course not," Alice replied very readily: "but that's because it stays the same year for such a long time together."

"Which is just the case with *mine*," said the Hatter.

Alice felt dreadfully puzzled. The Hatter's remark seemed to her to have no sort of meaning in it, and yet it was certainly English. "I don't quite understand you," she said, as politely as she could.

"The Dormouse is asleep again," said the Hatter, and he poured a little hot tea upon its nose.

The Dormouse shook its head impatiently, and said, without opening its eyes, "Of course, of course: just what I was going to remark myself."

"Have you guessed the riddle yet?" the Hatter said, turning to Alice again.

"No, I give it up," Alice replied. "What's the answer?"

"I haven't the slightest idea," said the Hatter.

"Nor I," said the March Hare.

Alice sighed wearily. "I think you might do something better with the time," she said, "than wasting it in asking riddles that have no answers."

"If you knew Time as well as I do," said the Hatter, "you wouldn't talk about wasting *it*. It's *him*."

"I don't know what you mean," said Alice.

"Of course you don't!" the Hatter said, tossing his head contemptuously. "I dare say you never even spoke to Time!"

"Perhaps not," Alice cautiously replied; "but I know I have to beat time when I learn music."

"Ah! That accounts for it," said the Hatter. "He won't stand beating. Now, if you only kept on good terms with him, he'd do almost anything you liked with the clock. For instance, suppose it were nine o'clock in the morning, just time to begin lessons: you'd only have to whisper a hint to Time, and round goes the clock in a twinkling! Half past one, time for dinner!"

("I only wish it was," the March Hare said to itself in a whisper.)

"That would be grand, certainly," said Alice thoughtfully; "but then—I shouldn't be hungry for it, you know."

"Not at first, perhaps," said the Hatter: "but you could keep it to half past one as long as you liked."

"Is that the way *you* manage?" Alice asked.

The Hatter shook his head mournfully. "Not I!" he replied. "We quarreled last March—just before *he* went mad, you know—" (pointing with his teaspoon at the March Hare) "—it was at the great concert given by the Queen of Hearts, and I had to sing

> *'Twinkle, twinkle, little bat!*
> *How I wonder what you're at!'*

You know the song, perhaps?"

"I've heard something like it," said Alice.

"It goes on, you know," the Hatter continued, "in this way:

> *'Up above the world you fly,*
> *Like a tea tray in the sky.*
> *Twinkle, twinkle—'* "

Here the Dormouse shook itself, and began singing in
its sleep, "*Twinkle, twinkle, twinkle, twinkle—*" and went
on so long that they had to pinch it to make it stop.

"Well, I'd hardly finished the first verse," said the Hatter, "when the Queen bawled out, 'He's murdering the
time! Off with his head!' "

"How dreadfully savage!" exclaimed Alice.

"And ever since that," the Hatter went on in a mournful tone, "he won't do a thing I ask! It's always six o'clock
now."

A bright idea came into Alice's head. "Is that the reason so many tea things are put out here?" she asked.

"Yes, that's it," said the Hatter with a sigh: "it's always
tea time, and we've no time to wash the things between
whiles."

"Then you keep moving round, I suppose?" said Alice.

"Exactly so," said the Hatter: "as the things get used
up."

"But what happens when you come to the beginning
again?" Alice ventured to ask.

"Suppose we change the subject," the March Hare interrupted, yawning. "I'm getting tired of this. I vote the
young lady tells us a story."

"I'm afraid I don't know one," said Alice, rather
alarmed at the proposal.

"Then the Dormouse shall!" they both cried. "Wake
up, Dormouse!" And they pinched it on both sides at
once.

The Dormouse slowly opened its eyes. "I wasn't
asleep," it said in a hoarse, feeble voice, "I heard every
word you fellows were saying."

"Tell us a story!" said the March Hare.

"Yes, please do!" pleaded Alice.

"And be quick about it," added the Hatter, "or you'll be asleep again before it's done."

"Once upon a time there were three little sisters," the Dormouse began in a great hurry; "and their names were Elsie, Lacie, and Tillie; and they lived at the bottom of a well—"

"What did they live on?" said Alice, who always took a great interest in questions of eating and drinking.

"They lived on treacle," said the Dormouse, after thinking a minute or two.

"They couldn't have done that, you know," Alice gently remarked. "They'd have been ill."

"So they were," said the Dormouse; "*very* ill."

Alice tried a little to fancy to herself what such an extraordinary way of living would be like, but it puzzled her too much: so she went on: "But why did they live at the bottom of a well?"

"Take some more tea," the March Hare said to Alice, very earnestly.

"I've had nothing yet," Alice replied in an offended tone: "so I can't take more."

"You mean you can't take *less*," said the Hatter: "it's very easy to take *more* than nothing."

"Nobody asked *your* opinion," said Alice.

"Who's making personal remarks now?" the Hatter asked triumphantly.

Alice did not quite know what to say to this: so she helped herself to some tea and bread and butter, and then turned to the Dormouse, and repeated her question. "Why did they live at the bottom of a well?"

The Dormouse again took a minute or two to think

about it, and then said, "It was a treacle well."

"There's no such thing!" Alice was beginning very angrily, but the Hatter and the March Hare went "Sh! Sh!" and the Dormouse sulkily remarked, "If you can't be civil, you'd better finish the story for yourself."

"No, please go on!" Alice said very humbly. "I won't interrupt you again. I dare say there may be *one*."

"One, indeed!" said the Dormouse indignantly. However, he consented to go on. "And so these three little sisters—they were learning to draw, you know—"

"What did they draw?" said Alice, quite forgetting her promise.

"Treacle," said the Dormouse, without considering at all, this time.

"I want a clean cup," interrupted the Hatter: "let's all move one place on."

He moved on as he spoke, and the Dormouse followed him: the March Hare moved into the Dormouse's place, and Alice rather unwillingly took the place of the March Hare. The Hatter was the only one who got any advantage from the change; and Alice was a good deal worse off than before, as the March Hare had just upset the milk jug into his plate.

Alice did not wish to offend the Dormouse again, so she began very cautiously: "But I don't understand. Where did they draw the treacle from?"

"You can draw water out of a water well," said the Hatter; "so I should think you could draw treacle out of a treacle well—eh, stupid?"

"But they were *in* the well," Alice said to the Dormouse, not choosing to notice this last remark.

"Of course they were," said the Dormouse: "well in."

The answer so confused poor Alice, that she let the Dormouse go on for some time without interrupting it.

"They were learning to draw," the Dormouse went on, yawning and rubbing its eyes, for it was getting very sleepy; "and they drew all manner of things—everything that begins with an M—"

"Why with an M?" said Alice.

"Why not?" said the March Hare.

Alice was silent.

The Dormouse had closed its eyes by this time, and was going off into a doze; but, on being pinched by the Hatter, it woke up again with a little shriek, and went on: "—that begins with an M, such as mousetraps, and the moon, and memory, and muchness—you know you say things are 'much of a muchness'—did you ever see such a thing as a drawing of a muchness!"

"Really, now you ask me," said Alice, very much confused, "I don't think—"

"Then you shouldn't talk," said the Hatter.

This piece of rudeness was more than Alice could bear: she got up in great disgust, and walked off: the Dormouse fell asleep instantly, and neither of the others took the least notice of her going, though she looked back once or twice, half hoping that they would call after her: the last time she saw them, they were trying to put the Dormouse into the teapot.

"At any rate I'll never go *there* again!" said Alice, as she picked her way through the wood. "It's the stupidest tea party I ever was at in all my life!"

"Whoever shall climb to the top of that mountain . . . and shall cast into the stream at its source three drops of holy water, for him, and for him only, the river shall turn to gold."

THE KING OF THE GOLDEN RIVER

John Ruskin

Chapter 1

In a secluded and mountainous part of Stiria there was, in old time, a valley of the most surprising and luxuriant fertility. It was surrounded on all sides by steep and rocky mountains, rising into peaks, which were always covered with snow, and from which a number of torrents descended in constant cataracts. One of these fell westward over the face of a crag so high that, when the sun had set to everything else, and all below was darkness, his beams still shone full upon this waterfall, so that it looked like a shower of gold. It was, therefore, called by the people of the neighborhood, the Golden River.

It was strange that none of these streams fell into the valley itself. They all descended on the other side of the mountains and wound away through broad plains and by populous cities. But the clouds were drawn so constantly to the snowy hills and rested so softly in the circular hol-

170   low that in time of drought and heat, when all the county round was burnt up, there was still rain in the little valley; and its crops were so heavy, and its hay so high, and its apples so red, and its grapes so blue, and its wine so rich, and its honey so sweet, that it was a marvel to everyone who beheld it and was commonly called the Treasure Valley.

The whole of this little valley belonged to three brothers called Schwartz, Hans, and Gluck. Schwartz and Hans, the two elder brothers, were very ugly men with overhanging eyebrows and small dull eyes, which were always half shut so that you couldn't see into *them* and always fancied they saw very far into *you.*

They lived by farming the Treasure Valley, and very good farmers they were. They killed everything that did not pay for its eating. They shot the blackbirds because they pecked the fruit, and killed the hedgehogs lest they should suck the cows; they poisoned the crickets for eating the crumbs in the kitchen, and smothered the cicadas which used to sing all summer in the lime trees. They worked their servants without any wages till they would not work any more, and then quarreled with them and turned them out of doors without paying them.

It would have been very odd if, with such a farm and such a system of farming, they hadn't got very rich; and very rich they *did* get. They generally contrived to keep their corn by them till it was very dear and then sell it for twice its value; they had heaps of gold lying about on their floors, yet it was never known that they had given so much as a penny or a crust to charity; they never went to mass; grumbled perpetually at paying tithes; and were, in a word, of so cruel and grinding a temper, as to receive from all those with whom they had any dealings the nickname of the "Black Brothers."

The youngest brother, Gluck, was as completely opposed in both appearance and character to his seniors as could possibly be imagined or desired. He was not above twelve years old, fair, blue-eyed, and kind in temper to every living thing. He did not, of course, agree particularly well with his brothers, or rather they did not agree with *him*. He was usually appointed to the honorable office of turnspit when there was anything to roast, which was not often; for to do the brothers justice, they were hardly less sparing upon themselves than upon other people. At other times he used to clean the shoes, floors, and sometimes the plates, occasionally getting what was left on them by way of encouragement, and a wholesome quantity of dry blows by way of education.

Things went on in this manner for a long time. At last came a very wet summer, and everything went wrong in the country round. The hay had hardly been got in when the haystacks were floated bodily down to the sea by an inundation, the vines were cut to pieces with the hail, the corn was all killed by a black blight; only in the Treasure Valley, as usual, all was safe. As it had rain when there was rain nowhere else, so it had sun when there was sun nowhere else. Everybody came to buy corn at the farm and went away pouring maledictions on the Black Brothers. They asked what they liked and got it, except from the poor people who could only beg, and several of whom were starved at their very door without the slightest regard or notice.

It was drawing towards winter and very cold weather, when one day the two elder brothers had gone out, with their usual warning to little Gluck, who was left to mind the roast, that he was to let nobody in and give nothing out. Gluck sat down quite close to the fire, for it was raining very hard, and the kitchen walls were by no means dry or comfortable looking. He turned and turned, and the roast got nice and brown. "What a pity," thought Gluck, "my brothers never ask anybody to dinner. I'm sure, when they've got such a nice piece of mutton as this, and nobody else has got so much as a piece of dry bread, it would do their hearts good to have somebody to eat it with them."

Just as he spoke, there came a double knock at the house door, yet heavy and dull, as though the knocker had been tied up—more like a puff than a knock. "It must be the wind," said Gluck; "nobody else would venture to knock double knocks at our door." No, it wasn't the wind: there it came again very hard, and what was particularly astounding, the knocker seemed to be in a hurry and not to be in the least afraid of the consequences.

Gluck went to the window, opened it, and put his head out to see who it was. It was the most extraordinary-looking little gentleman he had ever seen in his life. He had a very long nose, slightly brass-colored, and expanding towards its termination into a development not unlike the lower extremity of a key bugle. His cheeks were very round and very red and might have warranted a supposition that he had been blowing a refractory fire for the last eight-and-forty hours. His eyes twinkled merrily through long, silky eyelashes, his mustaches curled twice round like a corkscrew on each side of his mouth, and his hair, of a curious mixed pepper-and-salt color, descended far over his shoulders.

He was about four feet six in height and wore a conical pointed cap of nearly the same altitude, decorated with a black feather some three feet long. His doublet was prolonged behind into something resembling a violent exaggeration of what is now termed a "swallow tail," but was much obscured by the swelling folds of an enormous, glossy-looking cloak, which must have been very much too long in calm weather as the wind, whistling round the old house, carried it clear out from the wearer's shoulders to about four times his own length.

Gluck was so perfectly paralyzed by the singular appearance of his visitor that he remained fixed without uttering a word until the old gentleman, having performed another and a more energetic concerto on the knocker, turned round to look after his flyaway cloak. In so doing he caught sight of Gluck's little yellow head jammed in the window, with his mouth and eyes very wide open indeed.

"Hallo!" said the little gentleman, "that's not the way to answer the door: I'm wet, let me in."

To do the little gentleman justice, he *was* wet. His feather hung down between his legs like a beaten puppy's tail, dripping like an umbrella; and from the ends of his mustaches the water was running into his waistcoat pockets and out again like a millstream.

"I beg pardon, sir," said Gluck, "I'm very sorry, but I really can't."

"Can't what?" said the old gentleman.

"I can't let you in, sir—I can't indeed; my brothers would beat me to death, sir, if I thought of such a thing.

174   What do you want, sir?"

"Want?" said the old gentleman petulantly. "I want fire and shelter; and there's your great fire there blazing, crackling, and dancing on the walls with nobody to feel it. Let me in, I say; I only want to warm myself."

Gluck had had his head, by this time, so long out of the window that he began to feel it was really unpleasantly cold, and when he turned and saw the beautiful fire rustling and roaring and throwing long bright tongues up the chimney, as if it were licking its chops at the savory smell of the leg of mutton, his heart melted within him that it should be burned away for nothing. "He does look *very* wet," said little Gluck; "I'll just let him in for a quarter of an hour." Round he went to the door and opened it; and as the little gentleman walked in, there came a gust of wind through the house that made the chimney totter.

"That's a good boy," said the little gentleman. "Never mind your brothers. I'll talk to them."

"Pray, sir, don't do any such thing," said Gluck. "I can't let you stay till they come; they'd be the death of me."

"Dear me," said the old gentleman, "I'm very sorry to hear that. How long may I stay?"

"Only till the mutton's done, sir," replied Gluck, "and it's very brown."

Then the old gentleman walked into the kitchen and sat himself down on the hob, with the top of his cap accommodated up the chimney, for it was a great deal too high for the roof.

"You'll soon dry there, sir," said Gluck and sat down again to turn the mutton. But the old gentleman did *not* dry there, but went on drip, drip, dripping among the cinders, and the fire fizzled and sputtered and began to look very black and uncomfortable; never was there such a cloak; every fold in it ran like a gutter.

"I beg pardon, sir," said Gluck at length, after watching the water spreading in long, quicksilverlike streams over the floor for a quarter of an hour; "Mayn't I take your cloak?"

"No, thank you," said the old gentleman.

"Your cap, sir?"

"I am all right, thank you," said the old gentleman rather gruffly.

"But—sir—I'm very sorry," said Gluck, hesitatingly; "but—really, sir—you're—putting the fire out."

"It'll take longer to do the mutton then," replied his visitor dryly.

Gluck was very much puzzled by the behavior of his guest; it was such a strange mixture of coolness and humility. He turned away at the string meditatively for another five minutes.

"That mutton looks very nice," said the old gentleman at length. "Can't you give me a little bit?"

"Impossible, sir," said Gluck.

"I'm very hungry," continued the old gentleman. "I've had nothing to eat yesterday nor today. They surely couldn't miss a bit from the knuckle!"

He spoke in so very melancholy a tone that it quite melted Gluck's heart. "They promised me one slice today, sir," said he. "I can give you that but not a bit more."

"That's a good boy," said the old gentleman again.

Then Gluck warmed a plate and sharpened a knife. "I

don't care if I do get beaten for it," thought he. Just as he had cut a large slice out of the mutton, there came a tremendous rap at the door. The old gentleman jumped off the hob as if it had suddenly become inconveniently warm. Gluck fitted the slice into the mutton again, with desperate efforts at exactitude, and ran to open the door.

"What did you keep us waiting in the rain for?" said Schwartz as he walked in, throwing his umbrella in Gluck's face. "Ay! what for, indeed, you little vagabond?" said Hans, administering an education box on the ear as he followed his brother into the kitchen.

"Bless my soul!" said Schwartz when he opened the door.

"Amen," said the little gentleman, who had taken his cap off and was standing in the middle of the kitchen, bowing with the utmost possible velocity.

"Who's that?" said Schwartz, catching up a rolling pin and turning to Gluck with a fierce frown.

"I don't know, indeed, brother," said Gluck in great terror.

"How did he get in?" roared Schwartz.

"My dear brother," said Gluck deprecatingly, "he was so *very* wet!"

The rolling pin was descending on Gluck's head; but, at the instant, the old gentleman interposed his conical cap, on which it crashed with a shock that shook the water out of it all over the room. What was very odd, the rolling pin no sooner touched the cap than it flew out of Schwartz's hand, spinning like a straw in a high wind, and fell into the corner at the farther end of the room.

"Who are you, sir?" demanded Schwartz, turning upon him.

"What's your business?" snarled Hans.

"I'm a poor old man, sir," the little gentleman began very modestly, "and I saw your fire through the window and begged shelter for a quarter of an hour."

"Have the goodness to walk out again, then," said Schwartz. "We've quite enough water in our house without making it a drying house."

"It is a cold day to turn an old man out in, sir; look at my gray hairs." They hung down to his shoulders, as I told you before.

"Ay!" said Hans, "there are enough of them to keep you warm. Walk!"

"I'm very, very hungry, sir; couldn't you spare me a bit of bread before I go?"

"Bread, indeed!" said Schwartz; "do you suppose we've nothing to do with our bread but to give it to such red-nosed fellows as you?"

"Why don't you sell your feather?" said Hans, sneeringly. "Out with you."

"A little bit," said the old gentleman.

"Be off!" said Schwartz.

"Pray, gentlemen."

"Off, and be hanged!" cried Hans, seizing him by the collar. But he had no sooner touched the old gentleman's collar than away he went after the rolling pin, spinning round and round till he fell into the corner on the top of it. Then Schwartz was very angry and ran at the old gentleman to turn him out; but he also had hardly touched him when away he went after Hans and the rolling pin and hit his head against the wall as he tumbled into the corner. And so there they lay, all three.

Then the old gentleman spun himself round with ve-

78 locity in the opposite direction; continued to spin until his long cloak was all wound neatly about him; clapped his cap on his head, very much on one side (for it could not stand upright without going through the ceiling); gave an additional twist to his corkscrew mustaches; and replied with perfect coolness: "Gentlemen, I wish you a very good morning. At twelve o'clock tonight I'll call again; after such a refusal of hospitality as I have just experienced, you will not be surprised if that visit is the last I ever pay you."

"If ever I catch you here again," muttered Schwartz, coming half-frightened out of the corner—but before he could finish his sentence, the old gentleman had shut the house door behind him with a great bang; and there drove past the window at the same instant a wreath of ragged cloud that whirled and rolled away down the valley in all manner of shapes, turning over and over in the air, and melting away at last in a gush of rain.

"A very pretty business, indeed, Mr. Gluck!" said Schwartz. "Dish the mutton, sir. If ever I catch you at such a trick again—bless me, why the mutton's been cut!"

"You promised me one slice, brother, you know," said Gluck.

"Oh! and you were cutting it hot, I suppose, and going to catch all the gravy. It'll be long before I promise you such a thing again. Leave the room, sir; and have the kindness to wait in the coal cellar till I call you."

Gluck left the room, melancholy enough. The brothers ate as much mutton as they could, locked the rest in the cupboard, and proceeded to get very drunk after dinner.

Such a night it was! Howling wind and rushing rain

without intermission. The brothers had just sense enough left to put up all the shutters and double bar the door before they went to bed. They usually slept in the same room. As the clock struck twelve they were both awakened by a tremendous crash. Their door burst open with a violence that shook the house from top to bottom.

"What's that?" cried Schwartz, starting up in his bed.

"Only I," said the little gentleman.

The two brothers sat up on their bolster and stared into the darkness. The room was full of water, and by a misty moonbeam, which found its way through a hole in the shutter, they could see in the midst of it an enormous foam globe, spinning round and bobbing up and down like a cork, on which, as on a most luxurious cushion, reclined the little old gentleman, cap and all. There was plenty of room for it now, for the roof was off.

"Sorry to incommode you," said their visitor, ironically. "I'm afraid your beds are dampish; perhaps you had better go to your brother's room: I've left the ceiling on, there."

They required no second admonition but rushed into Gluck's room, wet through, and in an agony of terror.

"You'll find my card on the kitchen table," the old gentleman called after them. "Remember, the *last* visit."

"Pray Heaven it may!" said Schwartz, shuddering. And the foam globe disappeared.

Dawn came at last, and the two brothers looked out of Gluck's little window in the morning. The Treasure Valley was one mass of ruin and desolation. The inundation had swept away trees, crops, and cattle and left in their stead a waste of red sand and gray mud. The two brothers

180 crept shivering and horror-struck into the kitchen. The
water had gutted the whole first floor; corn, money, almost every movable thing, had been swept away, and
there was left only a small white card on the kitchen
table. On it, in large breezy, long-legged letters, were en-
graved the words:

Chapter 2

Southwest Wind, Esquire, was as good as his word. After
the momentous visit above related, he entered the Treasure Valley no more; and, what was worse, he had so
much influence with his relations, the West Winds in
general, and used it so effectually, that they all adopted a
similar line of conduct. So no rain fell in the valley from
one year's end to another. Though everything remained
green and flourishing in the plains below, the inheritance
of the Three Brothers was a desert. What had once been
the richest soil in the kingdom became a shifting heap of

red sand; and the brothers, unable longer to contend with
the adverse skies, abandoned their valueless patrimony in
despair to seek some means of gaining a livelihood among
the cities and people of the plains. All their money was
gone, and they had nothing left but some curious, old-
fashioned pieces of gold plate, the last remnants of their
ill-gotten wealth.

"Suppose we turn goldsmiths?" said Schwartz to Hans,
as they entered the large city. "It is a good knaves' trade;
we can put a great deal of copper into the gold without
anyone's finding it out."

The thought was agreed to be a very good one; they
hired a furnace and turned goldsmiths. But two slight circumstances affected their trade: the first, that people did
not approve of the coppered gold; the second, that the
two elder brothers, whenever they had sold anything,
used to leave little Gluck to mind the furnace and go and
drink out the money in the alehouse next door. So they
melted all their gold without making money enough to
buy more and were at last reduced to one large drinking
mug, which an uncle of his had given to little Gluck and
which he was very fond of and would not have parted
with for the world, though he never drank anything out
of it but milk and water. The mug was a very odd mug to
look at. The handle was formed of two wreaths of flowing golden hair, so finely spun that it looked more like
silk than metal, and these wreaths descended into and
mixed with a beard and whiskers of the same exquisite
workmanship, which surrounded and decorated a very
fierce little face of the reddest gold imaginable, right in
front of the mug, with a pair of eyes in it which seemed

182 to command its whole circumference. It was impossible to drink out of the mug without being subjected to an intense gaze out of the side of these eyes; and Schwartz positively averred that once, after emptying it, full of Rhenish, seventeen times, he had seen them wink! When it came to the mug's turn to be made into spoons, it half broke poor little Gluck's heart; but the brothers only laughed at him, tossed the mug into the melting pot, and staggered out to the alehouse, leaving him, as usual, to pour the gold into bars when it was all ready.

When they were gone, Gluck took a farewell look at his old friend in the melting pot. The flowing hair was all gone; nothing remained but the red nose and the sparkling eyes, which looked more malicious than ever. "And no wonder," thought Gluck, "after being treated in that way." He sauntered disconsolately to the window and sat himself down to catch the fresh evening air and escape the hot breath of the furnace. Now this window commanded a direct view of the range of mountains, which, as I told you before, overhung the Treasure Valley, and more especially of the peak from which fell the Golden River. It was just at the close of the day, and, when Gluck sat down at the window, he saw the rocks of the mountain tops all crimson and purple with the sunset; and there were bright tongues of fiery cloud burning and quivering about them; and the river, brighter than all, fell in a waving column of pure gold from precipice to precipice, with the double arch of a broad purple rainbow stretched across it, flushing and fading alternately in the wreaths of spray.

"Ah!" said Gluck aloud, after he had looked at it for a

little while, "if that river were really all gold, what a nice thing it would be."

"No it wouldn't, Gluck," said a clear, metallic voice close at his ear.

"Bless me, what's that?" exclaimed Gluck, jumping up. There was nobody there. He looked round the room and under the table and a great many times behind him, but there was certainly nobody there, and he sat down again at the window. This time he didn't speak, but he couldn't help thinking again that it would be very convenient if the river was really all gold.

"Not at all, my boy," said the same voice, louder than before.

"Bless me!" said Gluck again, "what *is* that?" He looked again into all the corners and cupboards, and then began turning round and round as fast as he could in the middle of the room, thinking there was somebody behind him, when the same voice struck again on his ear. It was singing now very merrily "Lala-lira-la"; no words, only a soft, running, effervescent melody, something like that of a kettle on the boil. Gluck looked out of the window. No, it was certainly in the house. Upstairs and downstairs. No, it was certainly in that very room, coming in quicker time and clearer notes every moment. "Lala-lira-la." All at once it struck Gluck that it sounded louder near the furnace. He ran to the opening and looked in: yes, he was right, it seemed to be coming not only out of the furnace but out of the pot. He uncovered it and ran back in a great fright, for the pot was certainly singing! He stood in the farthest corner of the room with his hands up and his mouth open for a minute or two, when the singing

184 stopped and the voice became clear and pronunciative.

"Hallo!" said the voice.

Gluck made no answer.

"Hallo, Gluck, my boy!" said the pot again.

Gluck summoned all his energies, walked straight up to the crucible, drew it out of the furnace, and looked in. The gold was all melted and its surface as smooth and polished as a river; but instead of reflecting little Gluck's head, as he looked in he saw, meeting his glance from beneath the gold, the red nose and sharp eyes of his friend of the mug, a thousand times redder and sharper than ever he had seen them in his life.

"Come, Gluck, my boy," said the voice out of the pot again, "I'm all right; pour me out."

But Gluck was too much astonished to do anything of the kind.

"Pour me out, I say," said the voice rather gruffly.

Still Gluck couldn't move.

"*Will* you pour me out?" said the voice passionately; "I'm too hot."

By a violent effort, Gluck recovered the use of his limbs, took hold of the crucible, and sloped it so as to pour out the gold. But instead of a liquid stream, there came out first a pair of pretty little yellow legs, then some coattails, then a pair of arms stuck akimbo, and, finally, the well-known head of his friend the mug; all which articles, uniting as they rolled out, stood up energetically on the floor in the shape of a little golden dwarf about a foot and a half high.

"That's right!" said the dwarf, stretching out first his legs and then his arms, and then shaking his head up and down and as far round as it would go, for five minutes without stopping, apparently with the view of ascertaining if he were quite correctly put together, while Gluck stood contemplating him in speechless amazement. He was dressed in a slashed doublet of spun gold, so fine in its texture that the prismatic colors gleamed over it as if on a surface of mother-of-pearl; and over this brilliant doublet, his hair and beard fell full halfway to the ground, in waving curls so exquisitely delicate that Gluck could hardly tell where they ended; they seemed to melt into air. The features of the face, however, were by no means finished with the same delicacy; they were rather coarse, slightly inclining to coppery in complexion, and indicative, in expression, of a very pertinacious and intractable disposition in their small proprietor. When the dwarf had finished his self-examination, he turned his small sharp eyes full on Gluck and stared at him deliberately for a minute or two. "No it wouldn't, Gluck, my boy," said the little man.

This was certainly rather an abrupt and unconnected mode of commencing conversation. It might indeed be supposed to refer to the course of Gluck's thoughts, which had first produced the dwarf's observations out of the pot; but whatever it referred to, Gluck had no inclination to dispute the dictum.

"Wouldn't it, sir?" said Gluck, very mildly and submissively indeed.

"No," said the dwarf conclusively. "No, it wouldn't." And with that, the dwarf pulled his cap hard over his brows, and took two turns of three feet long up and down the room, lifting his legs up very high and setting them down very hard. This pause gave time for Gluck to collect his thoughts a little; and seeing no great reason to

186 view his diminutive visitor with dread, and feeling his curiosity overcome his amazement, he ventured on a question of peculiar delicacy.

"Pray, sir," said Gluck rather hesitatingly, "were you my mug?"

On which the little man turned sharp round, walked straight up to Gluck, and drew himself up to his full height. "I," said the little man, "am the King of the Golden River." Whereupon he turned about again, and took two more turns some six feet long, in order to allow time for the consternation which this announcement produced in his auditor to evaporate. After which he again walked up to Gluck and stood still as if expecting some comment on his communication.

Gluck determined to say something at all events. "I hope your majesty is very well," said Gluck.

"Listen!" said the little man, deigning no reply to this polite inquiry. "I am the King of what you mortals call the Golden River. The shape you saw me in was owing to the malice of a stronger king, from whose enchantments you have this instant freed me. What I have seen of you and your conduct to your wicked brothers renders me willing to serve you; therefore attend to what I tell you. Whoever shall climb to the top of that mountain from which you see the Golden River issue and shall cast into the stream at its source three drops of holy water, for him, and for him only, the river shall turn to gold. But no one failing in his first can succeed in a second attempt; and if anyone shall cast unholy water into the river, it will overwhelm him, and he will become a black stone." So saying, the King of the Golden River turned away and

deliberately walked into the center of the hottest flame of
the furnace. His figure became red, white, transparent,
dazzling—a blaze of intense light—rose, trembled, and
disappeared. The King of the Golden River had evaporated.

"Oh!" cried poor Gluck, running to look up the chimney after him. "Oh dear, dear, dear me! My mug! My
mug! My mug!"

Chapter 3

The King of the Golden River had hardly made the extraordinary exit related in the last chapter before Hans
and Schwartz came roaring into the house, very savagely
drunk. The discovery of the total loss of their last piece of
plate had the effect of sobering them just enough to en-
able them to stand over Gluck, beating him very steadily
for a quarter of an hour; at the expiration of which period
they dropped into a couple of chairs and requested to
know what he had got to say for himself. Gluck told them
his story, of which of course they did not believe a word.
They beat him again till their arms were tired, and staggered to bed. In the morning, however, the steadiness
with which he adhered to his story obtained him some
degree of credence; the immediate consequence of which
was that the two brothers, after wrangling a long time on
the knotty question which of them should try his fortune
first, drew their swords and began fighting. The noise of
the fray alarmed the neighbors who, finding they could

188 not pacify the combatants, sent for the constable.

Hans, on hearing this, contrived to escape and hid himself; but Schwartz was taken before the magistrate, fined for breaking the peace, and, having drunk out his last penny the evening before, was thrown into prison till he should pay.

When Hans heard this, he was much delighted and determined to set out immediately for the Golden River. How to get the holy water was the question. He went to the priest, but the priest could not give any holy water to so abandoned a character. So Hans went to vespers in the evening for the first time in his life, and, under pretense of crossing himself, stole a cupful and returned home in triumph.

Next morning he got up before the sun rose, put the holy water into a strong flask and two bottles of wine and some meat in a basket, slung them over his back, took his alpine staff in his hand, and set off for the mountains.

On his way out of the town, he had to pass the prison, and as he looked in at the windows, whom should he see but Schwartz himself peeping out of the bars and looking very disconsolate.

"Good morning, brother," said Hans; "have you any message for the King of the Golden River?"

Schwartz gnashed his teeth with rage and shook the bars with all his strength; but Hans only laughed at him, and, advising him to make himself comfortable till he came back again, shouldering his basket, shook the bottle of holy water in Schwartz's face till it frothed again, and marched off in the highest spirits in the world.

It was, indeed, a morning that might have made anyone happy, even with no Golden River to seek for. Level lines of dewy mist lay stretched along the valley, out of which rose the massy mountains—their lower cliffs in pale gray shadow, hardly distinguishable from the floating vapor, but gradually ascending till they caught the sunlight which ran in sharp touches of ruddy color along the angular crags, and pierced in long level rays through their fringes of spearlike pine. Far above shot up red splintered masses of castellated rock, jagged and shivered into myriads of fantastic forms, with here and there a streak of sunlit snow traced down their chasms like a line of forked lightning; and far beyond and far above all these, fainter than the morning cloud but purer and changeless, slept in the blue sky the utmost peaks of the eternal snow.

The Golden River, which sprang from one of the lower and snowless elevations, was now nearly in shadow; all but the uppermost jets of spray, which rose like slow smoke above the undulating line of the cataract, and floated away in feeble wreaths upon the morning wind.

On this object and on this alone Hans's eyes and thoughts were fixed; forgetting the distance he had to traverse, he set off at an imprudent rate of walking, which greatly exhausted him before he had scaled the first range of the green and low hills. He was, moreover, surprised, on surmounting them, to find that a large glacier, of whose existence, notwithstanding his previous knowledge of the mountains, he had been absolutely ignorant, lay between him and the source of the Golden River. He entered on it with the boldness of a practiced mountaineer; yet he thought he had never traversed so strange or so dangerous a glacier in his life.

The ice was excessively slippery; and out of all its

190 chasms came wild sounds of gushing water, not monotonous or low, but changeful and loud, rising occasionally into drifting passages of wild melody, then breaking off into short, melancholy tones, or sudden shrieks resembling those of human voices in distress or pain.

The ice was broken into thousands of confused shapes, but none, Hans thought, like the ordinary forms of splintered ice. There seemed a curious *expression* about all their outlines—a perpetual resemblance to living features, distorted and scornful. Myriads of deceitful shadows and lurid lights played and floated about and through the pale blue pinnacles, dazzling and confusing the sight of the traveler; while his ears grew dull and his head giddy with the constant gush and roar of the concealed waters. These painful circumstances increased upon him as he advanced; the ice crashed and yawned into fresh chasms at his feet; tottering spires nodded around him and fell thundering across his path; and though he had repeatedly faced these dangers on the most terrific glaciers and in the wildest weather, it was with a new and oppressive feeling of panic terror that he leaped the last chasm and flung himself, exhausted and shuddering, on the firm turf of the mountain.

He had been compelled to abandon his basket of food, which became a perilous encumbrance on the glacier, and had now no means of refreshing himself but by breaking off and eating some of the pieces of ice. This, however, relieved his thirst; an hour's repose recruited his hardy frame; and, with the indomitable spirit of avarice, he resumed his laborious journey.

His way now lay straight up a ridge of bare red rocks, without a blade of grass to ease the foot or a projecting angle to afford an inch of shade from the south sun. It was past noon, and the rays beat intensely upon the steep path, while the whole atmosphere was motionless and penetrated with heat. Intense thirst was soon added to the bodily fatigue with which Hans was now afflicted; glance after glance he cast on the flask of water which hung at his belt. "Three drops are enough," at last thought he; "I may, at least, cool my lips with it."

He opened the flask and was raising it to his lips when his eye fell on an object lying on the rock beside him; he thought it moved. It was a small dog, apparently in the last agony of death from thirst. Its tongue was out, its jaws dry, its limbs extended lifelessly, and a swarm of black ants were crawling about its lips and throat. Its eye moved to the bottle which Hans held in his hand. He raised it, drank, spurned the animal with his foot, and passed on. And he did not know how it was, but he thought that a strange shadow had suddenly come across the blue sky.

The path became steeper and more rugged every moment; and the high hill air, instead of refreshing him, seemed to throw his blood into a fever. The noise of the hill cataracts sounded like mockery in his ears: they were all distant, and his thirst increased every moment. Another hour passed, and he again looked down to the flask at his side; it was half empty, but there was much more than three drops in it. He stopped to open it, and again, as he did so, something moved in the path above him. It was a fair child, stretched nearly lifeless on the rock, its breast heaving with thirst, its eyes closed, and its lips parched and burning. Hans eyed it deliberately, drank, and passed on. And a dark gray cloud came over the sun,

192 and long, snakelike shadows crept up along the mountainsides. Hans struggled on. The sun was sinking, but its descent seemed to bring no coolness; the leaden weight of the dead air pressed upon his brow and heart, but the goal was near. He saw the cataract of the Golden River springing from the hillside scarcely five hundred feet above him. He paused for a moment to breathe, and sprang on to complete his task.

At this instant a faint cry fell on his ear. He turned and saw a gray-haired old man extended on the rocks. His eyes were sunk, his features deadly pale and gathered into an expression of despair. "Water!" He stretched his arms to Hans and cried feebly: "Water! I am dying."

"I have none," replied Hans; "thou hast had thy share of life." He strode over the prostrate body and darted on. And a flash of blue lightning rose out of the East, shaped like a sword; it shook thrice over the whole heaven, and left it dark with one heavy, impenetrable shade. The sun was setting; it plunged towards the horizon like a red-hot ball.

The roar of the Golden River rose on Hans's ear. He stood at the brink of the chasm through which it ran. Its waves were filled with the red glory of the sunset; they shook their crests like tongues of fire, and flashes of blood-red light gleamed along their foam. Their sound came mightier and mightier on his senses; his brain grew giddy with the prolonged thunder. Shuddering, he drew the flask from his girdle and hurled it into the center of the torrent. As he did so, an icy chill shot through his limbs; he staggered, shrieked, and fell. The water closed over his cry. And the moaning of the river rose wildly into the night as it gushed over **The Black Stone.**

Chapter 4

Poor little Gluck waited very anxiously alone in the house for Hans's return. Finding he did not come back, he was terribly frightened, and went and told Schwartz in the prison all that had happened. Then Schwartz was very much pleased and said that Hans must certainly have been turned into a black stone, and he should have all the gold to himself. But Gluck was very sorry and cried all night. When he got up in the morning there was no bread in the house, nor any money; so Gluck went and hired himself to another goldsmith, and he worked so hard, and so neatly, and so long every day, that he soon got money enough together to pay his brother's fine; and he went and gave it all to Schwartz, and Schwartz got out of prison. Then Schwartz was quite pleased and said he should have some of the gold of the river. But Gluck only begged that he would go and see what had become of Hans.

Now when Schwartz had heard that Hans had stolen the holy water, he thought to himself that such a proceeding might not be considered altogether correct by the King of the Golden River and determined to manage matters better. So he took some more of Gluck's money and went to a bad priest who gave him some holy water very readily for it. Then Schwartz was sure it was all quite right. So Schwartz got up early in the morning before the sun rose, and took some bread and wine in a basket, and put his holy water in a flask, and set off for the mountains. Like his brother he was much surprised at the sight of the glacier and had great difficulty in crossing it, even after leaving his basket behind him. The day was cloudless but not bright: there was a heavy purple haze hanging over the sky, and the hills looked lowering and gloomy. And as Schwartz climbed the steep rock path, the thirst came upon him, as it had upon his brother, until he lifted his flask to his lips to drink. Then he saw the fair child lying near him on the rocks, and it cried to him and moaned for water.

"Water, indeed," said Schwartz; "I haven't half enough for myself," and passed on. And as he went he thought the sunbeams grew more dim, and he saw a low bank of black cloud rising out of the west; and, when he had climbed for another hour, the thirst overcame him again, and he would have drunk. Then he saw the old man lying before him on the path and heard him cry out for water.

"Water, indeed," said Schwartz; "I haven't half enough for myself," and on he went.

Then again the light seemed to fade from before his eyes, and he looked up, and behold, a mist of the color of blood had come over the sun; and the bank of black cloud had risen very high, and its edges were tossing and tumbling like the waves of the angry sea. And they cast long shadows, which flickered over Schwartz's path.

Then Schwartz climbed for another hour, and again his thirst returned; and as he lifted his flask to his lips, he thought he saw his brother Hans lying exhausted on the path before him, and as he gazed, the figure stretched its arms to him and cried for water. "Ha, ha," laughed Schwartz, "are you there? Remember the prison bars, my boy. Water, indeed! Do you suppose I carried it all the way up here for *you?*" And he strode over the figure; yet, as he passed, he thought he saw a strange expression of

mockery about its lips. And when he had gone a few
yards farther, he looked back; but the figure was not
there.

And a sudden horror came over Schwartz, he knew not
why; but the thirst for gold prevailed over his fear, and
he rushed on. And the bank of black cloud rose to the
zenith, and out of it came bursts of spiry lightning, and
waves of darkness seemed to heave and float, between
their flashes, over the whole heavens. And the sky where
the sun was setting was all level and like a lake of blood;
and a strong wind came out of that sky, tearing its crimson clouds into fragments and scattering them far into the
darkness. And when Schwartz stood by the brink of the
Golden River, its waves were black like thunder clouds,
but their foam was like fire; and the roar of the waters below and the thunder above met as he cast the flask into
the stream. And as he did so, the lightning glared in his
eyes, and the earth gave way beneath him, and the waters
closed over his cry. And the moaning of the river rose
wildly into the night, as it gushed over **The Two Black
Stones.**

Chapter 5

When Gluck found that Schwartz did not come back, he
was very sorry and did not know what to do. He had no
money and was obliged to go and hire himself again to
the goldsmith, who worked him very hard and gave him
very little money. So after a month or two, Gluck grew
tired and made up his mind to go and try his fortune with

the Golden River. "The little King looked very kind," thought he. "I don't think he will turn me into a black stone." So he went to the priest, and the priest gave him some holy water as soon as he asked for it. Then Gluck took some bread in his basket and the bottle of water and set off very early for the mountains.

If the glacier had occasioned a great deal of fatigue to his brothers, it was twenty times worse for him, who was neither so strong nor so practiced on the mountains. He had several very bad falls, lost his basket and bread, and was very much frightened at the strange noises under the ice. He lay a long time to rest on the grass, after he had got over, and began to climb the hill just in the hottest part of the day. When he had climbed for an hour he got dreadfully thirsty and was going to drink like his brothers when he saw an old man coming down the path above him, looking very feeble and leaning on a staff. "My son," said the old man, "I am faint with thirst—give me some of that water." Then Gluck looked at him, and when he saw that he was pale and weary, he gave him the water: "Only pray don't drink it all," said Gluck. But the old man drank a great deal and gave him back the bottle two-thirds empty. Then he bade him good speed, and Gluck went on again merrily. And the path became easier to his feet, and two or three blades of grass appeared upon it, and some grasshoppers began singing on the bank beside it; and Gluck thought he had never heard such merry singing.

Then he went on for another hour, and the thirst increased on him so that he thought he should be forced to drink. But, as he raised the flask, he saw a little child lying panting by the roadside, and it cried out piteously for

water. Then Gluck struggled with himself and determined to bear the thirst a little longer; and he put the
bottle to the child's lips, and it drank it all but a few
drops. Then it smiled on him, and got up, and ran down
the hill; and Gluck looked after it till it became as small
as a little star, and then turned and began climbing again.
And then there were all kinds of sweet flowers growing
on the rocks, bright green moss with pale pink starry
flowers, and soft-belled gentians more blue than the sky
at its deepest, and pure white transparent lilies. And
crimson and purple butterflies darted hither and thither,
and the sky sent down such pure light that Gluck had
never felt so happy in his life.

Yet, when he had climbed for another hour, his thirst
became intolerable again; and when he looked at his
bottle, he saw that there were only five or six drops left in
it, and he could not venture to drink. And, as he was
hanging the flask to his belt again, he saw a little dog lying on the rocks, gasping for breath—just as Hans had
seen it on the day of his ascent. And Gluck stopped and
looked at it and then at the Golden River, not five hundred yards above him; and he thought of the dwarf's
words, "that no one could succeed except in their first attempt"; and he tried to pass the dog, but it whined piteously, and Gluck stopped again. "Poor beastie," said
Gluck, "it'll be dead when I come down again if I don't
help it." Then he looked closer and closer at it, and its
eye turned on him so mournfully that he could not stand
it. "Confound the King and his gold too," said Gluck; and
he opened the flask and poured all the water into the
dog's mouth.

The dog sprang up and stood on its hind legs. Its tail

disappeared, its ears became long, longer, silky, golden; its nose became very red, its eyes became very twinkling; in three seconds the dog was gone, and before Gluck stood his old acquaintance, the King of the Golden River.

"Thank you," said the monarch, "but don't be frightened, it's all right"; for Gluck showed manifest symptoms of consternation at this unlooked-for reply to his last observation. "Why didn't you come before," continued the dwarf, "instead of sending me those rascally brothers of yours for me to have the trouble of turning into stones? Very hard stones they make too."

"Oh dear me!" said Gluck. "Have you really been so cruel?"

"Cruel!" said the dwarf. "They poured unholy water into my stream: do you suppose I'm going to allow that?"

"Why," said Gluck, "I am sure, sir—your majesty, I mean—they got the water out of the church font."

"Very probably," replied the dwarf; "but"—and his countenance grew stern as he spoke—"the water which has been refused to the cry of the weary and dying is unholy, though it has been blessed by every saint in heaven; and the water which is found in the vessel of mercy is holy, though it had been defiled with corpses."

So saying, the dwarf stooped and plucked a lily that grew at his feet. On its white leaves there hung three drops of clear dew. And the dwarf shook them into the flask which Gluck held in his hand. "Cast these into the river," he said, "and descend on the other side of the mountains into the Treasure Valley. And so good speed."

As he spoke, the figure of the dwarf became indistinct. The playing colors of his robe formed themselves into a prismatic mist of dewy light: he stood for an instant veiled with them as with the belt of a broad rainbow. The colors grew faint, the mist rose into the air; the monarch had evaporated.

And Gluck climbed to the brink of the Golden River, and its waves were as clear as crystal and as brilliant as the sun. And when he cast the three drops of dew into the stream, there opened where they fell a small circular whirlpool into which the waters descended with a musical noise. Gluck stood watching it for some time, very much disappointed, because not only was the river not turned into gold but its waters seemed much diminished in quantity. Yet he obeyed his friend the dwarf and descended the other side of the mountains towards the Treasure Valley; and as he went, he thought he heard the noise of water working its way under the ground. And when he came in sight of the Treasure Valley, behold, a river, like the Golden River, was springing from a new cleft of the rocks above it and was flowing in innumerable streams among the dry heaps of red sand. And as Gluck gazed, fresh grass sprang beside the new streams, and creeping plants grew and climbed among the moistening soil. Young flowers opened suddenly along the riversides as stars leap out when twilight is deepening, and thickets of myrtle and tendrils of vine cast lengthening shadows over the valley as they grew.

And thus the Treasure Valley became a garden again, and the inheritance, which had been lost by cruelty, was regained by love. And Gluck went and dwelt in the valley, and the poor were never driven from his door; so that his barns became full of corn and his house of treasure.

200 And for him the river had, according to the dwarf's promise, become a River of Gold. And to this day the inhabitants of the valley point to the place where the three drops of holy dew were cast into the stream, and trace the course of the Golden River under the ground until it emerges in the Treasure Valley. And at the top of the cataract of the Golden River are still to be seen two Black Stones, round which the waters howl mournfully every day at sunset; and these stones are still called by the people of the valley **The Black Brothers.**

SCIENCE FICTION

Science Fiction, like fantasy, asks *What if?* But unlike fantasy, it cannot make its own rules. It must abide by scientific data, by what is known about natural laws. If a science fiction story introduces a flying carpet, the carpet must be explained by the laws of aerodynamics.

In science fiction, science and imagination work hand in hand. Many science fiction writers present a good deal of data to convince their readers that what occurs is or may be possible, scientifically speaking. But the artistic imagination is also at work, touching on people's hopes, dreams, and fears.

In its speculations, science fiction suggests many possibilities. It can depict a world in which machines are marvelous servants—or a world in which machines become people's masters. It can speculate about wonderful changes in society that may result from new inventions, drugs, or animal or plant mutations—or horrible changes that may result from them.

As science fiction follows assumptions to their consequences, it makes people think about what is happening and about what might happen. It awakens minds to the possibilities of the universe.

Death! ... Why alone of all mortals have you cast me from your sheltering fold? Oh, for the peace of the grave!

THE MORTAL IMMORTAL

Mary Shelley

July 16, 1833—This is a memorable anniversary for me; on it I complete my three hundred and twenty-third year! The Wandering Jew?—certainly not. More than eighteen centuries have passed over his head. In comparison with him, I am a very young Immortal.

Am I, then, immortal? This is a question which I have asked myself, by day and night, for now three hundred and three years, and yet cannot answer it. I detected a gray hair amidst my brown locks this very day—that surely signifies decay. Yet it may have remained concealed there for three hundred years—for some persons have become entirely white-headed before twenty years of age.

I will tell my story, and my reader shall judge for me. I will tell my story, and so contrive to pass some few hours of a long eternity, become so wearisome to me. Forever! Can it be? to live forever! I have heard of enchantments, in which the victims were plunged into a deep sleep, to wake after a hundred years, as fresh as ever: I have heard of the Seven Sleepers—thus to be immortal would not be so burdensome: but, oh! the weight of never-ending time—the tedious passage of the still-succeeding hours! How happy was the fabled Nourjahad!—but to my task.

All the world has heard of Cornelius Agrippa. His memory is as immortal as his arts have made me. All the world has also heard of his scholar, who, unawares, raised the foul fiend during his master's absence, and was destroyed by him. The report, true or false, of this accident was attended with many inconveniences to the renowned philosopher. All his scholars at once deserted him—his servants disappeared. He had no one near him to put coals on his ever-burning fires while he slept, or to attend to the changeful colors of his medicines while he studied. Experiment after experiment failed, because one pair of hands was insufficient to complete them: the dark spirits laughed at him for not being able to retain a single mortal in his service.

I was then very young—very poor—and very much in love. I had been for about a year the pupil of Cornelius, though I was absent when this accident took place. On my return, my friends implored me not to return to the alchemist's abode. I trembled as I listened to the dire tale they told; I required no second warning; and when Cornelius came and offered me a purse of gold if I would remain under his roof, I felt as if Satan himself tempted me. My teeth chattered—my hair stood on end: I ran off as fast as my trembling knees would permit.

My failing steps were directed whither for two years they had every evening been attracted—a gently bubbling spring of pure living waters, beside which lingered a dark-haired girl, whose beaming eyes were fixed on the path I was accustomed each night to tread. I cannot remember the hour when I did not love Bertha; we had been neighbors and playmates from infancy—her parents, like mine, were of humble life, yet respectable—our attachment had been a source of pleasure to them. In an evil hour a malignant fever carried off both her father and mother, and Bertha became an orphan. She would have found a home beneath my paternal roof, but unfortunately, the old lady of the near castle, rich, childless, and solitary, declared her intention to adopt her. Henceforth Bertha was clad in silk—inhabited a marble palace—and was looked on as being highly favored by fortune. But in her new situation among her new associates, Bertha remained true to the friend of her humbler days; she often visited the cottage of my father, and when forbidden to go thither, she would stray towards the neighboring wood, and meet me beside its shady fountain.

She often declared that she owed no duty to her new protectress equal in sanctity to that which bound us. Yet still I was too poor to marry, and she grew weary of being tormented on my account. She had a haughty but an impatient spirit, and grew angry at the obstacles that prevented our union. We met now after an absence, and she had been sorely beset while I was away; she complained bitterly, and almost reproached me for being poor. I replied hastily:

"I am honest, if I am poor—were I not, I might soon become rich!"

This explanation produced a thousand questions. I feared to shock her by owning the truth, but she drew it from me: and then, casting a look of disdain on me, she said:

"You pretend to love, and you fear to face the Devil for my sake!"

I protested that I had only dreaded to offend her—while she dwelt on the magnitude of the reward that I should receive. Thus encouraged—shamed by her—led on by love and hope, laughing at my late fears, with quick steps and a light heart I returned to accept the offers of the alchemist, and was instantly installed in my office.

A year passed away. I became possessed of no insignificant sum of money. Custom had banished my fears. In spite of the most painful vigilance, I had never detected the trace of a cloven foot; nor was the studious silence of our abode ever disturbed by demoniac howls. I still continued my stolen interviews with Bertha, and hope dawned on me—hope—but not perfect joy; for Bertha fancied that love and securities were enemies, and her pleasure was to divide them in my bosom. Though true of heart, she was somewhat of a coquette in manner; and I was jealous as a Turk. She slighted me in a thousand ways, yet would never acknowledge herself to be in the wrong. She would drive me mad with anger, and then force me to beg her pardon. Sometimes she fancied that I was not sufficiently submissive, and then she had some story of a rival, favored by her protectress. She was surrounded by silk-clad youths—the rich and gay—What chance had the sad-robed scholar of Cornelius compared with these?

On one occasion the philosopher made such large demands upon my time that I was unable to meet her as I was wont. He was engaged in some mighty work, and I was forced to remain, day and night, feeding his furnaces and watching his chemical preparations. Bertha waited for me in vain at the fountain. Her haughty spirit fired at this neglect; and when at last I stole out during the few short minutes allotted to me for slumber, and hoped to be consoled by her, she received me with disdain, dismissed me in scorn, and vowed that any man should possess her hand rather than he who could not be in two places at once for her sake. She would be revenged!—And truly she was. In my dingy retreat I heard that she had been hunting, attended by Albert Hoffer. Albert Hoffer was favored by her protectress, and the three passed in cavalcade before my smoky window. Methought that they mentioned my name—it was followed by a laugh of derision, as her dark eyes glanced contemptuously towards my abode.

Jealousy, with all its vemon and all its misery, entered my breast. Now I shed a torrent of tears, to think that I should never call her mine; and, anon, I imprecated a thousand curses on her inconstancy. Yet still I must stir the fires of the alchemist, still attend on the changes of his unintelligible medicines.

Cornelius had watched for three days and nights, nor closed his eyes. The progress of his alembics was slower than he expected: in spite of his anxiety, sleep weighted upon his eyelids. Again and again he threw off drowsiness with more than human energy; again and again it stole away his senses. He eyed his crucibles wistfully. "Not ready yet," he murmured; "will another night pass before the work is accomplished? Winzy, you are vigilant—you are faithful—you have slept, my boy—you slept last night. Look at that glass vessel. The liquid it contains is of a soft rose color; the moment it begins to change its hue, awaken me—till then I may close my eyes. First, it will turn white, and then emit golden flashes: but wait not till then; when the rose color fades, rouse me." I scarcely heard the last words muttered as they were in sleep. Even then he did not quite yield to nature. "Winzy, my boy," he again said, "do not touch the vessel—do not put it to your lips; it's a philter—a philter to cure love; you would not cease to love your Bertha—beware to drink!"

And he slept. His venerable head sunk on his breast, and I scarce heard his regular breathing. For a few minutes I watched the vessel—the rosy hue of the liquid remained unchanged. Then my thoughts wandered—they visited the fountain, and dwelt on a thousand charming scenes never to be renewed—never! Serpents and adders were in my heart as the word "Never!" half formed itself on my lips. False girl!—false and cruel! Never more would she smile on me as that evening she smiled on Albert. Worthless, detested woman! I would not remain unrevenged—she should see Albert expire at her feet—she should die beneath my vengeance. She had smiled in disdain and triumph—she knew my wretchedness and her power. Yet what power had she?—the power of exciting my hate—my utter scorn—my—oh, all but indifference. Could I attain that—could I regard her with careless eyes, transferring my *rejected* love to one fairer and more true, that were indeed a victory!

A bright flash darted before my eyes. I had forgotten the medicine of the adept; I gazed on it with wonder: flashes of admirable beauty, more bright than those which the diamond emits when the sun's rays are on it, glanced from the surface of the liquid; an odor the most fragrant and grateful stole over my sense; the vessel seemed one globe of living radiance, lovely to the eye, and most inviting to the taste. The first thought, instinctively inspired by the grosser sense, was, I will—I

208 must drink. I raised the vessel to my lips. "It will cure me of love—of torture!" Already I had quaffed half of the most delicious liquor ever tasted by the palate of man, when the philosopher stirred. I started—I dropped the glass—the fluid flamed and glanced along the floor, while I felt Cornelius's grip at my throat, as he shrieked aloud, "Wretch! you have destroyed the labor of my life!"

The philosopher was totally unaware that I had drunk any portion of his drug. His idea was, and I gave a tacit assent to it, that I had raised the vessel from curiosity, and that, frighted at its brightness, and the flashes of intense light it gave forth, I had let it fall. I never undeceived him. The fire of the medicine was quenched—the fragrance died away—he grew calm, as a philosopher should under the heaviest trials, and dismissed me to rest.

I will not attempt to describe the sleep of glory and bliss which bathed my soul in paradise during the remaining hours of that memorable night. Words would be faint and shallow types of my enjoyment, or of the gladness that possessed my bosom when I woke. I trod air—my thoughts were in heaven. Earth appeared heaven, and my inheritance upon it was to be one trance of delight. "This it is to be cured of love," I thought; "I will see Bertha this day, and she will find her lover cold and regardless; too happy to be disdainful, yet how utterly indifferent to her!"

The hours danced away. The philosopher secure that he had once succeeded, and believing that he might again, began to concoct the same medicine once more. He was shut up with his books and drugs, and I had a holiday. I dressed myself with care; I looked in an old but polished shield, which served me for a mirror; methought my good looks had wonderfully improved. I hurried beyond the precincts of the town, joy in my soul, the beauty of heaven and earth around me. I turned my steps toward the castle—I could look on its lofty turrets with lightness of heart, for I was cured of love. My Bertha saw me afar off, as I came up the avenue. I know not what sudden impulse animated her bosom, but at the sight she sprung with a light fawn-like bound down the marble steps, and was hastening towards me. But I had been perceived by another person. The old high-born hag, who called herself her protectress, and was her tyrant, had seen me also; she hobbled, panting, up the terrace; a page, as ugly as herself, held up her train, and fanned her as she hurried along, and stopped my fair girl with a "How, now, my bold mistress? whither so fast? Back to your cage—hawks are abroad!"

Bertha clasped her hands—her eyes were still bent on my approaching figure. I saw the contest. How I abhorred the old crone who checked the kind impulses of my Bertha's softening heart. Hitherto, respect for her rank had caused me to avoid the lady of the castle; now I disdained such trivial considerations. I was cured of love and lifted above all human fears; I hastened forwards, and soon reached the terrace. How lovely Bertha looked! her eyes flashing fire, her cheeks glowing with impatience and anger, she was a thousand times more graceful and charming than ever—I no longer loved—Oh! no, I adored—worshipped—idolized her!

She had that morning been persecuted, with more than usual vehemence, to consent to an immediate marriage with my rival. She was reproached with the encouragement that she had shown him—she was threatened

210 with being turned out of doors with disgrace and shame. Her proud spirit rose in arms at the threat; but when she remembered the scorn that she had heaped upon me, and how, perhaps, she had thus lost one whom she now regarded as her only friend, she wept with remorse and rage. At that moment I appeared. "O, Winzy!" she exclaimed, "take me to your mother's cot; swiftly let me leave the detested luxuries and wretchedness of this noble dwelling—take me to poverty and happiness."

I clasped her in my arms with transport. The old lady was speechless with fury, and broke forth into invective only when we were far on our road to my natal cottage. My mother received the fair fugitive, escaped from a gilt cage to nature and liberty, with tenderness and joy; my father who loved her, welcomed her heartily; it was a day of rejoicing, which did not need the addition of the celestial potion of the alchemist to steep me in delight.

Soon after this eventful day I became the husband of Bertha. I ceased to be the scholar of Cornelius, but I continued his friend. I always felt grateful to him for having, unawares, procured me that delicious draught of a divine elixir, which instead of curing me of love (sad cure! solitary and joyless remedy for evils which seem blessings to the memory), had inspired me with courage and resolution, thus winning for me an inestimable treasure in my Bertha.

I often called to mind that period of trance-like inebriation with wonder. The drink of Cornelius had not fulfilled the task for which he affirmed that it had been prepared, but its effects were more potent and blissful than words can express. They had faded by degrees, yet they lingered long—and painted life in hues of splendor.

Bertha often wondered at my lightness of heart and unaccustomed gaiety; for, before, I had been rather serious, or even sad, in my disposition. She loved me the better for my cheerful temper, and our days were winged by joy.

Five years afterwards I was suddenly summoned to the bedside of the dying Cornelius. He had sent for me in haste, conjuring my instant presence. I found him stretched on his pallet, enfeebled even to death; all of life that yet remained animated his piercing eyes, and they were fixed on a glass vessel, full of a roseate liquid.

"Behold," he said, in a broken and inward voice, "the vanity of human wishes! a second time my hopes are about to be crowned, a second time they are destroyed. Look at that liquor—you remember five years ago I had prepared the same, with the same success; then, as now, my thirsting lips expected to taste the immortal elixir—you dashed it from me! and at present it is too late."

He spoke with difficulty, and fell back on his pillow. I could not help saying:

"How, revered master, can a cure for love restore you to life?"

A faint smile gleamed across his face as I listened earnestly to his scarcely intelligible answer.

"A cure for love and for all things—the Elixir of Immortality. Ah! if now I might drink, I should live forever!"

As he spoke, a golden flash gleamed from the fluid; a well-remembered fragrance stole over the air; he raised himself, all weak as he was—strength seemed miraculously to reenter his frame—he stretched forth his hand—a loud explosion startled me—a ray of fire shot up from the elixir, and the glass vessel which contained it was shiv-

212 ered to atoms! I turned my eyes towards the philosopher;
he had fallen back—his eyes were glassy—his features
rigid—he was dead!

But I lived, and was to live forever! So said the unfortunate alchemist, and for a few days I believed his
words. I remembered the glorious drunkenness that had
followed my stolen draught. I reflected on the change I
had felt in my frame—in my soul. The bounding elasticity
of the one—the buoyant lightness of the other. I surveyed
myself in a mirror, and could perceive no change in my
features during the space of the five years which had
elapsed. I remembered the radiant hues and grateful
scent of that delicious beverage—worthy the gift it was
capable of bestowing—I was, then, *Immortal!*

A few days after I laughed at my credulity. The old
proverb, that "a prophet is least regarded in his own
country," was true with respect to me and my defunct
master. I loved him as a man—I respected him as a sage—
but I derided the notion that he could command the powers of darkness, and laughed at the superstitious fears
with which he was regarded by the vulgar. He was a wise
philosopher, but had no acquaintance with any spirits but
those clad in flesh and blood. His science was simply human; and human science, I persuaded myself, could never
conquer nature's laws so far as to imprison the soul for
ever within its carnal habitation. Cornelius had brewed a
soul-refreshing drink—more inebriating than wine—
sweeter and more fragrant than any fruit: it possessed
probably strong medicinal powers, imparting gladness to
the heart and vigor to the limbs; but its effects would
wear out; already were they diminished in my frame. I
was a lucky fellow to have quaffed health and joyous spir-

its, and perhaps long life, at my master's hands; but my good fortune ended there: longevity was far different from immortality.

I continued to entertain this belief for many years. Sometimes a thought stole across me—Was the alchemist indeed deceived? But my habitual credence was, that I should meet the fate of all the children of Adam at my appointed time—a little late, but still at a natural age. Yet it was certain that I retained a wonderfully youthful look. I was laughed at for my vanity in consulting the mirror so often, but I consulted it in vain—my brow was untrenched—my cheeks—my eyes—my whole person continued as untarnished as in my twentieth year.

I was troubled. I looked at the faded beauty of Bertha—I seemed more like her son. By degrees our neighbors began to make similar observations, and I found at last that I went by the name of the scholar bewitched. Bertha herself grew uneasy. She became jealous and peevish, and at length she began to question me. We had no children; we were all in all to each other; and though, as she grew older, her vivacious spirit became a little allied to ill temper, and her beauty sadly diminished. I cherished her in my heart as the mistress I had idolized, the wife I had sought and won with such perfect love.

At last our situation became intolerable: Bertha was fifty—I twenty years of age. I had in very shame, in some measure adopted the habits of a more advanced age; I no longer mingled in the dance among the young and gay, but my heart bounded along with them while I restrained my feet; and a sorry figure I cut among the Nestors of our village. But before the time I mention things were altered—we were universally shunned; we were—at least I was—reported to have kept up an iniquitous acquaintance with some of my former master's supposed friends. Poor Bertha was pitied, but deserted. I was regarded with horror and detestation.

What was to be done? we sat by our winter fire—poverty had made itself felt, for none would buy the produce of my farm; and often I had been forced to journey twenty miles, to some place where I was not known, to dispose of our property. It was true we had saved something for an evil day—that day was come.

We sat by our lone fireside—the old-hearted youth and his antiquated wife. Again Bertha insisted on knowing the truth; she recapitulated all she had ever heard said about me, and added her own observations. She conjured me to cast off the spell; she described how much more comely gray hairs were than my chestnut locks; she descanted on the reverence and respect due to age—how preferable to the slight regard paid to mere children: could I imagine that the despicable gifts of youth and good looks outweighed disgrace, hatred, and scorn? Nay, in the end I should be burned as a dealer in the black art, while she, to whom I had not deigned to communicate any portion of my good fortune, might be stoned as my accomplice. At length she insinuated that I must share my secret with her, and bestow on her like benefits to those I myself enjoyed, or she would denounce me—and then she burst into tears.

Thus beset, methought it was the best way to tell the truth. I revealed it as tenderly as I could, and spoke only of a *very long life*, not of immortality—which representation, indeed, coincided best with my own ideas. When I ended, I rose and and said:

"And now, my Bertha, will you denounce the lover of your youth?—You will not, I know. But it is too hard, my poor wife, that you should suffer from my ill luck and the accursed arts of Cornelius. I will leave you—you have wealth enough, and friends will return in my absence. I will go; young as I seem, and strong as I am, I can work and gain my bread among strangers, unsuspected and unknown. I loved you in youth; God is my witness that I would not desert you in age, but that your safety and happiness require it."

I took my cap and moved towards the door; in a moment Bertha's arms were round my neck, and her lips were pressed to mine. "No, my husband, my Winzy," she said, "you shall not go alone—take me with you; we will remove from this place, and, as you say, among strangers we shall be unsuspected and safe. I am not so very old as quite to shame you, my Winzy; and I dare say the charm will soon wear off, and, with the blessing of God, you will become more elderly-looking, as is fitting; you shall not leave me."

I returned the good soul's embrace heartily. "I will not, my Bertha; but for your sake, I had not thought of such a thing. I will be your true, faithful husband while you are spared to me, and do my duty by you to the last."

The next day we prepared secretly for our emigration. We were obliged to make great pecuniary sacrifices—it could not be helped. We realized a sum sufficient, at least, to maintain us while Bertha lived; and without saying adieu to any one, quitted our native country to take refuge in a remote part of western France.

It was a cruel thing to transport poor Bertha from her native village, and the friends of her youth, to a new

216 country, new language, new customs. The strange secret
of my destiny rendered this removal immaterial to me;
but I compassionated her deeply, and was glad to perceive that she found compensation for her misfortunes in
a variety of little ridiculous circumstances. Away from all
tell-tale chroniclers, she sought to decrease the apparent
disparity of our ages by a thousand feminine arts—rouge,
youthful dress, and assumed juvenility of manner. I could
not be angry—Did not I myself wear a mask? Why quar-
rel with hers, because it was less successful? I grieved
deeply when I remembered that this was my Bertha,
whom I had loved so fondly, and won with such transport—the dark-eyed, dark-haired girl, with smiles of en-
chanting archness and a step like a fawn—this mincing,
simpering, jealous old woman. I should have revered her
gray locks and withered cheeks; but thus?—It was my
work, I knew; but I did not the less deplore this type of
human weakness.

Her jealousy never slept. Her chief occupation was to
discover that, in spite of outward appearances, I was myself growing old. I verily believed that the poor soul
loved me truly in her heart, but never had woman so tor-
menting a mode of displaying fondness. She would dis-
cern wrinkles in my face and decrepitude in my walk,
while I bounded along in youthful vigor, the youngest
looking of twenty youths. I never dared address another
woman: on one occasion, fancying that the belle of the
village regarded me with favoring eyes, she brought me a
gray wig. Her constant discourse among her acquaintances was, that though I looked so young, there was ruin
at work within my frame; and she affirmed that the worst
symptom about me was my apparent health. My youth

was a disease, she said, and I ought at all times to prepare for a sudden and awful death, at least to awake some morning white-headed, and bowed down with all the marks of advanced years. I let her talk—I often joined in her conjectures. Her warnings chimed in with my never-ceasing speculations concerning my state, and I took an earnest, though painful, interest in listening to all that her quick wit and excited imagination could say on the subject.

Why dwell on these minute circumstances? We lived on for many long years. Bertha became bed-ridden and paralytic; I nursed her as a mother might a child. She grew peevish, and still harped upon one string—of how long I should survive her. It has ever been a source of consolation to me, that I performed my duty scrupulously towards her. She had been mine in youth, she was mine in age, and at last, when I heaped the sod over her corpse, I wept to feel that I had lost all that really bound me to humanity.

Since then how many have been my cares and woes, how few and empty my enjoyments! I pause here in my history—I will pursue it no further. A sailor without rudder or compass, tossed on a stormy sea—a traveler lost on a widespread heath, without landmark or stone to guide him—such have I been: more lost, more hopeless than either. A nearing ship, a gleam from some far cot, may save them; but I have no beacon except the hope of death.

Death! mysterious, ill-visaged friend of weak humanity! Why alone of all mortals have you cast me from your sheltering fold? Oh, for the peace of the grave! the deep silence of the iron-bound tomb! that thought would cease

218 to work in my brain, and my heart beat no more with emotions varied only by new forms of sadness!

Am I immortal? I return to my first question. In the first place, is it not more probable that the beverage of the alchemist was fraught rather with longevity than eternal life? Such is my hope. And then be it remembered, that I only drank *half* of the potion prepared by him. Was not the whole necessary to complete the charm? To have drained half the Elixir of Immortality is but to be half immortal—my Forever is thus truncated and null.

But again, who shall number the years of the half of eternity? I often try to imagine by what rule the infinite may be divided. Sometimes I fancy age advancing upon me. One gray hair I have found. Fool! do I lament? Yes, the fear of age and death often creeps coldly into my heart; and the more I live, the more I dread death, even while I abhor life. Such an enigma is man—born to perish—when he wars, as I do, against the established laws of his nature.

But for this anomaly of feeling surely I might die: the medicine of the alchemist would not be proof against fire—sword—and the strangling waters. I have gazed upon the blue depths of many a placid lake, and the tumultuous rushing of many a mighty river, and have said, Peace inhabits those waters; yet I have turned my steps away, to live yet another day. I have asked myself, whether suicide would be a crime in one to whom thus only the portals of the other world could be open. I have done all, except presenting myself as a soldier or duelist, an object of destruction to my—no, *not* my fellow-mortals, and therefore I have shrunk away. They are not my fellows. The inextinguishable power of life in my frame, and their ephemeral existence, places us wide as the poles asunder. I could not raise a hand against the meanest or the most powerful among them.

Thus I have lived on for many a year—alone and weary of myself—desirous of death, yet never dying—a mortal immortal. Neither ambition nor avarice can enter my mind, and the ardent love that gnaws at my heart, never to be returned—never to find an equal on which to expend itself—lives there only to torment me.

This very day I conceived a design by which I may end all—without self-slaughter, without making another man a Cain—an expedition, which mortal frame can never survive, even endued with the youth and strength that inhabits mine. Thus I shall put my immortality to the test, and rest forever—or return, the wonder and benefactor of the human species.

Before I go, a miserable vanity has caused me to pen these pages. I would not die, and leave no name behind. Three centuries have passed since I quaffed the fatal beverage; another year shall not elapse before, encountering gigantic dangers—warring with the powers of frost in their home—beset by famine, toil, and tempest—I yield this body, too tenacious a cage for a soul which thirsts for freedom, to the destructive elements of air and water—or, if I survive, my name shall be recorded as one of the most famous among the sons of men; and, my task achieved, I shall adopt more resolute means, and, by scattering and annihilating the atoms that compose my frame set at liberty the life imprisoned within, and so cruelly prevented from soaring from this dim earth to a sphere more congenial to its immortal essence.

*Moxon tried to throw himself backward out of reach, but
he was too late: I saw the horrible thing's hands close
upon his throat. . . .*

MOXON'S MASTER

Ambrose Bierce

"Are you serious?—do you really believe that a machine
thinks?"

I got no immediate reply; Moxon was apparently intent upon the coals in the grate, touching them deftly
here and there with the fire poker till they signified a
sense of his attention by a brighter glow. For several
weeks I had been observing in him a growing habit of delay in answering even the most trivial of commonplace
questions. His air, however, was that of preoccupation
rather than deliberation: one might have said that he had
"something on his mind."

Presently he said:

"What is a 'machine'? The word has been variously de-
fined. Here is one definition from a popular dictionary:
'Any instrument or organization by which power is applied and made effective, or a desired effect produced.'
Well, then, is not a man a machine? And you will admit
that he thinks—or thinks he thinks."

"If you do not wish to answer my question," I said,

rather testily, "why not say so?—all that you say is mere evasion. You know well enough that when I say 'machine' I do not mean a man, but something that man has made and controls."

"When it does not control him," he said, rising abruptly and looking out of a window, whence nothing was visible in the blackness of a stormy night. A moment later he turned about and with a smile said:

"I beg your pardon; I had no thought of evasion. I considered the dictionary man's unconscious testimony suggestive and worth something in the discussion. I can give your question a direct answer easily enough: I do believe that a machine thinks about the work that it is doing."

That was direct enough, certainly. It was not altogether pleasing, for it tended to confirm a sad suspicion that Moxon's devotion to study and work in his machine shop had not been good for him. I knew, for one thing, that he suffered from insomnia, and that is no light affliction. Had it affected his mind? His reply to my question seemed to me then evidence that it had; perhaps I should think differently about it now. I was younger then, and among the blessings that are not denied to youth is ignorance. Incited by that great stimulant to controversy, I said:

"And what, pray, does it think with—in the absence of a brain?"

The reply, coming with less than his customary delay, took his favorite form of counter interrogation:

"With what does a plant think—in the absence of a brain?"

"Ah, plants also belong to the philosopher class! I should be pleased to know some of their conclusions; you

222 may omit the premises."

"Perhaps," he replied, apparently unaffected by my foolish irony, "you may be able to infer their convictions from their acts. I will spare you the familiar examples of the sensitive mimosa, the several insectivorous flowers, and those whose stamens bend down and shake their pollen upon the entering bee in order that he may fertilize their distant mates. But observe this. In an open spot in my garden I planted a climbing vine. When it was barely above the surface I set a stake into the soil a yard away. The vine at once made for it, but as it was about to reach it after several days I removed it a few feet. The vine at once altered its course, making an acute angle, and again made for the stake. This maneuver was repeated several times, but finally, as if discouraged, the vine abandoned the pursuit and ignoring further attempts to divert it traveled to a small tree, further away, which it climbed.

"Roots of the eucalyptus will prolong themselves incredibly in search of moisture. A well-known horticulturist relates that one entered an old drain pipe and followed it until it came to a break, where a section of the pipe had been removed to make way for a stone wall that had been built across its course. The root left the drain and followed the wall until it found an opening where a stone had fallen out. It crept through and following the other side of the wall back to the drain, entered the unexplored part and resumed its journey."

"And all this?"

"Can you miss the significance of it? It shows the consciousness of plants. It proves that they think."

"Even if it did—what then? We were speaking, not of plants, but of machines. They may be composed partly of wood—wood that has no longer vitality—or wholly of metal. Is thought an attribute also of the mineral kingdom?"

"How else do you explain the phenomena, for example, of crystalization?"

"I do not explain them."

"Because you cannot without affirming what you wish to deny, namely, intelligent cooperation among the constituent elements of the crystals. When soldiers form lines, or hollow squares, you call it reason. When wild geese in flight take the form of a letter V you say instinct. When the homogeneous atoms of a mineral, moving freely in solution, arrange themselves into shapes mathematically perfect, or particles of frozen moisture into the symmetrical and beautiful forms of snowflakes, you have nothing to say. You have not even invented a name to conceal your heroic unreason."

Moxon was speaking with unusual animation and earnestness. As he paused I heard in an adjoining room known to me as his "machine shop," which no one but himself was permitted to enter, a singular thumping sound, as of some one pounding upon a table with an open hand. Moxon heard it at the same moment and, visibly agitated, rose and hurriedly passed into the room whence it came. I thought it odd that anyone else should be in there, and my interest in my friend—with doubtless a touch of unwarrantable curiosity—led me to listen intently, though, I am happy to say, not at the keyhole. There were confused sounds, as of a struggle or scuffle; the floor shook. I distinctly heard hard breathing and a hoarse whisper which said "Damn you!" Then all was silent, and presently Moxon reappeared and said, with a rather sorry smile:

"Pardon me for leaving you so abruptly. I have a machine in there that lost its temper and cut up rough."

Fixing my eyes steadily upon his left cheek, which was traversed by four parellel excoriations showing blood, I said:

"How would it do to trim its nails?"

I could have spared myself the jest; he gave it no attention, but seated himself in the chair that he had left and resumed the interrupted monologue as if nothing had occurred:

"Doubtless you do not hold with those (I need not name them to a man of your reading) who have taught that all matter is sentient, that every atom is a living, feeling, conscious being. *I* do. There is no such thing as dead, inert matter: it is all alive; all instinct with force, actual and potential; all sensitive to the same forces in its environment and susceptible to the contagion of higher and subtler ones residing in such superior organisms as it may be brought into relation with, as those of man when he is fashioning it into an instrument of his will. It absorbs something of his intelligence and purpose—more of them in proportion to the complexity of the resulting machine and that of its work.

"Do you happen to recall Herbert Spencer's definition of 'Life'? I read it thirty years ago. He may have altered it afterward, for anything I know, but in all that time I have been unable to think of a single word that could profitably be changed or added or removed. It seems to me not only the best definition, but the only possible one.

" 'Life,' he says, 'is a definite combination of heterogeneous changes, both simultaneous and successive, in correspondence with external coexistences and sequences.'"

"That defines the phenomenon," I said, "but gives no hint of its cause."

"That," he replied, "is all that any definition can do. As Mill points out, we know nothing of cause except as an antecedent—nothing of effect except as a consequent. Of certain phenomena, one never occurs without another, which is dissimilar: the first in point of time we call cause, the second, effect. One who had many times seen a rabbit pursued by a dog, and had never seen rabbits and dogs otherwise, would think the rabbit the cause of the dog.

"But I fear," he added, laughing naturally enough, "that my rabbit is leading me a long way from the track of my legitimate quarry: I'm indulging in the pleasure of the chase for its own sake. What I want you to observe is that in Herbert Spencer's definition of 'life' the activity of a machine is included—there is nothing in the definition that is not applicable to it. According to this sharpest of observers and deepest of thinkers, if a man during his period of activity is alive, so is a machine when in operation. As an inventor and constructor of machines I know that to be true."

Moxon was silent for a long time, gazing absently into the fire. It was growing late and I thought it time to be going, but somehow I did not like the notion of leaving him in that isolated house, all alone except for the presence of some person of whose nature my conjectures could go no further than that it was unfriendly, perhaps

226 malign. Leaning toward him and looking earnestly into his eyes while making a motion with my hand through the door of his workshop, I said:

"Moxon, whom have you in there?"

Somewhat to my surprise he laughed lightly and answered without hesitation:

"Nobody; the incident that you have in mind was caused by my folly in leaving a machine in action with nothing to act upon, while I undertook the interminable task of enlightening your understanding. Do you happen to know that Consciousness is the creature of Rhythm?"

"Oh bother them both!" I replied, rising and laying hold of my overcoat. "I'm going to wish you good night; and I'll add the hope that the machine which you inadvertently left in action will have her gloves on the next time you think it needful to stop her."

Without waiting to observe the effect of my shot I left the house.

Rain was falling, and the darkness was intense. In the sky beyond the crest of a hill toward which I groped my way along precarious plank sidewalks and across miry, unpaved streets I could see the faint glow of the city's lights, but behind me nothing was visible but a single window of Moxon's house. It glowed with what seemed to me a mysterious and fateful meaning. I knew it was an uncurtained aperture in my friend's "machine shop," and I had little doubt that he had resumed the studies interrupted by his duties as my instructor in mechanical consciousness and the fatherhood of Rhythm. Odd, and in some degree humorous, as his convictions seemed to me at that time, I could not wholly divest myself of the feeling that they had some tragic relation to his life and

character—perhaps to his destiny—although I no longer
entertained the notion that they were the vagaries of a
disordered mind. Whatever might be thought of his
views, his exposition of them was too logical for that.
Over and over, his last words came back to me: "Consciousness is the creature of Rhythm." Bald and terse as
the statement was, I now found it infinitely alluring. At
each recurrence it broadened in meaning and deepened
in suggestion. Why, here (I thought) is something upon
which to found a philosophy. If consciousness is the product of rhythm all things *are* conscious, for all have motion, and all motion is rhythmic. I wondered if Moxon
knew the significance and breadth of his thought—the
scope of this momentous generalization; or had he arrived at his philosophic faith by the tortuous and uncer-
tain road of observation?

That faith was then new to me, and all Moxon's ex-
pounding had failed to make me a convert; but now it
seemed as if a great light shone about me, like that which
fell upon Saul of Tarsus; and out there in the storm and
darkness and solitude I experienced what Lewes calls
"The endless variety and excitement of philosophic
thought." I exulted in a new sense of knowledge, a new
pride of reason. My feet seemed hardly to touch the
earth; it was as if I were uplifted and borne through the
air by invisible wings.

Yielding to an impulse to seek further light from him
whom I now recognized as my master and guide, I had
unconsciously turned about, and almost before I was
aware of having done so found myself again at Moxon's
door. I was drenched with rain, but felt no discomfort.
Unable in my excitement to find the doorbell I in-

228 stinctively tried the knob. It turned and, entering, I mounted the stairs to the room that I had so recently left. All was dark and silent; Moxon, as I had supposed, was in the adjoining room—the "machine shop." Groping along the wall until I found the communicating door I knocked loudly several times, but got no response, which I attributed to the uproar outside, for the wind was blowing a gale and dashing the rain against the thin walls in sheets. The drumming upon the shingle roof spanning the unceiled room was loud and incessant.

I had never been invited into the machine shop—had, indeed, been denied admittance, as had all others, with one exception, a skilled metal worker, of whom no one knew anything except that his name was Haley and his habit silence. But in my spiritual exaltation, discretion and civility were alike forgotten and I opened the door. What I saw took all philosophical speculation out of me in short order.

Moxon sat facing me at the farther side of a small table upon which a single candle made all the light that was in the room. Opposite him, his back toward me, sat another person. On the table between the two was a chessboard; the men were playing. I knew little of chess, but as only a few pieces were on the board it was obvious that the game was near its close. Moxon was intensely interested—not so much, it seemed to me, in the game as in his antagonist, upon whom he had fixed so intent a look that, standing though I did directly in the line of his vision, I was altogether unobserved. His face was ghastly white, and his eyes glittered like diamonds. Of his antagonist I had only a back view, but that was sufficient; I should not have cared to see his face.

He was apparently not more than five feet in height, with proportions suggesting those of a gorilla—a tremendous breadth of shoulders, thick, short neck and broad, squat head, which had a tangled growth of black hair and was topped with a crimson fez. A tunic of the same color, belted tightly to the waist, reached the seat— apparently a box—upon which he sat; his legs and feet were not seen. His left forearm appeared to rest in his lap; he moved his pieces with his right hand, which seemed disproportionately long.

I had shrunk back and now stood a little to one side of the doorway and in shadow. If Moxon had looked farther than the face of his opponent he could have observed nothing now, except that the door was open. Something forbade me either to enter or to retire, a feeling—I know not how it came—that I was in the presence of an imminent tragedy and might serve my friend by remaining. With a scarcely conscious rebellion against the indelicacy of the act I remained.

The play was rapid. Moxon hardly glanced at the board before making his moves, and to my unskilled eye seemed to move the piece most convenient to his hand, his motions in doing so being quick, nervous and lacking in precision. The response of his antagonist, while equally prompt in the inception, was made with a slow, uniform, mechanical and, I thought, somewhat theatrical movement of the arm, that was a sore trial to my patience. There was something unearthly about it all, and I caught myself shuddering. But I was wet and cold.

Two or three times after moving a piece the stranger

230   slightly inclined his head, and each time I observed that Moxon shifted his king. All at once the thought came to me that the man was dumb. And then that he was a machine—an automaton chess-player! Then I remembered that Moxon had once spoken to me of having invented such a piece of mechanism, though I did not understand that it had actually been constructed. Was all his talk about the consciousness and intelligence of machines merely a prelude to eventual exhibition of this device— only a trick to intensify the effect of its mechanical action upon me in my ignorance of its secret?

A fine end, this, of all my intellectual transports—my "endless variety and excitement of philosophic thought!" I was about to retire in disgust when something occurred to hold my curiosity. I observed a shrug of the thing's great shoulders, as if it were irritated: and so natural was this—so entirely human—that in my new view of the matter it startled me. Nor was that all, for a moment later it struck the table sharply with its clenched hand. At that gesture Moxon seemed even more startled than I: he pushed his chair a little backward, as in alarm.

Presently Moxon, whose play it was, raised his hand high above the board, pounced upon one of his pieces like a sparrow hawk and with the exclamation "checkmate!" rose quickly to his feet and stepped behind his chair. The automaton sat motionless.

The wind had now gone down, but I heard, at lessening intervals and progressively louder, the rumble and roll of thunder. In the pauses between I now became conscious of a low humming or buzzing which, like the thunder, grew momentarily louder and more distinct. It seemed to come from the body of the automaton, and was unmistakably a whirring of wheels. It gave me the impression of a disordered mechanism which had escaped the repressive and regulating action of some controlling part—an effect such as might be expected if a pawl should be jostled from the teeth of a ratchet wheel. But before I had time for much conjecture as to its nature my attention was taken by the strange motions of the automaton itself. A slight but continuous convulsion appeared to have possession of it. In body and head it shook like a man with palsy or an ague chill, and the motion augmented every moment until the entire figure was in violent agitation. Suddenly it sprang to its feet and with a movement almost too quick for the eye to follow shot forward across table and chair, with both arms thrust forth to their full length—the posture and lunge of a diver. Moxon tried to throw himself backward out of reach, but he was too late: I saw the horrible thing's hands close upon his throat, his own clutch its wrists. Then the table was overturned, the candle thrown to the floor and extinguished, and all was black dark. But the noise of the struggle was dreadfully distinct, and most terrible of all were the raucous, squawking sounds made by the strangled man's efforts to breathe. Guided by the infernal hubbub, I sprang to the rescue of my friend, but had hardly taken a stride in the darkness when the whole room blazed with a blinding white light that burned into my brain and heart and memory a vivid picture of the combatants on the floor. Moxon underneath, his throat still in the clutch of those iron hands, his head forced backward, his eyes protruding, his mouth wide open and his tongue thrust out; and—horrible contrast!—upon the painted face of his assassin an expression of tranquil and profound thought, as in the

232 solution of a problem in chess! This I observed, then all was blackness and silence.

Three days later I recovered consciousness in a hospital. As the memory of that tragic night slowly evolved in my ailing brain I recognized in my attendant Moxon's confidential workman, Haley. Responding to a look he approached, smiling.

"Tell me about it," I managed to say, faintly—"all about it."

"Certainly," he said; "you were carried unconscious from a burning house—Moxon's. Nobody knows how you came to be there. You may have to do a little explaining. The origin of the fire is a bit mysterious, too. My own notion is that the house was struck by lightning."

"And Moxon?"

"Buried yesterday—what was left of him."

Apparently this reticent person could unfold himself on occasion. When imparting shocking intelligence to the sick he was affable enough. After some moments of the keenest mental suffering I ventured to ask another question:

"Who rescued me?"

"Well, if that interests you—I did."

"Thank you, Mr. Haley, and may God bless you for it. Did you rescue, also, that charming product of your skill, the automaton chess-player that murdered its inventor?"

The man was silent a long time, looking away from me. Presently he turned and gravely said:

"Do you know that?"

"I do," I replied; "I saw it done."

That was many years ago. If asked today I should answer less confidently.

———

FROM THE EARTH TO THE MOON

from *From the Earth to the Moon* and *Round the Moon*

Jules Verne

Preliminary Chapter

During the year 186—, the whole world was greatly excited by a scientific experiment unprecedented in the annals of science. The members of the Gun Club, a circle of artillerymen formed at Baltimore after the American war, conceived the idea of putting themselves in communication with the moon!—yes, with the moon—by sending to her a projectile. Their president, Barbicane, the promoter of the enterprise, having consulted the astronomers of the Cambridge Observatory upon the subject, took all necessary means to ensure the success of this extraordinary enterprise, which had been declared practicable by the majority of competent judges. After setting on foot a public subscription, which realized nearly £1,200,000, they began the gigantic work.

According to the advice forwarded from the members of the Observatory, the gun destined to launch the projectile had to be fixed in a country situated between the 0 and 28th degrees of north or south latitude, in order to aim at the moon when at the zenith; and its initiatory velocity was fixed at twelve thousand yards to the second. Launched on the 1st of December, at 10hrs. 46m. 40s. P.M., it ought to reach the moon four days after its departure, that is on the 5th of December, at midnight precisely, at the moment of her attaining her perigee, that is her nearest distance from the earth, which is exactly 86,410 leagues (French), or 238,833 miles mean distance (English).

The principal members of the Gun Club, President Barbicane, Major Elphinstone, the secretary Joseph T. Maston, and other learned men, held several meetings, at which the shape and composition of the projectile were discussed, also the position and nature of the gun, and the quality and quantity of the powder to be used. It was decided: First, that the projectile should be a shell made of aluminum with a diameter of 108 inches and a thickness of twelve inches to its walls; and should weigh 19,250 pounds. Second, that the gun should be a Columbiad cast in iron, 900 feet long, and run perpendicularly into the earth. Third, that the charge should contain 400,000 pounds of guncotton, which, giving out six billions of liters of gas in rear of the projectile, would easily carry it toward the orb of night.

These questions determined President Barbicane, assisted by Murchison the engineer, to choose a spot situated in Florida, in 27° 7′ North latitude, and 77° 3′ West (Greenwich) longitude. It was on this spot, after stupendous labor, that the Columbiad was cast with full success. Things stood thus, when an incident took place which increased the interest attached to this great enterprise a hundredfold.

A Frenchman, an enthusiastic Parisian, as witty as he was bold, asked to be enclosed in the projectile, in order that he might reach the moon and reconnoiter this terrestrial satellite. The name of this intrepid adventurer was Michel Ardan. He landed in America, was received with enthusiasm, held meetings, saw himself carried in triumph, reconciled President Barbicane to his mortal enemy, Captain Nicholl, and, as a token of reconciliation, persuaded them both to start with him in the projectile. The proposition being accepted, the shape of the projectile was slightly altered. It was made of cylindro-conical form. This species of aerial car was lined with strong springs and partitions to deaden the shock of departure. It was provided with food for a year, water for some months, and gas for some days. A self-acting apparatus supplied the three travelers with air to breathe. At the same time, on one of the highest points of the Rocky Mountains, the Gun Club had a gigantic telescope erected, in order that they might be able to follow the course of the projectile through space. All was then ready.

Fire!

The moon advanced upward in a heaven of the purest clearness, outshining in her passage the twinkling light of the stars. She passed over the constellation of the Twins, and was now nearing the halfway point between the hori-

236 zon and the zenith. A terrible silence weighed upon the entire scene! Not a breath of wind upon the earth! not a sound of breathing from the countless chests of the spectators! Their hearts seemed afraid to beat! All eyes were fixed upon the yawning mouth of the Columbiad.

Murchison followed with his eye the hand of his chronometer. It wanted scarce forty seconds to the moment of departure, but each second seemed to last an age! At the twentieth there was a general shudder, as it occurred to the minds of that vast assemblage that the bold travelers shut up within the projectile were also counting those terrible seconds. Some few cries here and there escaped the crowd.

"Thirty-five!—thirty-six!—thirty-seven!—thirty-eight!— thirty-nine!—forty! FIRE!!!"

Instantly Murchison pressed with his finger the key of the electric battery, restored the current of the fluid, and discharged the spark into the breech of the Columbiad.

An appalling, unearthly report followed instantly, such as can be compared to nothing whatever known, not even to the roar of thunder, or the blast of volcanic explosions! No words can convey the slightest idea of the terrific sound! An immense spout of fire shot up from the bowels of the earth as from a crater. The earth heaved up, and with great difficulty some few spectators obtained a momentary glimpse of the projectile victoriously cleaving the air in the midst of the fiery vapors!

At the moment when that pyramid of fire rose to a prodigious height into the air, the glare of the flame lit up the whole of Florida; and for a moment day superseded night over a considerable extent of the country. This immense canopy of fire was perceived at a distance of one hundred miles out at sea, and more than one ship's captain entered in his log the appearance of this gigantic meteor.

The discharge of the Columbiad was accompanied by a perfect earthquake. Florida was shaken to its very depths. The gases of the powder, expanded by heat, forced back the atmospheric strata with tremendous violence, and this artificial hurricane rushed like a waterspout through the air.

Not a single spectator remained on his feet! Men, women, children, all lay prostrate like ears of corn under a tempest. There ensued a terrible tumult; a large number of persons were seriously injured. J. T. Maston, who, despite all dietates of prudence, had kept in advance of the mass, was pitched back 120 feet, shooting like a projectile over the heads of his fellow citizens. Three hundred thousand persons remained deaf for a time, and as though struck stupefied.

As soon as the first effects were over, the injured, the deaf, and lastly, the crowd in general, woke up with frenzied cries. "Hurrah for Ardan! Hurrah for Barbicane! Hurrah for Nicholl!" rose to the skies. Thousands of persons, noses in air, armed with telescopes and race glasses, were questioning space, forgetting all contusions and emotions in the one idea of watching for the projectile. They looked in vain! It was no longer to be seen, and they were obliged to wait for telegrams from Long's Peak. The director of the Cambridge Observatory was at his post on the Rocky Mountains; and to him, as a skillful

238 and persevering astronomer, all observations had been confided.

But an unforseen phenomenon came in to subject the public impatience to a severe trial.

The weather, hitherto so fine, suddenly changed; the sky became heavy with clouds. It could not have been otherwise after the terrible derangement of the atmospheric strata, and the dispersion of the enormous quantity of vapor arising from the combustion of 200,000 pounds of pyroxyle!

On the morrow the horizon was covered with clouds— a thick and impenetrable curtain between earth and sky, which unhappily extended as far as the Rocky Mountains. It was a fatality! But since man had chosen so to disturb the atmosphere, he was bound to accept the consequences of his experiment.

Supposing, now, that the experiment had succeeded, the travelers having started on the 1st of December, at 10h. 46m. 40s. P.M., were due on the 4th at 0h. P.M. at their destination. So that up to that time it would have been very difficult after all to have observed, under such conditions, a body so small as the shell. Therefore they waited with what patience they might.

From the 4th to the 6th of December inclusive, the weather remaining much the same in America, the great European instruments of Herschel, Rosse, and Foucault, were constantly directed toward the moon, for the weather was then magnificent; but the comparative weakness of their glasses prevented any trustworthy observations being made.

On the 7th the sky seemed to lighten. They were in hopes now, but their hope was of but short duration, and at night again thick clouds hid the starry vault from all eyes.

Matters were now becoming serious, when on the 9th the sun reappeared for an instant, as if for the purpose of teasing the Americans. It was received with hisses; and wounded, no doubt, by such a reception, showed itself very sparing of its rays.

On the 10th, no change! J. T. Maston went nearly mad, and great fears were entertained regarding the brain of this worthy individual, which had hitherto been so well preserved within his gutta-percha cranium.

But on the 11th one of those inexplicable tempests peculiar to those intertropical regions was let loose in the atmosphere. A terrific east wind swept away the groups of clouds which had been so long gathering, and at night the semidisc of the orb of night rode majestically amid the soft constellations of the sky.

A New Star

That very night, the startling news so impatiently awaited, burst like a thunderbolt over the United States of the Union, and thence, darting across the ocean, ran through all the telegraphic wires of the globe. The projectile had been detected, thanks to the gigantic reflector of Long's Peak! Here is the note received by the director of the Observatory of Cambridge. It contains the scientific conclusion regarding this great experiment of the Gun Club.

LONG'S PEAK, December 12.

To the Officers of the Observatory of Cambridge.

The projectile discharged by the Columbiad at Stones Hill has been detected by Messrs. Belfast and J. T. Maston, 12th of December, at 8:47 P.M., the moon having entered her last quarter. This projectile has not arrived at its destination. It has passed by the side; but sufficiently near to be retained by the lunar attraction.

The rectilinear movement has thus become changed into a circular motion of extreme velocity, and it is now pursuing an elliptical orbit round the moon, of which it has become a true satellite.

The elements of this new star we have as yet been unable to determine; we do not yet know the velocity of its passage. The distance which separates it from the surface of the moon may be estimated at about 2,833 miles.

However, two hypotheses come here into our consideration.

1. Either the attraction of the moon will end by drawing them into itself, and the travelers will attain their destination; or,

2. The projectile, following an immutable law, will continue to gravitate round the moon till the end of time.

At some future time, our observations will be able to determine this point, but till then the experiment of the Gun Club can have no other result than to have provided our solar system with a new star.

J. BELFAST

To how many questions did this unexpected *dénouement* give rise? What mysterious results was the future reserving for the investigation of science? At all events, the names of Nicholl, Barbicane, and Michel Ardan were certain to be immortalized in the annals of astronomy!

When the dispatch from Long's Peak had once become known, there was but one universal feeling of surprise and alarm. Was it possible to go the aid of these bold travelers? No! for they had placed themselves beyond the pale of humanity, by crossing the limits imposed by the Creator on his earthly creatures. They had air enough for *two* months; they had victuals enough for *twelve;—but after that?* There was only one man who would not admit that the situation was desperate—he alone had confidence; and that was their devoted friend J. T. Maston.

Besides, he never let them get out of sight. His home was henceforth the post at Long's Peak; his horizon, the mirror of that immense reflector. As soon as the moon rose above the horizon, he immediately caught her in the field of the telescope; he never let her go for an instant out of his sight, and followed her assiduously in her course through the stellar spaces. He watched with untiring patience the passage of the projectile across her silvery disc, and really the worthy man remained in perpetual communication with his three friends, whom he did not despair of seeing again some day.

"Those three men," said he, "have carried into space all the resources of art, science, and industry. With that, one can do anything; and you will see that, some day, they will come out all right."

Round The Moon

The three travelers—the Frenchman Michel Ardan, the Americans Barbicane and Nicholl—become accustomed to their spacecraft, gaslit, comfortably furnished with a circular divan, windows, and games to while away the time. They feel a terrible shock at blast-off and wonder why they have not heard the explosion. At last they conclude that the velocity of blast-off was greater than the speed of sound.

Once in space, they see from the window an enormous disc, an asteroid, approaching. It misses them by only a few hundred yards. After recovering from the fright, they speculate on what it would be like to go outside the projectile but realize that they could not breathe in the near-vacuum of space.

"If Barbicane had only thought of furnishing us with a diving apparatus and an air pump, I could have ventured out and assumed fanciful attitudes of feigned monsters on top of the projectile!" says Michel.

The three travelers discuss the fact that as they get farther from the earth and nearer the moon, a point will be reached when the two attractions will neutralize each other, and the projectile will no longer be subject to the laws of weight.

Up to this time, the travelers, while admitting that this action [earth's attraction] was constantly decreasing, had not yet become sensible to its total absence.

But that day, about eleven o'clock in the morning, Nicholl having accidentally let a glass slip from his hand, the glass, instead of falling, remained suspended in the air.

"Ah!" exclaimed Michel Ardan, "that is rather an amusing piece of natural philosophy."

And immediately divers other objects, firearms and bottles, abandoned to themselves, held themselves up as by enchantment. . . .

The three adventurous companions were surprised and stupefied, despite their scientific reasonings. They felt themselves being carried into the domain of wonders! they felt that weight was really wanting to their bodies. If they stretched out their arms, they did not attempt to fall. Their heads shook on their shoulders. Their feet no longer clung to the floor of the projectile. They were like drunken men having no stability in themselves.

Fancy has depicted men without reflection, others without shadow. But here reality, by the neutralizations of attractive forces, produced men in whom nothing had any weight, and who weighed nothing themselves.

Suddenly Michel, taking a spring, left the floor and remained suspended in the air, like Murillo's monk of the *Cusine des Anges.*

The two friends joined him instantly, and all three formed a miraculous "Ascension" in the center of the projectile.

As the attraction of the moon increases, the three men come back to the floor. They begin to discuss the Selenites, or moon people, they hope to find on a moon whose mass is one-sixth that of the earth and where, therefore, any object will weigh six times less than on the earth.

"But we shall be regular Herculeses," exclaims Michel.

"Yes," replies Nicholl, "for if the height of the Selenites is in proportion to the density of their globe, they will be scarcely a foot high."

But soon Captain Nicholl realizes that the asteroid that passed so near the projectile has pulled them off course. They will miss the moon!

What will happen to the three men? Eventually, certainly, they will run out of air. But their thoughts are only for the moon they have come so far and through so much danger to see.

"My friends," says Barbicane, "I do not know whither we are going; I do not know if we shall ever see the terrestrial globe again. Nevertheless, let us proceed as if our work would one day be useful to our fellow men. Let us keep our minds free from every other consideration. We are astronomers; and this projectile is a room in the Cambridge University, carried into space. Let us make our observations!"

As they approach the moon, they are amazed by its appearance.

The moon having no atmosphere, the consequences arising from the absence of this gaseous envelope have already been shown. No twilight on her surface; night following day and day following night with the suddenness of a lamp which is extinguished or lighted amid profound darkness—no transition from cold to heat, the temperature falling in an instant from boiling point to the cold of space.

Another consequence of this want of air is that absolute darkness reigns where the sun's rays do not pene-

trate. That which on earth is called diffusion of light, that
luminous matter which the air holds in suspension, which
creates the twilight and the daybreak, which produces
the *umbrae* and *penumbrae,* and all the magic of *chiaro-
oscuro,* does not exist on the moon. Hence the harshness
of contrasts, which only admit of two colors, black and
white. If a Selenite were to shade his eyes from the sun's
rays, the sky would seem absolutely black, and the stars
would shine to him as on the darkest night. Judge of the
impression produced on Barbicane and his two friends by
this strange scene! Their eyes were confused. They could
no longer grasp the respective distances of the different
plains. A lunar landscape without the softening of the
phenomena of *chiaro-oscuro* could not be rendered by an
earthly landscape painter: it would be spots of ink on a
white page—nothing more.

This aspect was not altered even when the projectile,
at the height of 80°, was only separated from the moon
by a distance of fifty miles; nor even when, at five in the
morning, it passed at less than twenty-five miles from the
mountain of Gioja, a distance reduced by the glasses to a
quarter of a mile. It seemed as if the moon might be
touched by the hand! It seemed impossible that, before
long, the projectile would not strike her, if only at the
north pole, the brilliant arch of which was so distinctly
visible on the black sky.

Michel Ardan wanted to open one of the scuttles and
throw himself onto the moon's surface! A very useless attempt; for if the projectile could not attain any point
whatever of the satellite, Michel, carried along by its
motion, could not attain it either.

At that moment, at six o'clock, the lunar pole

246 appeared. The disc only presented to the travelers' gaze one half brilliantly lit up, while the other disappeared in the darkness. Suddenly the projectile passed the line of demarcation between intense light and absolute darkness, and was plunged in profound night!

The travelers are in orbit around the moon and are transversing the dark side of the moon. They are subject not only to total darkness but also—being cut off from the sun's rays—to bitter cold.

"The devil!" exclaims Michel, "it is cold enough to freeze a white bear!"

"A hundred and forty degrees Centigrade below zero!" calculates Barbicane.

On the black horizon of the moon, the travelers see a point of brightness, a reddish incandescense that increases in size as they approach it.

"A volcano! it is a volcano in action!" cried Nicholl; "a disemboweling of the interior fires of the moon! That world is not quite extinguished."

"Yes, an eruption," replied Barbicane, who was carefully studying the phenomenon through his night glass. "What should it be, if not a volcano?"

"But, then," said Michel Ardan, "in order to maintain that combustion, there must be air. So the atmosphere does surround that part of the moon."

"Perhaps so," replied Barbicane, "but not necessarily. The volcano, by the decomposition of certain substances, can provide its own oxygen, and thus throw flames into space. It seems to me that the deflagration, by the intense brilliancy of the substances in combustion, is produced in pure oxygen. We must not be in a hurry to proclaim the existence of a lunar atmosphere." . . .

Suddenly, in the midst of the ether, in the profound darkness, an enormous mass appeared. It was like a moon, but an incandescent moon whose brilliancy was all the more intolerable as it cut sharply on the frightful darkness of space. This mass, of a circular form, threw a light which filled the projectile. The forms of Barbicane, Nicholl, and Michel Ardan, bathed in its white sheets, assumed that livid spectral appearance which physicians produce with the fictitious light of alcohol impregnated with salt.

"By Jove!" cried Michel Ardan, "we are hideous. What is that ill-conditioned moon?"

"A meteor," replied Barbicane.

"A meteor burning in space?"

"Yes."

This shooting globe suddenly appearing in shadow at a distance of at most 200 miles, ought, according to Barbicane, to have a diameter of 2,000 yards. It advanced at a speed of about one mile and a half per second. It cut the projectile's path and must reach it in some minutes. As it approached it grew to enormous proportions.

Imagine, if possible, the situation of the travelers! It is impossible to describe it. In spite of their courage, their *sangfroid,* their carelessness of danger, they were mute, motionless with stiffened limbs, a prey to frightful terror. Their projectile, the course of which they could not alter, was rushing straight on this ignited mass, more intense than the open mouth of an oven. It seemed as though they were being precipitated toward an abyss of fire.

Barbicane had seized the hands of his two companions,

and all three looked through their half-open eyelids upon that asteroid heated to a white heat. If thought was not destroyed within them, if their brains still worked amid all this awe, they must have given themselves up for lost.

Two minutes after the sudden appearance of the meteor (to them two centuries of anguish) the projectile seemed almost about to strike it, when the globe of fire burst like a bomb, but without making any noise in that void where sound, which is but the agitation of the layers of air, could not be generated.

Nicholl uttered a cry, and he and his companions rushed to the scuttle. What a sight! What pen can describe it? What palette is rich enough in colors to reproduce so magnificent a spectacle?

It was like the opening of a crater, like the scattering of an immense conflagration. Thousands of luminous fragments lit up and irradiated space with their fires. Every size, every color, was there intermingled. There were rays of yellow and pale yellow, red, green, gray—a crown of fireworks of all colors. Of the enormous and much-dreaded globe there remained nothing but these fragments carried in all directions, now become asteroids in their turn, some flaming like a sword, some surrounded by a whitish cloud, and others leaving behind them trains of brilliant cosmical dust.

These incandescent blocks crossed and struck each other, scattering still smaller fragments, some of which struck the projectile. Its left scuttle was even cracked by a violent shock. It seemed to be floating amid a hail of howitzer shells, the smallest of which might destroy it instantly.

The light which saturated the ether was so wonderfully intense, that Michel, drawing Barbicane and Nicholl to his window, exclaimed, "The invisible moon, visible at last!"

And through a luminous emanation, which lasted some seconds, the whole three caught a glimpse of that mysterious disc which the eye of man now saw for the first time. What could they distinguish at a distance which they could not estimate? Some lengthened bands along the disc, real clouds formed in the midst of a very confined atmosphere, from which emerged not only all the mountains, but also projections of less importance; its circles, its yawning craters, as capriciously placed as on the visible surface. Then immense spaces, no longer arid plains, but real seas, oceans, widely distributed, reflecting on their liquid surface all the dazzling magic of the fires of space; and, lastly, on the surface of the continents, large dark masses, looking like immense forests under the rapid illumination of a brilliance.

Was it an illusion, a mistake, an optical illusion? Could they give a scientific assent to an observation so superficially obtained? Dared they pronounce upon the question of its habitability after so slight a glimpse of the invisible disc?

But the lightnings in space subsided by degrees; its accidental brilliancy died away; the asteroids dispersed in different directions and were extinguished in the distance. The ether returned to its accustomed darkness; the stars, eclipsed for a moment, again twinkled in the firmament, and the disc, so hastily discerned, was again buried in impenetrable night.

250 *At last, the projectile emerges from the dark to the lighted side of the moon. From their observations of the moon's reduced atmosphere, insufficient water and vegetation, sudden alternations of hot and cold, days and nights of 364 hours, Barbicane concludes that life as we understand it cannot exist on the moon.*

Now, their elliptical orbit is swinging them away from the moon toward the earth. Barbicane calculates that if their speed is not great enough, they may be caught and held stationary between the pull of earth and moon forever, and if their speed is great enough, they will continue in orbit around the moon.

Is there no escape?

Perhaps. The projectile has small rockets at one end. They were to have been fired toward the surface of the moon to ease a landing there. But now, Michel thinks of another use for the rockets: to fire the projectile out of orbit and onto the moon.

"By Jove!" he exclaimed, "I must admit we are downright simpletons!"

"I do not say we are not," replied Barbicane; "but why?"

"Because we have a very simple means of checking this speed which is bearing us from the moon, and we do not use it!"

"And what is the means?"

"To use the recoil contained in our rockets."

"Done!" said Nicholl.

"We have not used this force yet," said Barbicane, "it is true, but we will do so."

"When?" asked Michel.

"When the time comes. Observe, my friends, that in the position occupied by the projectile, an oblique position with regard to the lunar disc, our rockets, in slightly altering its direction, might turn it from the moon instead of drawing it nearer?"

"Just so," replied Michel.

"Let us wait, then. By some inexplicable influence, the projectile is turning its base toward the earth. It is probable that at the point of equal attraction, its conical cap will be directed rigidly toward the moon; at that moment we may hope that its speed will be *nil*; then will be the moment to act, and with the influence of our rockets we may perhaps provoke a fall directly on the surface of the lunar disc."

"Bravo!" said Michel. "What we did not do, what we could not do on our first passage at the dead point, because the projectile was then endowed with too great a speed."

"Very well reasoned," said Nichol.

"Let us wait patiently," continued Barbicane. "Putting every chance on our side, and after having so much despaired, I may say I think that we shall gain our end."

This conclusion was a signal for Michel Ardan's hips and hurrahs. And none of the audacious boobies remembered the question that they themselves had solved in the negative. No! the moon is not inhabited; no! the moon is probably not habitable. And yet they were going to try everything to reach her.

One single question remained to be solved. At what precise moment the projectile would reach the point of equal attraction, on which the travelers must play their last card. In order to calculate this to within a few seconds, Barbicane had only to refer to his notes, and to reckon the different heights taken on the lunar parallels. Thus the time necessary to travel over the distance between the dead point and the south pole would be equal to the distance separating the north pole from the dead point. The hours representing the time traveled over were carefully noted, and the calculation was easy. Barbicane found that this point would be reached at one in the morning on the night of the 7th—8th of December. So that, if nothing interfered with its course, it would reach the given point in twenty-two hours.

The rockets had primarily been placed to check the fall of the projectile upon the moon, and now they were going to employ them for a directly contrary purpose. In any case they were ready, and they had only to wait for the moment to set fire to them.

"Since there is nothing else to be done," said Nicholl, "I make a proposition."

"What is it?" asked Barbicane.

"I propose to go to sleep."

"What a motion!" exclaimed Michel Ardan.

"It is forty hours since we closed our eyes," said Nicholl. "Some hours of sleep will restore our strength."

"Never," interrupted Michel.

"Well," continued Nicholl, "every one to his taste; I shall go to sleep." And stretching himself on the divan, he soon snored like a forty-eight pounder.

"That Nicholl has a good deal of sense," said Barbicane; "presently I shall follow his example." Some moments after his continued bass supported the captain's baritone.

"Certainly," said Michel Ardan, finding himself alone, "these practical people have sometimes most opportune ideas."

And with his long legs stretched out, and his great arms folded under his head, Michel slept in his turn.

But this sleep could be neither peaceful nor lasting, the minds of these three men were too much occupied, and some hours after, about seven in the morning, all three were on foot at the same instant.

The projectile was still leaving the moon, and turning its conical part more and more toward her.

An explicable phenomenon, but one which happily served Barbicane's ends.

Seventeen hours more, and the moment for action would have arrived.

The day seemed long. However bold the travelers might be, they were greatly impressed by the approach of that moment which would decide all—either precipitate their fall onto the moon, or forever chain them in an immutable orbit. They counted the hours as they passed too slow for their wish; Barbicane and Nicholl were obstinately plunged in their calculations, Michel going and coming between the narrow walls, and watching that impassive moon with a longing eye.

At times recollections of the earth crossed their minds. They saw once more their friends of the Gun Club, and the dearest of all, J. T. Maston. At that moment, the honorable secretary must be filling his post on the Rocky Mountains. If he could see the projectile through the glass of his gigantic telescope, what would he think? After seeing it disappear behind the moon's south pole, he

254 would see them reappear by the north pole! They must therefore be a satellite of a satellite! Had J. T. Maston given this unexpected news to the world? Was this the *dénouement* of this great enterprise?

But the day passed without incident. The terrestrial midnight arrived. The 8th of December was beginning. One hour more, and the point of equal attraction would be reached. What speed would then animate the projectile? They could not estimate it. But no error could vitiate Barbicane's calculations. At one in the morning this speed ought to be and would be *nil*.

Besides, another phenomenon would mark the projectile's stopping point on the neutral line. At that spot the two attractions, lunar and terrestrial, would be annulled. Objects would "weigh" no more. This singular fact, which had surprised Barbicane and his companions so much in going, would be repeated on their return under the very same conditions. At this precise moment they must act.

Already the projectile's conical top was sensibly turned toward the lunar disc, presented in such a way as to utilize the whole of the recoil produced by the pressure of the rocket apparatus. The chances were in favor of the travelers. If its speed was utterly annulled on this dead point, a decided movement toward the moon would suffice, however slight, to determine its fall.

"Five minutes to one," said Nicholl.

"All is ready," replied Michel Ardan, directing a lighted match to the flame of the gas.

"Wait!" said Barbicane, holding his chronometer in his hand.

At that moment weight had no effect. The travelers

felt in themselves the entire disappearance of it. They were very near the neutral point, if they did not touch it.

"One o'clock," said Barbicane.

Michel Ardan applied the lighted match to a train in communication with the rockets. No detonation was heard in the inside, for there was no air. But, through the scuttles, Barbicane saw a prolonged smoke, the flames of which were immediately extinguished.

The projectile sustained a certain shock, which was sensibly felt in the interior.

The three friends looked and listened without speaking, and scarcely breathing. One might have heard the beating of their hearts amid this perfect silence.

"Are we falling?" asked Michel Ardan, at length.

"No," said Nicholl, "since the bottom of the projectile is not turning to the lunar disc!"

At this moment, Barbicane, quitting the scuttle, turned to his two companions. He was frightfully pale, his forehead wrinkled, and his lips contracted.

"We are falling!" said he.

"Ah!" cried Michel Ardan, "onto the moon?"

"Onto the earth!"

"The devil!" exclaimed Michel Ardan, adding philosophically, "well, when we came into this projectile we were very doubtful as to the ease with which we should get out of it!"

And now this fearful fall had begun. The speed retained had borne the projectile beyond the dead point. The explosion of the rockets could not divert its course. This speed in going had carried it over the neutral line, and in returning had done the same thing. The laws of physics condemned it *to pass through every point which it*

256 *had already gone through.* It was a terrible fall, from a height of 160,000 miles, and no springs to break it. According to the laws of gunnery, the projectile must strike the earth with a speed equal to that with which it left the mouth of the Columbiad, a speed of 16,000 yards in the last second.

But to give some figures of comparison, it has been reckoned that an object thrown from the top of the towers of Notre Dame, the height of which is only 200 feet, will arrive on the pavement at a speed of 240 miles per hour. Here the projectile must strike the earth with a speed of 115,200 miles per hour.

"We are lost!" said Michel coolly.

"Very well! if we die," answered Barbicane, with a sort of religious enthusiasm, "the result of our travels will be magnificently spread. It is His own secret that God will tell us! In the other life the soul will want to know nothing, either of machines or engines! It will be identified with eternal wisdom!"

"In fact," interrupted Michel Ardan, "the whole of the other world may well console us for the loss of that inferior orb called the moon!"

Barbicane crossed his arms on his breast, with a motion of sublime resignation, saying at the same time:

"The will of heaven be done!"

Back on earth, the crew of a U.S. navy ship, a corvette called Susquehanna, *is at work taking soundings in the Pacific Ocean about 200 miles off the American coast. They are all wondering, as is almost everyone on the earth, what has become of the three moon voyagers.*

At that moment (it was seventeen minutes past one in the morning) Lieutenant Bronsfield was preparing to leave the watch and return to his cabin, when his attention was attracted by a distant hissing noise. His comrades and himself first thought that this hissing was caused by the letting off of steam; but lifting their heads, they found that the noise was produced in the highest regions of the air. They had not time to question each other before the hissing became frightfully intense, and suddenly there appeared to their dazzled eyes an enormous meteor, ignited by the rapidity of its course and its friction through the atmospheric strata.

This fiery mass grew larger to their eyes, and fell, with the noise of thunder, upon the bowsprit, which it smashed close to the stem, and buried itself in the waves with a deafening roar!

A few feet nearer, and the *Susquehanna* would have foundered with all on board!

At this instant Captain Blomsberry appeared, half dressed, and rushing on to the forecastle deck, whither all the officers had hurried, exclaimed, "With your permission, gentlemen, what has happened?"

And the midshipman, making himself as it were the echo of the body, cried, "Commander, it is 'they' come back again!"

Are the three men suffocated or burned? Dead or alive? The Susquehanna *hasn't the proper equipment to try to haul up the projectile. They set a buoy to mark the spot and steam back to San Francisco for help. J. T. Maston hurries to the Pacific Coast to join the rescue dive.*

258 The descent was rapid. At seventeen minutes past two, J. T. Maston and his companions had reached the bottom of the Pacific; but they saw nothing but an arid desert, no longer animated by either fauna or flora. By the light of their lamps, furnished with powerful reflectors, they could see the dark beds of the ocean for a considerable extent of view, but the projectile was nowhere to be seen.

The impatience of these bold divers cannot be described, and having an electrical communication with the corvette, they made a signal already agreed upon, and for the space of a mile the *Susquehanna* moved their chamber along some yards above the bottom.

Thus they explored the whole submarine plain, deceived at every turn by optical illusions which almost broke their hearts. Here a rock, there a projection from the ground, seemed to be the much-sought-for projectile; but their mistake was soon discovered, and then they were in despair.

"But where are they? where are they?" cried J. T. Maston. And the poor man called loudly upon Nicholl, Barbicane, and Michel Ardan, as if his unfortunate friends could either hear or answer him through such an impenetrable medium! The search continued under these conditions until the vitiated air compelled the divers to ascend.

The hauling in began about six in the evening, and was not ended before midnight.

"Tomorrow," said J. T. Maston, as he set foot on the bridge of the corvette.

"Yes," answered Captain Blomsberry.

"And on another spot?"

"Yes."

J. T. Maston did not doubt of their final success, but his 259 companions, no longer upheld by the excitement of the first hours, understood all the difficulty of the enterprise. What seemed easy at San Francisco, seemed here in the wide ocean almost impossible. The chances of success diminished in rapid proportion; and it was from chance alone that the meeting with the projectile might be expected.

The next day, the 24th, in spite of the fatigue of the previous day, the operation was renewed. The corvette advanced some minutes to westward, and the apparatus, provided with air, bore the same explorers to the depths of the ocean.

The whole day passed in fruitless research; the bed of the sea was a desert. The 25th brought no other result, nor the 26th.

It was disheartening. They thought of those unfortunates shut up in the projectile for twenty-six days. Perhaps at that moment they were experiencing the first approach of suffocation; that is, if they had escaped the dangers of their fall. The air was spent, and doubtless with the air all their *morale*.

"The air, possibly," answered J. T. Maston resolutely, "but their *morale* never!"

On the 28th, after two more days of search, all hope was gone. This projectile was but an atom in the immensity of the ocean. They must give up all idea of finding it.

But J. T. Maston would not hear of going away. He would not abandon the place without at least discovering the tomb of his friends. But Commander Blomsberry could no longer persist, and in spite of the exclamations of the worthy secretary, was obliged to give the order to sail.

On the 29th of December, at nine A.M., the *Susquehanna,* heading northeast, resumed her course to the bay of San Francisco.

It was ten in the morning; the corvette was under half steam, as if regretting to leave the spot where the catastrophe had taken place, when a sailor, perched on the main-top-gallant crosstrees, watching the sea, cried suddenly:

"A buoy on the lee bow!"

The officers looked in the direction indicated, and by the help of their glasses saw that the object signaled had the appearance of one of those bouys which are used to mark the passages of bays or rivers. But, singularly to say, a flag floating on the wind surmounted its cone, which emerged five or six feet out of water. This buoy shone under the rays of the sun as if it had been made of plates of silver. Commander Blomsberry, J. T. Maston, and the delegates of the Gun Club were mounted on the bridge, examining this object straying at random on the waves.

All looked with feverish anxiety, but in silence. None dared give expression to the thoughts which came to the minds of all.

The corvette approached to within two cables' lengths of the object.

A shudder ran through the whole crew. That flag was the American flag!

At this moment a perfect howling was heard; it was the brave J. T. Maston, who had just fallen all in a heap. Forgetting on the one hand that his right arm had been replaced by an iron hook, and on the other that a simple gutta-percha cap covered his brain box, he had given himself a formidable blow.

They hurried toward him, picked him up, restored him to life. And what were his first words?

"Ah! trebly brutes! quadruply idiots! quintuply boobies that we are!"

"What is it?" exclaimed everyone around him.

"What is it?"

"Come, speak!"

"It is, simpletons," howled the terrible secretary, "it is that the projectile only weighs 19,250 pounds!"

"Well?"

"And that it displaces twenty-eight tons, or in other words 56,000 pounds, and that consequently *it floats!*"

Ah! what stress the worthy man laid on the verb "float"! And it was true! All, yes! all these savants had forgotten this fundamental law, namely, that on account of its specific lightness, the projectile, after having been drawn by its fall to the greatest depths of the ocean, must naturally return to the surface. And now it was floating quietly at the mercy of the waves.

The boats were put to sea. J. T. Maston and his friends had rushed into them! Excitement was at its height! Every heart beat loudly while they advanced to the projectile. What did it contain? Living or dead?

Living, yes! living, at least unless death had struck Barbicane and his two friends since they had hoisted the flag. Profound silence reigned on the boats. All were breathless. Eyes no longer saw. One of the scuttles of the projectile was open. Some pieces of glass remained in the

262 frame, showing that it had been broken. This scuttle was actually five feet above the water.

A boat came alongside, that of J. T. Maston, and J. T. Maston rushed to the broken window.

At that moment they heard a clear and merry voice, the voice of Michel Ardan, exclaiming in an accent of triumph:

"White all, Barbicane, white all!"

Barbicane, Michel Ardan, and Nicholl were playing at dominoes!

"Nothing ever does happen to me," Wedderburn remarked. "I wonder why? . . ."

THE STRANGE ORCHID

H.G. Wells

The buying of orchids always has in it a certain speculative flavor. You have before you the brown shriveled lump of tissue, and for the rest you must trust your judgment, or the auctioneer, or your good luck, as your taste may incline. The plant may be moribund or dead, or it may be just a respectable purchase, fair value for your money, or perhaps—for the thing has happened again and again—there slowly unfolds before the delighted eyes of the happy purchaser, day after day, some new variety, some novel richness, a strange twist of the labellum, or some subtler coloration or unexpected mimicry. Pride, beauty, and profit blossom together on one delicate green spike, and, it may be, even immortality. For the new miracle of Nature may stand in need of a new specific name, and what so convenient as that of its discoverer? "Johnsmithia"! There have been worse names.

It was perhaps the hope of some such happy discovery that made Winter-Wedderburn such a frequent attendant at these sales—that hope, and also, maybe, the fact that he had nothing else of the slightest interest to do in the world. He was a shy, lonely, rather ineffectual man, provided with just enough income to keep off the spur of necessity, and not enough nervous energy to make him seek any exacting employment. He might have collected stamps or coins, or translated Horace, or bound books, or invented new species of diatoms. But, as it happened, he grew orchids, and had one ambitious little hothouse.

"I have a fancy," he said over his coffee, "that something is going to happen to me today." He spoke—as he moved and thought—slowly.

"Oh, don't say *that!*" said his housekeeper—who was also his remote cousin. For "something happening" was a euphemism that meant only one thing to her.

"You misunderstand me. I mean nothing unpleasant ... though what I do mean I scarcely know.

"Today," he continued, after a pause, "Peters' are going to sell a batch of plants from the Andamans and the Indies. I shall go up and see what they have. It may be I shall buy something good, unawares. That may be it."

He passed his cup for his second cupful of coffee.

"Are those the things collected by that poor young fellow you told me of the other day?" asked his cousin as she filled his cup.

"Yes," he said, and became meditative over a piece of toast.

"Nothing ever does happen to me," he remarked presently, beginning to think aloud. "I wonder why? Things enough happen to other people. There is Harvey. Only the other week—on Monday he picked up sixpence, on Wednesday his chicks all had the staggers, on Friday his cousin came home from Australia, and on Saturday he broke his ankle. What a whirl of excitement!—compared to me."

"I think I would rather be without so much excitement," said his housekeeper. "It can't be good for you."

"I suppose it's troublesome. Still . . . you see, nothing ever happens to me. When I was a little boy I never had accidents. I never fell in love as I grew up. Never married. . . . I wonder how it feels to have something happen to you, something really remarkable.

"That orchid collector was only thirty-six—twenty years younger than myself—when he died. And he had been married twice and divorced once; he had had malarial fever four times, and once he broke his thigh. He killed a Malay once, and once he was wounded by a poisoned dart. And in the end he was killed by jungle leeches. It must have all been very troublesome, but then it must have been very interesting, you know—except, perhaps, the leeches."

"I am sure it was not good for him," said the lady, with conviction.

"Perhaps not." And then Wedderburn looked at his watch. "Twenty-three minutes past eight. I am going up by the quarter to twelve train, so that there is plenty of time. I think I shall wear my alpaca jacket—it is quite warm enough—and my grey felt hat and brown shoes. I suppose—"

He glanced out of the window at the serene sky and sunlit garden, and then nervously at his cousin's face.

"I think you had better take an umbrella if you are going to London," she said in a voice that admitted of no denial. "There's all between here and the station coming back."

When he returned he was in a state of mild excitement. He had made a purchase. It was rare that he could make up his mind quickly enough to buy, but this time he had done so.

"There are Vandas," he said, "and a Dendrobe and some Palaeonophis." He surveyed his purchases lovingly as he consumed his soup. They were laid out on the spotless tablecloth before him, and he was telling his cousin all about them as he slowly meandered through his dinner. It was his custom to live all his visits to London over again in the evening for her and his own entertainment.

"I knew something would happen today. And I have bought all these. Some of them—some of them—I feel sure, do you know, that some of them will be remarkable. I don't know how it is, but I feel just as sure as if someone had told me that some of these will turn out remarkable.

"That one"—he pointed to a shrivelled rhizome—"was not identified. It may be a Palaeonophis—or it may not. It may be a new species, or even a new genus. And it was the last that poor Batten ever collected."

"I don't like the look of it," said his housekeeper. "It's such an ugly shape."

"To me it scarcely seems to have a shape."

"I don't like those things that stick out," said his housekeeper.

"It shall be put away in a pot tomorrow."

"It looks," said the housekeeper, "like a spider shamming dead."

Wedderburn smiled and surveyed the root with his head on one side. "It is certainly not a pretty lump of stuff. But you can never judge of these things from their dry appearance. It may turn out to be a very beautiful orchid indeed. How busy I shall be tomorrow! I must see tonight just exactly what to do with these things, and tomorrow I shall set to work.

"They found poor Batten lying dead, or dying, in a mangrove swamp—I forget which," he began again presently, "with one of these very orchids crushed up under his body. He had been unwell for some days with some kind of native fever, and I suppose he fainted. These mangrove swamps are very unwholesome. Every drop of blood, they say, was taken out of him by the jungle leeches. It may be that very plant that cost him his life to obtain."

"I think none the better of it for that."

"Men must work though women may weep," said Wedderburn with profound gravity.

"Fancy dying away from every comfort in a nasty swamp! Fancy being ill of fever with nothing to take but chlorodyne and quinine—if men were left to themselves they would live on chlorodyne and quinine—and no one round you but horrible natives! They say the Andaman islanders are most disgusting wretches—and, anyhow, they can scarcely make good nurses, not having the necessary training. And just for people in England to have orchids!"

"I don't suppose it was comfortable, but some men seem to enjoy that kind of thing," said Wedderburn. "Anyhow, the natives of his party were sufficiently civilized to take care of all his collection until his colleague, who was an ornithologist, came back again from the interior; though they could not tell the species of the orchid and had let it wither. And it makes these things more interesting."

"It makes them disgusting. I should be afraid of some of the malaria clinging to them. And just think, there has been a dead body lying across that ugly thing! I never thought of that before. There! I declare I cannot eat another mouthful of dinner."

"I will take them off the table if you like, and put them in the window seat. I can see them just as well there."

The next few days he was indeed singularly busy in his steamy little hothouse, fussing about with charcoal, lumps of teak, moss, and all the other mysteries of the orchid cultivator. He considered he was having a wonderfully eventful time. In the evening he would talk about these new orchids to his friends, and over and over again he reverted to his expectation of something strange.

Several of the Vandas and the Dendrobium died under his care, but presently the strange orchid began to show signs of life. He was delighted and took his housekeeper right away from jam making to see it at once, directly he made the discovery.

"That is a bud," he said, "and presently there will be a lot of leaves there, and those little things coming out here are aerial rootlets."

"They look to me like little white fingers poking out of the brown," said his housekeeper. "I don't like them."

"Why not?"

"I don't know. They look like fingers trying to get at you. I can't help my likes and dislikes."

"I don't know for certain, but I don't *think* there are any orchids I know that have aerial rootlets quite like that. It may be my fancy, of course. You see they are a little flattened at the ends."

"I don't like 'em," said his housekeeper, suddenly shivering and turning away. "I know it's very silly of me—and I'm very sorry, particularly as you like the thing so much. But I can't help thinking of that corpse."

"But it may not be that particular plant. That was merely a guess of mine."

His housekeeper shrugged her shoulders. "Anyhow I don't like it," she said.

Wedderburn felt a little hurt at her dislike to the plant. But that did not prevent his talking to her about orchids generally, and this orchid in particular, whenever he felt inclined.

"There are such queer things about orchids," he said one day; "such possibilities of surprises. You know, Darwin studied their fertilization, and showed that the whole structure of an ordinary orchid flower was contrived in order that moths might carry the pollen from plant to plant. Well, it seems that there are lots of orchids known the flower of which cannot possibly be used for fertilization in that way. Some of the Cypripediums, for instance; there are no insects known that can possibly fertilize them, and some of them have never been found with seed."

"But how do they form new plants?"

"By runners and tubers, and that kind of outgrowth. That is easily explained. The puzzle is, what are the flowers for?

"Very likely," he added, "*my* orchid may be something extraordinary in that way. If so I shall study it. I have often thought of making researches as Darwin did. But hitherto I have not found the time, or something else has happened to prevent it. The leaves are beginning to unfold now. I do wish you would come and see them!"

But she said that the orchid house was so hot it gave her the headache. She had seen the plant once again, and the aerial rootlets, which were now some of them more than a foot long, had unfortunately reminded her of tentacles reaching out after something; and they got into her dreams, growing after her with incredible rapidity. So that she had settled to her entire satisfaction that she would not see that plant again, and Wedderburn had to admire its leaves alone. They were of the ordinary broad form, and a deep glossy green, with splashes and dots of deep red towards the base. He knew of no other leaves quite like them. The plant was placed on a low bench near the thermometer, and close by was a simple arrangement by which a tap dripped on the hot-water pipes and kept the air steamy. And he spent his afternoons now with some regularity meditating on the approaching flowering of this strange plant.

And at last the great thing happened. Directly he entered the little glass house he knew that the spike had burst out, although his great *Palaeonophis Lowii* hid the corner where his new darling stood. There was a new odor in the air, a rich, intensely sweet scent, that overpowered every other in that crowded, steaming little greenhouse.

Directly he noticed this he hurried down to the strange orchid. And, behold! the trailing green spikes bore now three great splashes of blossom, from which this overpowering sweetness proceeded. He stopped before them in an ecstasy of admiration.

The flowers were white, with streaks of golden orange upon the petals; the heavy labellum was coiled into an intricate projection, and a wonderful bluish purple mingled there with the gold. He could see at once that the genus was altogether a new one. And the insufferable scent! How hot the place was! The blossoms swam before his eyes.

He would see if the temperature was right. He made a step towards the thermometer. Suddenly everything appeared unsteady. The bricks on the floor were dancing up and down. Then the white blossoms, the green leaves behind them, the whole greenhouse, seemed to sweep sideways, and then in a curve upward.

* * *

At half past four his cousin made the tea, according to their invariable custom. But Wedderburn did not come in for his tea.

"He is worshipping that horrid orchid," she told herself, and waited ten minutes. "His watch must have stopped. I will go and call him."

She went straight to the hothouse, and, opening the door, called his name. There was no reply. She noticed that the air was very close, and loaded with an intense perfume. Then she saw something lying on the bricks between the hot-water pipes.

For a minute, perhaps, she stood motionless.

He was lying, face upward, at the foot of the strange orchid. The tentaclelike aerial rootlets no longer swayed freely in the air, but were crowded together, a tangle of grey ropes, and stretched tight with their ends closely applied to his chin and neck and hands.

She did not understand. Then she saw from under one of the exultant tentacles upon his cheek there trickled a little thread of blood.

272   With an inarticulate cry she ran towards him, and tried
to pull him away from the leechlike suckers. She snapped
two of these tentacles, and their sap dripped red.

Then the overpowering scent of the blossom began to
make her head reel. How they clung to him! She tore at
the tough ropes, and he and the white inflorescence swam
about her. She felt she was fainting, knew she must not.
She left him and hastily opened the nearest door, and, after she had panted for a moment in the fresh air, she had
a brilliant inspiration. She caught up a flower pot and
smashed in the windows at the end of the greenhouse.
Then she reentered. She tugged now with renewed
strength at Wedderburn's motionless body, and brought
the strange orchid crashing to the floor. It still clung with
the grimmest tenacity to its victim. In a frenzy, she
lugged it and him into the open air.

Then she thought of tearing through the sucker rootlets one by one, and in another minute she had released
him and was dragging him away from the horror.

He was white and bleeding from a dozen circular
patches.

The odd-job man was coming up the garden, amazed
at the smashing of glass, and saw her emerge, hauling the
inanimate body with red-stained hands. For a moment he
thought impossible things.

"Bring some water!" she cried, and her voice dispelled
his fancies. When, with unnatural alacrity, he returned
with the water, he found her weeping with excitement,
and with Wedderburn's head upon her knee, wiping the
blood from his face.

"What's the matter?" said Wedderburn, opening his
eyes feebly, and closing them again at once.

"Go and tell Annie to come out here to me, and then go for Doctor Haddon at once," she said to the odd-job man so soon as he brought the water; and added, seeing he hesitated, "I will tell you all about it when you come back."

Presently Wedderburn opened his eyes again, and, seeing that he was troubled by the puzzle of his position, she explained to him, "You fainted in the hothouse."

"And the orchid?"

"I will see to that," she said.

Wedderburn had lost a good deal of blood, but beyond that he had suffered no very great injury. They gave him brandy mixed with some pink extract of meat, and carried him upstairs to bed. His housekeeper told her incredible story in fragments to Dr. Haddon. "Come to the orchid house and see," she said.

The cold outer air was blowing in through the open door, and the sickly perfume was almost dispelled. Most of the torn aerial rootlets lay already withered amidst a number of dark stains upon the bricks. The stem of the inflorescence was broken by the fall of the plant, and the flowers were growing limp and brown at the edges of the petals. The doctor stooped towards it, then saw that one of the aerial rootlets still stirred feebly, and hesitated.

The next morning the strange orchid still lay there, black now and putrescent. The door banged intermittently in the morning breeze, and all the array of Wedderburn's orchids was shrivelled and prostrate. But Wedderburn himself was bright and garrulous upstairs in the glory of his strange adventure.

STUDY GUIDE
by
Bernard Brodsky
for
TALES OF IMAGINATION
AND SUSPENSE

A Note on the Study Guide "About the Author" and "About the Story" are intended to be used before the story, "Checkup Quiz" and "Interpreting the Story" after the story. Each group of four stories is followed by "Be a Writer," "Special Projects," and "Further Reading." Audiovisual resources are listed at the end.

TALES OF CRIME AND DETECTION

THE TELL-TALE HEART

About the Author

Edgar Allan Poe (1809–1849) was born in Boston, Massachusetts, the son of traveling actors. His father deserted the family, and his mother died when he was two. Poe's foster father was John Allan, a merchant of Richmond, Virginia. Poe attended the University of Virginia but dropped out and later was dismissed from West Point. Thereafter, he worked feverishly as a writer and an editor, supporting himself on small fees.

Despite poverty and illness, Poe achieved great things. Millions of readers are familiar with his poems, such as "The Raven" and "The Bells." Many of his stories, including "The Murders in the Rue Morgue," "The Gold Bug," and "The Pit and the Pendulum," are considered masterpieces of mystery and suspense.

About the Story

"The Tell-Tale Heart" is one of the most famous stories ever written about the mind of a criminal. The criminal tells his own story and insists that he is not mad. Is he right? You must judge for yourself.

death watches Small insects. Their ticking was believed to be a warning of death.

tattoo A rhythmic beating like that of a drum.

scantlings Timbers; part of the framework of a house.

Checkup Quiz (True or False)

1. The murderer kills his son.
2. The victim's eye offends the murderer.
3. The murderer buries the body under the floor.
4. A neighbor hears the victim shriek.
5. The police trick the murderer into a confession.

Interpreting the Story

1. The murderer is concerned with an eye, a lantern, and a beating heart. Why or in what way does each of these three concern him?
2. In many stories, narrators (in this story, the murderer) reveal more about themselves than they intend to. What does the narrator of "The Tell-Tale Heart" reveal about himself? Do you believe his claim that he is not mad? Why or why not?
3. The sound of the beating heart can be interpreted as ghostly revenge (the victim is haunting his killer) or as a delusion (the killer only *thinks* he hears it; it's all in his mind). Which interpretation do you prefer? Why?

A TERRIBLY STRANGE BED

About the Author

Wilkie Collins (1824–1889) was born in London, the son of a painter. He studied law and was admitted to the bar, but he had already begun writing novels and stories. Gradually, he became a full-time writer. Collins has been called "the most skillful plot constructor of the century." Nowhere is this skill more evident than in his classic detective novel *The Moonstone*.

About the Story

"A Terribly Strange Bed" is a tale of mystery and peril. A young man visits a Paris gambling den and wins a great deal of money but then falls into a situation of mortal danger. As you read, notice how cunningly the author arranges the trap for his hero and creates suspense about his fate.

Rouge et Noir French for "Red and Black," a card game.

napoleons French gold coins.

sacré mille bombes Sacred thousands bombs. (This and other expressions suggest rough military slang.)

mille tonnerres A thousand thunders.

sacré petit polisson de Napoleon Sacred little brat of Napoleon.

nom d'une pipe Name of a pipe.

vive le vin Long live wine.

Voyage autour de ma Chambre Voyage around my Room.

valance A short curtain around the top of a bed.

C4

First floor ... *entresol* In France, a floor above the ground floor is called the first floor. The *entresol* is a mezzanine, or intermediate, floor.

posse comitatus A posse; a search party.

procès verbal A statement; an official report.

au revoir Until we meet again; good-bye.

Checkup Quiz (True or False)

1. The hero wins a fortune on a lottery ticket.
2. He meets an old soldier.
3. In the bedroom, he falls into a deep sleep.
4. The police burst into the room to save him.
5. Those who tried to kill him are arrested.

Interpreting the Story

1. Step by step, the hero is led into a trap. Tell exactly how he gets into this dangerous situation.
2. What is "terribly strange" about the bed? Explain how its mechanism works. What object in the room helps make the hero aware of his danger? How?
3. Even after the hero escapes the bed, he is still not out of danger. Explain why not.
4. Does this story show that Wilkie Collins is a master of plots? (Points to consider: Is the situation believable? Does the story keep you in suspense? Do all the details help move the story to its outcome?) Give examples from the story to support your opinion.

THE MYSTERIOUS DEATH ON THE
UNDERGROUND RAILWAY

About the Author

Baroness Emmuska Orczy (1865–1947) was born in Hungary, but when she was fifteen her family settled in London. There she attended art school, and after working as a painter and illustrator, she began writing stories for magazines.

In her fiction, Baroness Orczy created two memorable characters. One is the Scarlet Pimpernel, the dashing, mysterious hero of a series of novels, who rescues French aristocrats from the guillotine in the period after the French Revolution. Her other popular character is the Old Man in the Corner, a detective.

About the Story

The Old Man in the Corner is an "armchair detective," one who never visits the scene of the crime but reasons out a solution based on newspaper reports. In each story, a reporter named Polly Burton encounters him in a restaurant where he sits at a corner table unraveling mysteries that baffle the police.

In this story, The Old Man solves the murder of pretty Mrs. Hazeldene. As usual in mysteries, things are not what they seem, and it takes a master detective to separate illusion from truth.

Underground Railway   Subway.

toxicologist   An expert on poisons.

au revoir   French for "until we meet again"; good-bye.

Checkup Quiz (True or False)

1. Mrs. Hazeldene was a wealthy woman.
2. Mr. Errington's hobby is taxidermy.
3. Andrew Scott witnesses the murder.
4. Mr. Errington is not indicted for murder.
5. The Old Man helps the police solve the murder.

Interpreting the Story

1. The Old Man asks Polly to "give me a description of the man who sat next to you." What point does he make about people's observations? How is this point important to the story?
2. At the inquest, Mr. Hazeldene says his wife had no friends he didn't approve of—carefully *not* mentioning Mr. Errington, the chief suspect. Why would Mr. Hazeldene try to protect Mr. Errington? Explain Mr. Hazeldene's behavior.
3. How do the words "*Au Revoir*! Don't be late tonight," lead to the mystery's solution?
4. Do you admire the Old Man in the Corner? Explain.

SILVER BLAZE

About the Author

Arthur Conan Doyle (1859–1930) was a young English doctor when he began writing stories about a master detective whom he named Sherlock Holmes. Holmes could solve crimes simply by observing things more keenly than anyone else. The stories became enormously popular.

The lasting popularity of Sherlock Holmes results not only from his cleverness but from his eccentric personality, his relationship with the admiring Dr. Watson (who tells the stories), and the wonderful atmosphere of gaslit London and of the English countryside in the late 1800s. To read a Sherlock Holmes story is not only to enjoy a good mystery, but to become caught up with fascinating people in a romantic time and place.

About the Story

All England is aghast. The famous racehorse Silver Blaze has vanished, his trainer found murdered. The police are baffled. The crime seems unsolvable—until Sherlock Holmes enters the case.

You the reader see everything through the eyes of Dr. Watson. (He sees everything Holmes sees but lacks his friend's immense powers of deduction.) Can you grasp what Watson does not? Can you match wits with Holmes and solve the mystery of "Silver Blaze" before he explains it? Read on.

touts   Men who sell tips on races.

ten-pound note   English paper money. (One pound then equaled about five dollars.)

vestas   Matches.

Cavendish   A brand of tobacco.

sovereign   A gold coin worth one pound.

guinea   A gold coin worth a bit more than a pound.

subcutaneously   Beneath the skin.

Checkup Quiz

G8   1. Straker is Silver Blaze's (a) owner, (b) trainer, (c) rider.
2. On Straker's body is found (a) a club, (b) a surgeon's knife, (c) a dagger.
3. Silver Blaze (a) wins a race, (b) breaks a leg, (c) is found dead.

Interpreting the Story

1. If you solved the mystery of "Silver Blaze," you probably used the following clues: (a) the dish of curried mutton, (b) the knife, (c) the candle and the match, (d) "the curious incident of the dog in the nighttime," and (e) the three lame sheep. How does each clue lead to the solution?
2. Dr. Watson is obviously not as bright as his friend Holmes. In your opinion, why did the author use Watson to tell the story? (Points to consider: As a reader, do you have more in common with Watson or with Holmes? How well would the story work with Holmes telling it instead of Watson?)

Be a Writer

A. Write a detective story. Think up an interesting detective (eccentric old woman; teenage super-brain). Choose a crime (murder; jewel robbery). Include three suspects who had a motive to commit the crime. Have a clue only the detective connects with the real criminal (footprint from shoe only one suspect wears; guard tied with knot only the former-Eagle-Scout suspect would know). End with the detective telling how he or she solved the crime or tricking the criminal into confessing.

B. A monologue is a speech. Like the killer in "The Tell-Tale Heart," the speaker often reveals his or her character or feelings unintentionally. Write a monologue in which the speaker reveals the opposite of what he or she means to. Examples: (1) "I wasn't invited to the party, but I don't care."—then reveals deep hurt; (2) "I never gossip."—then tells *all* about a friend. Use one of these ideas or make up your own.

Special Projects

A. Report on a famous solved or unsolved crime. Examples: (1) The Boston Strangler—Who was he? (2) Patty Hearst—her kidnapping and her trial; (3) Murph the Surf—the theft of the Star of India Sapphire; (4) Lizzie Borden—Did she kill her parents? A librarian can direct you to books and articles on these and other famous crimes. In your report, tell how the crime was committed, whether it was solved, what became of the criminal or suspect, and whether any mystery remains.

B. Draw or paint a dramatic scene from "The Tell-Tale Heart," "A Terribly Strange Bed," "The Mysterious Death on the Underground Railway," or "Silver Blaze." Write a caption for the illustration.

Further Reading

G10 Barzun, Jacques, editor. *The Delights of Detection.* A noted historian and detective-story buff presents seventeen classic and modern tales of detection. His introduction sets forth the standards by which he judges detective stories.

Haycraft, Howard, editor. *Fourteen Great Detective Stories.* A noted critic and historian of detective fiction collects tales of master detectives.

Liebman, Arthur, editor. *Quickie Thrillers: 25 Mini-Mysteries* (paperback). Short-short stories of crime, horror, and suspense, many with surprise endings.

Macdonald, Ross, editor. *Great Stories of Suspense.* Three novels (Kenneth Fearing's *The Big Clock*, Agatha Christie's *What Mrs. McGillicuddy Saw*, and Dick Francis's *Enquiry*), a novella, and eleven short stories.

Manley, Seon and Gogo Lewis, editors. *Grande Dames of Detection.* Stories by noted women mystery writers, including Baroness Orczy, Agatha Christie, and Margery Allingham.

GHOST STORIES

THE WIND IN THE ROSEBUSH

About the Author

Mary Wilkins Freeman (1852–1930) was born in Randolph, Massachusetts, into an old New England family. The life of New England towns became the setting and the subject of most of her novels and short stories. In all, she wrote 238 short stories and 12 novels. At her best, she was an acute observer of village people—especially women—and their hard, narrow lives.

About the Story

Many a ghost story is set at midnight in an old castle or
haunted house. But "The Wind in the Rosebush" is set in
an ordinary house in an ordinary village, and most of it
takes place in broad daylight.

Rebecca Flint arrives in Ford Village to take her niece
home to live with her. "Seems as if I ought to have told
her," a villager says as Rebecca sets off for the niece's
house. . . . Ought to have told her *what*? You may guess
long before Rebecca does.

froward Stubborn and contrary.

piazza A covered porch.

Checkup Quiz (True or False)

1. Rebecca Flint has come from Michigan.
2. Mrs. Dent is Agnes's stepmother.
3. Agnes is away at boarding school.
4. A telegram summons Rebecca back home.

Interpreting the Story

1. Now that you have finished the story, you probably
   understand certain incidents better. Explain why, in
   your opinion, (a) the woman on the ferry said, "Seems
   as if I ought to have told her"; (b) the rose bush
   trembled when there was no wind; (c) Mrs. Dent
   made excuses for Agnes's absence; (d) Rebecca saw
   someone pass by the window; (e) Rebecca heard the
   music; (f) Rebecca got the news from Michigan.

2. In many stories, ghosts are vividly described. But the ghost in this story remains vague, elusive. Why do you think the author chose not to give more details about the ghost?

3. Do you think that this story, with its ordinary, everyday setting, is more or less chilling than ghost stories that take place in haunted castles at midnight? Give reasons for your answer.

THE OPEN WINDOW

About the Author

Hector Hugh Munro (1870–1916) was born in Burma of British parents. When he was two, his mother died, and he was sent to England to be raised by two strict aunts, whom he came to detest. Later, he got his revenge by making aunts the villains of several stories.

Munro became a foreign correspondent, reporting from Paris, Russia, and the Balkans. When he began to write fiction, he adopted the pen name "Saki"—meaning "wine bearer"—from the *Rubaiyat* of Omar Khayyam, the Persian poet. His stories are noted for their clever plots, humor, biting satire, and—sometimes—cruelty.

Although Munro was forty-four when World War I began, he enlisted and was later killed in battle in France.

About the Story

"The Open Window"—a ghost story with a difference—is famous for its surprise ending. (Read the last sentence carefully.) There are clues to the ending throughout the story, but many readers miss them. You may want to read it *twice* to see how Saki sets up the surprise.

French window A tall window; a French door.

Ganges A river in India.

pariah dogs Wild dogs.

Checkup Quiz (True or False)

Answer only after reading the entire story!
1. The niece tells Nuttel about a tragedy.
2. The niece tells the story before the aunt comes in.
3. The French window has been open every evening for three years.
4. The three men who come at twilight are ghosts.
5. Mr. Nuttel was once attacked by dogs.

Interpreting the Story

1. What does the niece tell Nuttell? Why does he flee?
2. Consider the story's last sentence and the word *romance.* Definitions of *romance* include "an imaginative tale"; "invented details or incidents." How does the word help you understand the story?
3. Now that you have finished the story, you probably understand the niece better. (a) In light of what you know, why do you think she asked Nuttel, "Then you know practically nothing about my aunt?" (b) What does the story of the pariah dogs reveal about the niece? How? (c) What *really* happened to Mrs. Sappleton's husband and brothers?
4. Did you like the ending? Why or why not?

G14 About the Author

When Stephen Crane (1871–1900) was in college, he was offered a job as a professional baseball player. Instead, he became a journalist and fiction writer and led a more adventurous life than most athletes. Crane's years as a correspondent took him to Mexico, where he was nearly murdered by bandits, and to Cuba, where he covered the Spanish-American War. Being shipwrecked and having to row to safety in a ten-foot dinghy led him to write his most famous short story, "The Open Boat." But he is best known for *The Red Badge of Courage,* his classic novel about a young soldier in the Civil War.

Few writers—even those who lived long lives—have written as many important works as Stephen Crane; yet he was only 28 years old when he died.

About the Story

Ghostly lovers, dead sailors, a hound with burning eyes—unusual subjects for a newspaper article. This one first appeared in the New York Saturday *Press.*

Crane's journalism and his fiction are closely related. His fiction often seems as realistic as his journalism, and his journalism (including this story) often makes use of fiction-writing techniques. Can you tell how much of "Ghosts" is fact and how much is fiction?

stilettolike Like a knife or dagger.

impalpable Unfeelable.

perambulate Walk.

Checkup Quiz

1. Some young men stopped following one ghost because of his (a) weird glow, (b) glance, (c) cries.
2. Pirates lured ships to shore with (a) lights, (b) flags, (c) dogs.
3. The black hound belonged to (a) a shipwrecked young man, (b) an old miser, (c) a pirate.
4. A pirate wanted the dead man's (a) clothes, (b) gold, (c) gems.

Interpreting the Story

1. The first sentence suggests that Crane does not take all ghosts seriously. Quote two other phrases or sentences that show Crane's humorous style.
2. Where in "Ghosts" does Crane seem to function as a reporter (of facts)? Where does he seem to be using fiction-writing techniques? Give examples.
3. According to Crane, what kind of people and animals make "good" ghosts? What kind do not? Why?

THE WATER GHOST OF HARROWBY HALL

About the Author

John Kendrick Bangs (1862–1922), born in Yonkers, New York, was one of the most popular American humorists of his time. One of his books, *A Houseboat on the Styx*, is about a boat that houses real and fictional characters (including Sherlock Holmes and William Shakespeare) who have passed on to the other world. Their conversations and quarrels can still amuse modern readers. In this, as in other works, Bangs makes gentle fun of accepted ideas and traditions.

About the Story

An English country estate, the ghost of an unhappy young woman, the midnight appearances of the ghost—hundreds of ghost stories share these ingredients. But there is something hilariously different about the water ghost of Harrowby Hall—as you will see.

sine qua non Latin for "without which not"; a necessity.

aqueously Like water.

felicitating Congratulating.

shillings, pence, pounds English money.

guineas to hot cross buns The equivalent of a bet at fifty-to-one odds.

Checkup Quiz

1. The ghost appears every (a) Christmas, (b) May Day, (c) All Saints' Day.
2. When alive, the ghost was outraged by (a) a cruel husband, (b) her father's poverty, (c) the colors of her room.
3. The master of Harrowby Hall is named (a) Rochester, (b) Oglethorpe, (c) Heathcliff.
4. The heir's father dies of (a) fright, (b) a cold, (c) drowning.

Interpreting the Story

1. What is inconvenient about the ghost's visits? How G17 does the heir to Harrowby Hall finally stop her?
2. In ghost stories, the ghost often shows how it died; for example, a ghost that was beheaded carries its head, and a ghost that was stabbed or shot displays its wounds. A watery ghost that drenches its victims is a comic variation on this tradition. (a) How did the water ghost (as a young girl) die? (b) List at least five sentences that contain words or phrases showing the ghost's watery nature.
3. Not all people laugh at the same jokes. Explain why you did or did not find this story funny.

Be a Writer

A. Write a humorous variation on "Water Ghost." Make up a comic ghost that shows how it died. (Example: An ice-cream lover overdoses on pistachio sundaes. The ghost is green and cold and has whipped-cream hair.) Notice the funny situations Bangs puts his ghost in. (Near a fire, she puts it out; near a man, she soaks his clothes.) Use as many funny situations as you can think of to show off your ghost.

B. In "Ghosts on the Jersey Coast," notice the vivid details Stephen Crane uses in describing his unearthly hound: "There is a dreadful hatchet wound in the animal's head, and from it the phantom blood bubbles. His jaws drip angry foam, and his eyes are lit with crimson fire." Create your own ghost. Use vivid details to make the creature seem so real that your readers can imagine it floating, creeping, shuffling, or rushing toward them.

Special Projects

A. Exchange written ghost descriptions (see above) with another student. Draw pictures of each other's ghosts, and let the class judge which drawings best capture the writers' descriptions.

B. Ghosts are often more effective in radio plays than in movies or on television. The listener can imagine a scarier ghost than could be shown. Create a radio play. Adapt a favorite ghost story or write your own. Tape it to replay for the class. Remember that vivid words and details are important. But just as important for the radio play are sound effects and incomplete suggestions that leave something to the listener's imagination. (Example: *Sound effect*—creak, creak, clank. *Voice*—Ugh! It's coming toward us! It's ... Argh!)

Further Reading

Beagle, Peter. *A Fine and Private Place.* A man who lives in a cemetery converses with a raven, ghosts, and a woman who visits her husband's grave. A modern ghost story, both sad and funny.

Cerf, Bennett, editor. *Famous Ghost Stories.* Fifteen ghost stories including W. W. Jacobs's "The Monkey's Paw" and Rudyard Kipling's "The Phantom Rickshaw."

Lamb, Hugh, editor. *Victorian Tales of Terror.* For those who like their ghost stories old-fashioned, this collection includes fifteen ghost and horror stories by Charles Dickens, Ambrose Bierce, and others.

Macardle, Dorothy. *The Uninvited.* A young man meets a beautiful girl who appears to be haunted. He falls in love with the girl and tries to free her of her ghost. A modern ghost story.

FANTASY

THE UGLY DUCKLING

About the Author

Hans Christian Andersen (1805–1875) was born in Odense, Denmark. As a boy, he wanted to be an actor, a singer, a dancer—anything to do with the theater. Instead, he was apprenticed to a weaver and later was sent to work in a tobacco factory.

At fourteen, he fled Odense and went to Copenhagen in rags. He tried to get work in theaters but was turned down time after time. Eventually, a director of the Royal theater took an interest in the boy and made him go to school. For five years he attended grammar school, a gangling teenager much older than his classmates, poor at studies, scolded by the teacher.

He had already begun writing. In 1835, he wrote his first fairy tales to pay the rent. He continued writing tales to earn money but regarded himself as primarily a playwright and novelist. Readers saw what Andersen did not: that his true genius lay in his tales.

Andersen's tales made him world-famous. In 1867, he returned to Odense to be honored by his native town.

About the Story

G20   "The Ugly Duckling," possibly the most-loved fairy tale in all literature, is as popular with adults as with children. As you read—or reread—this story of the unlovely, unloved little duckling, think about how uncannily human Andersen's barnyard creatures are.

Checkup Quiz (True or False)

1. The grand old duck with the red rag on her leg knows there is something marvelous about the duckling.
2. The hen thinks the duckling is "the cleverest animal I know."
3. The peasant's children frighten the duckling.
4. The duckling turns out to be a gander.

Interpreting the Story

1. Through most of the story, what is the duckling's opinion of himself? Why does he have this opinion? What causes the change in him in the spring?
2. One writer has noted that Andersen's characters "live and breathe and become individuals." Which characters in this tale are like some people who think they are the best and what they do not know is not worth knowing? Quote a conversation in the story that reveals this attitude.
3. The hen tells the duckling, "I speak for your good. I tell you disagreeable things, and by that one may always know one's true friends!" *Is* this the mark of a true friend? Why or why not?

4. What human hopes, dreams, and fears is Andersen writing about in "The Ugly Duckling"? How do you account for its immense popularity?

5. Some readers see this tale as disguised autobiography. In fact, one biography of Andersen is titled *The Ugly Duckling*. From what you know of his life, explain why this tale might really be about Hans Christian Andersen.

THE DANCING DOLL

About the Author

Ernst Theodor Amadeus Hoffmann (1776–1822) was a lawyer, a composer, a conductor, a stage director, and a writer of plays, novels, and fantastic tales. Today, he is chiefly remembered for his tales, which are a remarkable combination of horror and humor, the supernatural and the everyday.

Several musical works are based on Hoffmann's tales; among them are Offenbach's opera *The Tales of Hoffmann,* Tchaikovsky's ballet *Nutcracker,* and Delibes's ballet *Coppélia. Coppélia* and part of *The Tales of Hoffmann* are based on the story of the dancing doll.

About the Story

Like many later writers—especially science fiction writers—Hoffmann was intrigued and horrified by the idea of being fooled by an automaton, or robot, so real it would seem human. As you read, observe how the hero of this strange story falls victim to just such a trick.

ducats Gold or silver coins.

legend of the dead bride A reference to Goethe's ballad "Bride of Corinth"; the hero unknowingly loves someone who has returned from the dead and therefore must himself die.

Checkup Quiz

1. Coppola tries to sell Nathanael (a) a book of magic, (b) a lamp, (c) eyeglasses.
2. Nathanael sees Olympia (a) at a tea party, (b) at a ball, (c) on an opera stage.
3. Nathanael finds that Olympia's hand is (a) cold, (b) hot, (c) moist.
4. When Nathanael asks Olympia if she loves him, she replies (a) "Ah, ah!" (b) "Yes, yes!" (c) "Dance, dance!"

Interpreting the Story

1. At first Nathanael is indifferent to Olympia. What changes his view of her?
2. Nathanael continually misunderstands Olympia's behavior. What details provide clues to her *real* nature?
3. "Coppola" means "eye socket" in Italian, and "Clara" comes from the Latin word for "clear." What other details suggest that the story is about seeing and about true and false perceptions?
4. One interpretation is that this is the story of a man going mad. Another interpretation is that this is the story of evil (Coppelius) overcoming good (Nathanael). Which interpretation would you choose? Why?

A MAD TEA PARTY

About the Author

Charles Lutwidge Dodgson (1832–1898) was a mathemetician and logician at Christ Church College, Oxford, England. For his lighter books, he used the name "Lewis Carroll," a version of his first two names reversed.

A lifelong bachelor, Carroll was enormously fond of children. Three of his particular friends were the Liddell girls, the young daughters of a friend. Alice Liddell was his special favorite. On a summer excursion, Carroll began telling the girls about Alice's adventures as she follows a rabbit down a hole.

In 1865, these adventures were published as *Alice's Adventures in Wonderland.* A sequel, *Through the Looking Glass,* followed in 1872. These books made Carroll one of the most popular authors of his day. Adults, even more than children, were fascinated by his Wonderland.

Charles Dodgson was a bit uneasy about the popularity. He wanted to be known for his serious mathematical and logical treatises. But it is chiefly for the Alice books that Lewis Carroll is remembered.

About the Story

"A Mad Tea Party" is from *Alice in Wonderland.* The Alice books are considered "nonsense" writing. But such nonsense does not mean "no sense." Carroll's world makes its own kind of sense, like reflections in a funhouse mirror, changed just enough to be funny. As you read, notice how the tea party is like a strange reflection of the real world.

dormouse A rodent resembling a squirrel.

treacle Molasses.

Checkup Quiz (True or False)

1. The March Hare pours Alice a glass of wine.
2. The Dormouse keeps falling asleep.
3. The March Hare put butter in a watch.
4. The Hatter sings about a bat.
5. The Hatter and the Hare try to shove the Dormouse into the teapot.

Interpreting the Story

1. At a tea party, the host and guests are usually very polite and make conversation even if they are bored. How is this tea party different from most? How is it curiously *like* ordinary tea parties?
2. A popular children's song begins, "Twinkle, twinkle, little star/How I wonder what you are/Up above the world so high/Like a diamond in the sky." How is the song at the tea party similar? How is it different? If you found it funny, can you explain why?
3. Carroll, a logician, has shifty fun with logic by changing the meanings of words from sentence to sentence. For example, Alice says, "I know I have to beat time when I learn music." The Hatter replies, "He won't stand beating." Explain what "beat time" means to Alice. Explain what it means to the Hatter. Explain one other example of shifting meaning, such as when Alice and the Dormouse talk about the girls in the treacle well who were learning "to draw."

THE KING OF THE GOLDEN RIVER

About the Author

John Ruskin (1819–1900) was born in London. As a boy, he accompanied his father, a wine merchant, on his travels. In this way Ruskin saw a good deal of the English countryside and came to love the beauties of nature, "the work and gift of a Living Spirit, greater than our own."

As an adult, he made a study of natural beauty as represented in works of art. He became the foremost art critic of his time. Ruskin argued that great art is more than just lines and color, that it expresses moral ideas. Ruskin also cared deeply about social problems. He criticized the materialism and the social injustices of his day. He admired skilled craftspeople and honest workers and argued "the dependence of all human work ... on the happy life of the workman."

About the Story

"The King of the Golden River," Ruskin's only work of fiction, draws on the traditions of German and Austrian folktales. But more than that, it is an expression of Ruskin's concern with the beauties of nature and with moral ideas.

Ruskin's rich, intricate, descriptive prose cannot be skimmed; like poetry, it demands—and rewards—a slow reading. You might enjoy reading parts of the story aloud. Watch, too, for Ruskin's ideas about people as represented by the three brothers who seek a treasure promised by the King of the Golden River.

Stiria An Austrian province (also Styria).

paying tithes The practice of giving a tenth of one's income to the church.

refractory Resisting heat.

doublet Jacket.

Rhenish Rhine wine.

Checkup Quiz

1. Gluck gives some mutton to (a) the King of the Golden River, (b) the Southwest Wind, (c) a hungry dog.
2. The King of the Golden River was imprisoned in (a) a lamp, (b) a glacier, (c) a mug.
3. Hans and Schwartz become (a) millionaires, (b) trees, (c) stones.

Interpreting the Story

1. On their trips to the mountain, whom do the brothers meet? How is Gluck's behavior different from that of Hans and Schwartz? How do changes in nature reflect their good or bad behavior? Give examples.
2. Folktales often include (a) gods or spirits disguised as humans, (b) spells that change creatures' shapes or imprison them, and (c) quests that test bravery and moral values. Explain how each of these traditional elements appears in this story.
3. "The King of the Golden River" can be enjoyed simply as a tale of fantastic events. But it can also be

understood as a serious moral tale. Explain what the author seems to be saying about (a) nature, its beauties, and how it should be treated; (b) honest and dishonest workmanship; (c) greed and the love of money; and (d) how people should behave toward those less fortunate. Give examples from the story.

4. In the end, does the river turn to gold? In what way does it become a "River of Gold"?

Be a Writer

A. "The King of the Golden River" is especially rich in dramatic and glowing descriptions of nature:

> And the sky where the sun was setting was all level and like a lake of blood; and a strong wind came out of that sky, tearing its crimson clouds into fragments and scattering them far into the darkness.

Write your own description of a beautiful natural sight, perhaps a sunset or a place you love. Use effective details to evoke its beauty.

B. Fantasies are frequently populated by animals with human quirks and foibles. Write a fantasy in which animals possess human faults and follies.

Special Projects

A. Two characters in "A Mad Tea Party" are based on phrases current in Lewis Carroll's time and still used today. "Mad as a hatter" comes from the fact that hatters often did appear to go mad. Hatters used mercury in curing felt. Mercury poisoning weakened their eyes and limbs and addled their speech. "Mad as a march hare" comes from the frenzied behavior of male hares in March, their mating season. Find and report on the origin of one of the following phrases:

go berserk	wolf in sheep's clothing
rain cats and dogs	from the horse's mouth
eat crow	with a grain of salt
wild-goose chase	Hobson's choice

(A good reference on origins of phrases is Charles E. Funk's *A Hog on Ice and Other Curious Expressions*.)

B. Hold a public reading of passages from the fantasies that you particularly admire. You might choose:

descriptions of natural beauty
dramatic passages
amusing or thought-provoking passages
passages in which animals behave like humans

Tape your readings to play for the class.

Further Reading

Beagle, Peter. *The Last Unicorn*. Learning that she may be the last of her kind, a beautiful unicorn sets off in search of her fellows. During her travels, she meets a magician, a bandit, a prince, a king, and a Red Bull.

Carroll, Lewis. *The Annotated Alice*. Contains *Alice in Wonderland* and *Through the Looking Glass*. Martin Gardner, a writer on mathematics and logic, comments on Carroll's fun with logic and explains humor that depends on a knowledge of the Victorian era.

Leguin, Ursula K. *The Tombs of Atuan.* Taken from her family G29 at the age of six, Tenar has to give up her own identity and become a high priestess to the Powers of the Earth. A wizard helps her realize the emptiness of her life and escape from the tombs of Atuan.

L'Engle, Madeleine. *A Wrinkle in Time.* A brother and sister, together with a friend, travel in time and space searching for their father, who is held prisoner on another planet.

Moskowitz, Samuel, and Roger Elwood, editors. *Strange Signposts: an Anthology of the Fantastic.* Fifteen fantasies by Edgar Allan Poe, Nathaniel Hawthorne, Mary Shelley, H.G. Wells, and others.

SCIENCE FICTION

THE MORTAL IMMORTAL

About the Author

Mary Wollstonecraft Shelley (1797–1851) was the daughter of famous parents. Her father was William Godwin, the English political philosopher. Her mother, Mary Wollstonecraft, was a champion of women's rights. When Percy Bysshe Shelley, the great English poet, came to study with Godwin, he met Mary and they ran off together. At the age of eighteen, while vacationing with Shelley in Switzerland, Mary wrote her masterpiece, *Frankenstein,* a novel about a man who experiments with the creation of life and produces a monster.

About the Story

To live forever would be wonderful—or would it? Like *Frankenstein,* the story of "The Mortal Immortal" can be interpreted as a warning not to overstep certain boundaries in the quest for knowledge. As you read the story, consider what boundaries are overstepped and what the consequences are.

mortal A human being with a limited life span.

immortal Undying; exempt from death.

Wandering Jew In a medieval legend, a Jew condemned to wander the earth until Jesus' second coming. References to the Wandering Jew may be considered antisemitic (anti-Jewish); but Mary Shelley was referring only to his eighteen centuries of life as compared to her character's 323 years.

Seven Sleepers ... Nourjahad Legendary characters who slept for many years.

Cornelius Agrippa A philosopher known for defending the study of magic and the supernatural (1486–1535).

alchemist A medieval chemist with three main concerns: transmuting base metals into gold, finding a remedy for all disease, and devising an elixir for perpetual life and youth.

cloven foot A sign or characteristic of the devil.

adept Alchemist.

cot Hut.

conjured Urged.

Nestors Nestor is an aged and wise warrior in the *Iliad,* Homer's ancient story of the Trojan War.

Cain A murderer. (In the Bible Cain killed his brother.)

Checkup Quiz

1. Winzy drinks the elixir, thinking it will (a) make him immortal, (b) make him sleepy, (c) cure love.
2. Winzy's wife (a) drowns herself, (b) dies of old age, (c) becomes immortal.
3. At the story's end, Winzy (a) drowns himself, (b) becomes ill, (c) goes off on an expedition.

Interpreting the Story

1. Over the years, how does Winzy's relationship with his wife change—and why?
2. At the end, Winzy plans to die. How?
3. Scientists are still trying to extend life, and many people would like to be immortal. Would you drink an elixir of immortality if you could? Explain.
4. The author seems to be warning us that new knowledge can be dangerous. Do you agree or disagree? To support your point of view, give examples of new knowledge or inventions of the last century.

MOXON'S MASTER

About the Author

Ambrose Bierce (1842–1914?) was born in Ohio. When the Civil War broke out, he enlisted as a drummer boy. By the end of the war, he was a major. Later, Bierce became a newspaper columnist, an editor, and a short-story writer. His best-known stories are of two types: stories of Civil War violence, and horror stories. In 1913, Bierce

went off to Mexico to cover a revolution and was last heard from in 1914. He was presumed to have been
killed, but his death remains a mystery.

About the Story

"Do you really believe that a machine thinks?" the narrator of the story asks Moxon. The real answer comes only at the end of this chilling tale.

People's relationship to machines has long pre-occupied science fiction writers. And since the future will almost certainly be an age of computers and robots, "Moxon's Master" has even more relevance to the future than to the age in which it was written.

excoriations Scratches.

Herbert Spencer An English philosopher (1820–1903).

Mill John Stuart Mill, an English philosopher (1806–1873).

Saul of Tarsus On the road to Damascus, Saul (St. Paul) saw a great light and heard a voice ask, "Saul, Saul, why persecutest thou me?" He became a convert to Christ. (See the Bible, Acts 9.)

Lewes George Henry Lewes, an English writer (1817–1878).

automaton A thing that moves by its own power; a robot.

Checkup Quiz (True or False)

1. Moxon's cheek is scratched by a machine.

2. The narrator secretly watches the chess game.
3. The machine cries, "Checkmate!" to show it has won.
4. Moxon junks the machine.

Interpreting the Story

1. To back up his argument that machines think, Moxon says that plants, crystals, and atoms also think. Choose one of these three examples and explain how—according to Moxon—its behavior shows it can think.
2. When the narrator finally sees the creature with Moxon, he doesn't realize what it is. What details does he *first* observe about it? What makes him realize that it is a machine? What does the machine do that shows it can think?
3. At the end, is the narrator *sure* who killed Moxon? If it wasn't the automaton, who could it have been?
4. Today, there are computers that play chess. If you played chess with one of these machines, could the outcome be the same for you as for Moxon? Explain.
5. The story's title suggests the question: *Will machines eventually rule the world? Be our masters?* What do you think?

FROM THE EARTH TO THE MOON

About the Author

The French writer Jules Verne (1828–1905) has been called the "father of science fiction." Writers before him wrote about marvelous inventions and space travel, but none presented so much scientific data.

Verne's novels of scientific speculation—including *From the Earth to the Moon* and *Twenty Thousand Leagues Under the Sea*—won him an international audience. Such was his fame that, after his death, more than five thousand people attended his funeral.

About the Story

From the Earth to the Moon and *Round the Moon*, its sequel, tell of space flight in the 1860s. In their time, these books were considered scientifically accurate. Modern readers can detect inaccuracies: a telescope powerful enough to see a spaceship in moon orbit (we still don't have such a telescope); the burning of the meteor in space (impossible without oxygen); sudden changes from day to night on the moon (the same side always faces the sun); the fact that the travelers would have been crushed by G-forces in the cannon-fired takeoff or burned on reentry into earth's atmosphere.

But it is astonishing how many *correct* guesses Verne made one hundred years before the first moon flight: the launch from Florida; the count before launch (but a count *up* instead of a countdown); weightlessness (but he thought it would be brief instead of through most of the flight); the possibility of a space walk outside the rocket (and the accurate description of how it would look); the contrast of light and shadow on the moon; the use of rockets to correct course; and reentry in the Pacific.

Note This story is condensed from two novels, *From the Earth to the Moon* and *Round the Moon*, published in 1865 and 1870. For the second novel Verne made some changes: In one book, the spaceship reaches moon orbit on December fourth (an error in calculation); in the other book on December fifth (correct). In one book, the space- ship is still in moon orbit on December eleventh; in the other, the spaceship begins its return to earth on December eighth. As you read, you may notice these and several other contradictory facts.

£1,200,000 One million two hundred thousand pounds English money; about six million dollars.

pyroxyle A combustible material.

gutta-percha A rubberlike substance. Apparently, Maston suffered a head wound in the Civil War and needed a covering for the top of his head.

dénouement Outcome or resolution.

Cuisine des Anges *Food of the Gods*, a painting by the Spanish artist Murillo.

umbra Shadow.

penumbra Partial light around a shadow.

chiar-oscuro A contrast between light and darkness.

deflagration Rapid, intense burning.

sangfroid Coolness, composure.

Checkup Quiz (True or False)

1. Three men are sent to the moon by a gun club.
2. They are captured by moon creatures.
3. They are threatened by a meteor.
4. They have not planned how to get back to Earth.
5. They are rescued from the bottom of the ocean.

Interpreting the Story

1. Space stories often convey a sense of wonder. What marvelous sights do Verne's travelers witness?
2. Why did they undertake such a dangerous journey? Were they brave or foolhardy? Explain your opinion.
3. Other than scientific errors, what struck you about the voyage of Verne's travelers as compared to the voyages of modern astronauts? If Verne's travelers could have watched the moon voyage of 1969 on television, what would have surprised them?

THE STRANGE ORCHID

About the Author

Herbert George Wells (1866–1946) was born in Kent, England. He wrote a number of science fiction classics, including *The Time Machine* and *The War of the Worlds*. In addition, he wrote many serious realistic novels about class relationships and social problems.

Wells was also a historian, and in his best-selling *Outline of History*, he saw humanity rising from primitive selfishness and superstition to a rational society working to everyone's benefit. But during World War II, Wells lost his optimism and began to despair for humanity's future. He died a disillusioned and bitter man.

About the Story

"The Strange Orchid" is a low-key horror story with an unexpected twist. The story is a speculation about

plants developing in a certain way. But it is also a p(
trait of a middle-aged man who says wistfully, "Nothin,
ever does happen to me."

As you read, notice how Wells blends scientific speculation with the telling of a good story.

labellum An orchid's longest, lowest petal.

rhizome A creeping stem.

ornithologist A zoologist who studies birds.

garrulous Talkative.

Checkup Quiz (True or False)

1. Mr. Wedderburn's housekeeper loves adventure.
2. Wedderburn is suspicious of the orchid.
3. Wedderburn saves the housekeeper's life.
4. Wedderburn is happy about the adventure.

Interpreting the Story

1. Why does Wedderburn feel that "nothing ever does
   happen to me"? Why does he envy Harvey?
2. When the odd-job man saw the housekeeper pulling
   Wedderburn out of the greenhouse "he thought impossible things." What did he think—and why?
3. Like much science fiction, this story presents scientific
   data to make what happens seem plausible. What
   facts about plants are presented? How are these facts
   related to Wedderburn's adventure?
4. Several of Wells's novels are about insignificant
   people, leading ordinary lives, who have their mo-

glory. What does "The Strange Orchid" have _ _mon with those novels?

_d you call "The Strange Orchid" a humorous _ry? Why or why not?

Be a Writer

A. Rewrite a part of Jules Verne's "From the Earth to the Moon" as Verne might write it today with a knowledge of modern astronautics. (Points to consider: How would Verne get his travelers to the moon? What might they find there? How would he resolve the problems of reentering the earth's atmosphere and landing the ship?)

B. In "Moxon's Master," the machine's actions reveal its feelings. Write a scene or a story about a robot that has feelings and how the robot's actions reveal these feelings—to its maker's surprise. Use one of these ideas or make up your own:

1. The robot falls in love with its maker.
2. The robot longs for freedom from the laboratory.
3. The robot is jealous of a newer-model robot.

Special Projects

A. Report on the Baltimore Gun Club's space program—which culminated in an 1860s flight around the moon—as if it were a recent event. Write a news or feature article about it, make drawings of importa[nt] moments, invent interviews with Verne's space trav[el]ers, and/or dramatize episodes in the flight.

B. Report on NASA's Apollo program—which resulted in Neil Armstrong's setting foot on the moon in 1969. Compile photos and articles about it and/or dramatize the historic moon landing. (A source is *Apollo Expeditions to the Moon*, edited by Edgar M. Cortwright, published by the National Aeronautics and Space Administration, Washington, D.C., 1975.)

C. Plan an advertising campaign for one of the following:

1. a resort hotel on the moon
2. a newly-developed plant that protects a house from burglars
3. a machine that solves personal problems
4. a new process for slowing down aging

The campaign can include print advertisements (with art) and broadcast commercials (which can be taped or dramatized for the class). Emphasize the main features and advantages.

Further Reading

Asimov, Isaac, editor. *Where Do We Go from Here?* Seventeen science fiction stories, chosen by a leading writer in the field.

Asimov, Isaac. *I, Robot.* Nine related stories about robots, the rules governing their creation (they may not harm people), and the problems caused when the rules have unforeseen results.

...bert. *The Past Through Tomorrow*. Heinlein ... history" of the future and wrote novels and sto-... ed on that history. This book includes most of the ... e history" series.

...ey, Mary. *The Annotated Frankenstein*. The famous novel about a scientist and the monster he created. Leonard Wolf, a scholar of horror fiction, provides a commentary and explains many references.

Verne, Jules. *A Journey to the Center of the Earth*. A band of explorers enters the funnel of a volcano and makes its way to the center of the earth.

Verne, Jules. *Twenty Thousand Leagues Under the Sea*. The mysterious Captain Nemo prowls the sea in the *Nautilus*, his powerful submarine, raiding ships and avenging wrongs.

Wells, H.G. *The Invisible Man*. A mad scientist experiments with light refraction, makes himself invisible, and terrorizes a town.

Wells, H.G. *The Time Machine*. A man travels into the future and proves that time is "the fourth dimension."

Wells, H.G. *The War of the Worlds*. Martians invade Earth. The most famous novel of interplanetary warfare.

☆ ★ ☆

Audiovisual Resources

Records and Cassettes

Alice in Wonderland—Carole Shelley, George Rose. CMS. 3 records.

Coppélia (ballet by Delibes, based on the dancing-doll portion of "The Sandman" by Hoffmann)—L'Orchestre de la Suisse Romande. London. 2 records.

Great Short Stories ("The Open Window" and others). Caedmon. Cassette.

The King of the Golden River—Robert Ryan. Spoken Arts.
2 cassettes.

Murray Hill Radio Theatre: More Sherlock Holmes ("Silver Blaze" and others)—Sir John Gielgud, Sir Ralph Richardson. Publishers Central Bureau. 3 records.

Nutcracker Suite (from the ballet by Tchaikovsky, based on Hoffmann tales)—L'Orchestre de la Suisse Romande. London. 2 records.

Silver Blaze—Basil Rathbone. Caedmon. Record, cassette.

Tales of Hoffman (excerpts from the opera by Offenbach)—L'Orchestre de la Suisse Romande, Joan Sutherland. London. Record.

The Tell-Tale Heart and *The Cask of Amontillado*—Alexander Scourby. Spoken Arts. Record.

A *Terribly Strange Bed* (and other horror stories). Spoken Arts. Record.

Films (16mm)°

Alice in Wonderland. Paramount Pictures, Indiana University. 44 min, b/w. Excerpted from feature film.

From the Earth to the Moon. Audio Brandon Films, Inc. 100 min, color. Revamped version of the Verne novel with Joseph Cotton, George Sanders, Debra Paget.

Hans Christian Andersen. Samuel Goldwyn, Audio Brandon Films. 104 min, color. Musical biography with Danny Kaye.

The Open Window. American Film Institute, Pyramid Films. 12 min, color.

Silver Blaze. Learning Corporation of America. 32 min, color. With Christopher Plummer.

Tales of Hoffmann. Centron Corporation. 52 min, color. Excerpted from full-length film of the opera, British cast.

G42 *The Tell-Tale Heart.* American Film Institute, Time-Life Films Multimedia Division. 26 min, b/w.

A Terribly Strange Bed. Anglia Films, Encyclopedia Britannica Educational Corporation. 24 min, color. Introduced by Orson Welles.

The Ugly Duckling. Woods, Weston, Studios. 15 min, color. Animated version, includes teacher's guide stressing themes of alienation, prejudice, true beauty.

Filmstrips (35mm)[*]

A Mad Tea-Party (from *Alice's Adventures in Wonderland* series). Teaching Resources Films. 66 frames, color, with record/cassette/script.

The Mortal Immortal (from *The Science Fiction Series*). Society for Visual Education. 62 frames, color, with record/cassette/script.

Silver Blaze (from *Sherlock Holmes Adventures* series). Brunswick Corporation, Educational Record Sales. 55 frames, color, with captions.

The Tell-Tale Heart (from *Works of Poe* series). Brunswick Corporation. 34 frames, color, with captions.

The Ugly Duckling (from *Andersen's Fairy Tales* series). Coronet Instructional Films. 34 frames, color, with captions, record/cassette.

---

[*] When two sources are listed, the first is the producer and the second is the distributor. To locate addresses of producers and distributors, use the *Index to 16mm Educational Films* and the *Index to 35mm Educational Filmstrips,* both published by the National Information Center of Educational Media at the University of Southern California. An alternate source of addresses is *Audiovisual Market Place,* published by R. R. Bowker Company. *The Educational Film Locator,* also published by Bowker, lists university libraries that are film rental centers. In addition, many of these audiovisual materials may be available through your local library.